Praise for Ca...

On *The Queer Principles of Kit Webb*

"Cat Sebastian is an author at the absolute top of her game."
—Erin Sterling, *New York Times* bestselling author of *The Ex Hex*

"With *The Queer Principles of Kit Webb*, Cat Sebastian's newest, we get the full Georgian-era experience: coffeehouses, lace cuffs, noblemen in pastel silks and ballad-worthy highwaymen whose thieving days are almost, almost behind them. . . . Highwayman, it turns out, is a pitch-perfect role for a queer historical hero. If you're already risking your neck to steal purses and harry the gentry, you'll think nothing of risking your neck for someone you love. . . . The book does not so much tear down class boundaries as dynamite the very idea of class itself, which is becoming a satisfying theme in Sebastian's work. Laws that exist only to hurt people are unjust; systems that depend on people's misery should be subverted and dismantled at every chance. The right to love and be loved as we are is a compass that always points toward justice."

—*New York Times Book Review*

"*The Queer Principles of Kit Webb* kept me up all night! I simply couldn't put it down."

—Tessa Dare, *New York Times* bestselling author

"Their sexual tension is a living, breathing thing on the page, but mercifully, Sebastian doesn't leave them in want for long. And there's plenty of sparkling dialogue to go with their physical connection. Kit has very clear opinions about the privilege Percy is fighting to protect, and their conversations about class and politics are uniformly excellent and fascinating. *Kit Webb* will surprise and delight not only fans of Sebastian and queer historical romance but also readers who are new to both."

—*BookPage* (starred review)

"Sebastian's prose is entertaining and delightful, with many steamy scenes. . . . It's also full of intelligent and thought-provoking political debates. . . . An irresistible story of love and adventure that will delight both newcomers and regular readers of queer romance."

—*Kirkus Reviews* (starred review)

"Cat Sebastian is one of my favorite writers in romance or any other genre. *The Queer Principles of Kit Webb*, like all her other books, is intelligent, wryly funny, deeply thoughtful, empathetic, and romantic as can be. I absolutely loved it."

—Olivia Dade, author of *Spoiler Alert*

"*The Queer Principles of Kit Webb* is by turns witty, heartfelt, sexy, and deeply emotional. I devoured it and am clamoring for more."

—Eva Leigh, author of *My Fake Rake*

"Wielding a rapier-sharp wit and displaying an exceptional gift for insightful characterization, Sebastian fashions another fiercely romantic, fabulously sexy M/M love story that not only delivers a delicious surfeit of slow-burn sexual chemistry but also deftly illustrates the true complexity of all human relationships."

—*Booklist*

Praise for Previous Books

"Sebastian crafts another enormously fun, sexy romp that is also touching, with two heroines who make each other better together than they were alone. This latest entry in the Turner series stands on its own and will make readers wish for more about the winsome duo. Highly recommended."

> —*Library Journal* (starred review) on *A Little Light Mischief*

"This book is a marvel and a gem."

> —*New York Times Book Review* on *Unmasked by the Marquess*

"The conflict . . . is . . . utterly new and refreshing for the genre. . . . Sebastian masters the plotting and emotions of an individual coming to grips with her gender queer identity, while also not falling into the trap of melodrama or maudlin afterschool special."

> —*Entertainment Weekly* on *Unmasked by the Marquess*

"Cat Sebastian sets a beautiful romance against a compelling story of blackmail, scandal and the impossibility of happily-everafter. . . . A reminder that love holds such power over us all."

> —*Washington Post* on *The Soldier's Scoundrel*

"A familiar Regency opposites-attract romance becomes something freshly seductive in the hands of a skilled newcomer . . . Sebastian deploys dialogue, especially the men's frequent disagreements, to great and often hilarious effect. . . . An accomplished, thoroughly winning debut."

> —*Kirkus Reviews* on *The Soldier's Scoundrel*

"Sweetly prim Oliver and the roguish Jack will quickly win the hearts of readers, while the mysterious blackmail investigation keeps them invested to the end. An excellent choice not just for M/M romance fans but also for Regency fans with a penchant for vigilante justice."

—*Library Journal* on *The Soldier's Scoundrel*

"Readers can expect angst-filled romance and scorching hot passion. Gentleman Oliver and Private Investigator Jack will check every box on your romance must-have list. I highly recommend this debut novel!"

—Bonnie Dee, *New York Times* bestselling author

"Cat Sebastian has a place on my keeper shelf!"

—Tessa Dare, *New York Times* bestselling author, on *The Ruin of a Rake*

"Sebastian might use the well-worn opposites-attract trope to get her lovers together, but her mastery of conflict, tension, and timing along with flawless characterization and sexual attraction turn *The Ruin of a Rake* into a unique and entrancing romance that touches the heart deeper than most."

—*Library Journal* (starred review) on *The Ruin of a Rake*

"Sebastian's character-driven novel is sensuously romantic yet grounded in its approach to human relationships. . . . [she] upends Regency romance conventions in this sensual, emotional, and upbeat take on the rake/wallflower trope."

—*Kirkus Reviews* on *The Ruin of a Rake*

"Cat Sebastian's debut sparkles with wit and sensuality. Not to be missed!"
—Lenora Bell, *USA Today* bestselling author, on *The Ruin of a Rake*

"Cat Sebastian writes an irresistible blend of wit, warmth, and passion."

—Cecilia Grant, author of *A Lady Awakened*

"Cat Sebastian's writing is a pure joy to read—it's engaging, romantic, witty, and positive. Reading one of her books always leaves me with a smile on my face and a warm, happy feeling in my heart."

—Avon Gale, author of the Scoring Chances series

"Cat Sebastian is already on my auto-buy list!"

—Summer Devon, coauthor of *The Gentleman and the Rogue*

"Sebastian's latest elegantly and eloquently written Regency historical . . . slowly unfolds into an unforgettable love story that manages to be both sweetly romantic and sizzlingly sensual at the same time, demonstrating once again why Sebastian is one of the brightest new stars in the romance genre."

—*Booklist* (starred review) on *It Takes Two to Tumble*

"The novel soars most in the moments where we see Phillip and Ben's love propel them to find understanding with other members of their families. . . . Sebastian's latest checks all the boxes for a delightful winter read."

—*Entertainment Weekly* on *It Takes Two to Tumble*

"This novel left our hearts bursting with happiness and it is a must-read for fans of historical romances."

—Bookish.com on *It Takes Two to Tumble*

"Achingly beautiful, heartbreakingly realistic, magnificently written; simply sublime!"

—Fresh Fiction on *It Takes Two to Tumble*

"There is something quicksilver and alive at the heart of this book that refuses to be pinned down to commonplace realism."

—Seattle Review of Books on *It Takes Two to Tumble*

"Sebastian sends out her Seducing the Sedgwicks series in style with this intimate Regency romance. . . . Sensual sex scenes and fully realized supporting characters enhance the tale, and though the conflict is minimal, Sebastian succeeds in making it feel momentous. This is a delight."

—*Publishers Weekly* (starred review) on *Two Rogues Make a Right*

"With this life-affirming final act to the trilogy, Sebastian delivers a fiercely joyous tale of two people fighting to give each other a home and learning to love well."

—*Library Journal* (starred review) on *Two Rogues Make a Right*

"With the latest swoon-worthy addition to her Regency-set Seducing the Sedgwicks series, Sebastian once again brings exquisite depth and nuance to her characters while at the same time striking the perfect balance between sweet romantic yearning and bold sensuality."

—*Booklist* on *Two Rogues Make a Right*

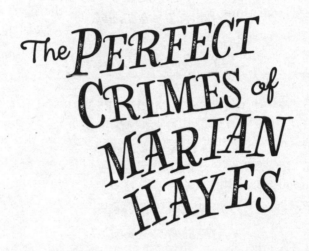

The PERFECT CRIMES of MARIAN HAYES

ALSO BY CAT SEBASTIAN

The Queer Principles of Kit Webb

THE SEDUCING THE SEDGWICKS SERIES
It Takes Two to Tumble
A Gentleman Never Keeps Score
Two Rogues Make a Right

THE REGENCY IMPOSTORS SERIES
Unmasked by the Marquess
A Duke in Disguise
A Delicate Deception

THE TURNER SERIES
The Soldier's Scoundrel
The Lawrence Browne Affair
The Ruin of a Rake
A Little Light Mischief (novella)

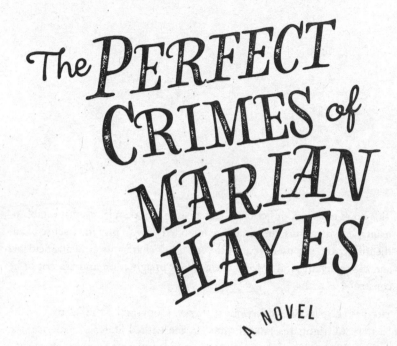

The PERFECT CRIMES of MARIAN HAYES

A NOVEL

CAT SEBASTIAN

AVON

An Imprint of HarperCollinsPublishers

THE PERFECT CRIMES OF MARIAN HAYES. Copyright © 2022 by Cat Sebastian. All rights reserved. Printed in the United States of America. No part of this book may be used or reproduced in any manner whatsoever without written permission except in the case of brief quotations embodied in critical articles and reviews. For information, address HarperCollins Publishers, 195 Broadway, New York, NY 10007.

HarperCollins books may be purchased for educational, business, or sales promotional use. For information, please email the Special Markets Department at SPsales@harpercollins.com.

FIRST EDITION

Designed by Diahann Sturge

Library of Congress Cataloging-in-Publication Data has been applied for.

ISBN 978-0-06-302625-4

22 23 24 25 26   LSC   10 9 8 7 6 5 4 3 2 1

Prologue

*R*ob Brooks had not survived to the age of five and twenty without having mastered the art of escape.

He had been arrested heaven only knew how many times and convicted rather more often than he cared to admit. He had been charged with robbery (true), burglary (false), smuggling (true, but he hadn't known what was in those barrels), counterfeiting (false), and horse theft (he had done that horse a favor). By the age of five and twenty he had visited so many of His Majesty's establishments that if any publisher wished to commission a travelers' guide to the prisons of Surrey, Oxfordshire, and Buckinghamshire, they could seek no author more qualified than Rob. On one memorable occasion, he progressed so far as to make the acquaintance of the hangman. He had been shot, stabbed, whipped, cudgeled, and thrown overboard.

And yet: here he was, quite thoroughly and unmistakably alive, not to mention intact and in the pink of health. He knew he was impulsive, maybe even reckless, and that this lack of caution had made his biography nothing but a string of narrowly avoided disasters.

The fact was that he had made something of a career out of close calls and near-run things. When people talked about Rob—which was to say Gladhand Jack, the nom de guerre he and his friend used when liberating coin from rich men's purses—they spoke of his escapes as much as his triumphs. He escaped, evaded, and wriggled out; he bribed, cajoled, and charmed.

It boiled down to this: people liked Rob and they wanted to help him. As luck would have it, Rob liked them right back and wished to return the favor. The world, as far as Rob could tell, was filled with people who were simply waiting for the chance to participate in an adventure, and Rob was willing to furnish them with precisely that. This transformed the difficulty of sneaking lockpicks, rasps, and files into prisons from the merely transactional and uninspiring business of bribery into a jolly time for everyone concerned. Everybody went home feeling good about themselves and their fellow man.

That was why it was especially galling that, try as he might, Rob could not see a way out of his current predicament. There was nobody to charm, nobody to bribe. No quantity of lockpicks, no number of rasps cunningly baked into cakes or sewn into cloaks could undo the trouble he was in. The sorry truth of it was that his mother—his beloved, inscrutable, maddening mother—had seen fit to marry the eldest son of a duke some months before Rob's arrival into the world. What could possibly have been going through the minds of his mother, the piece of aristocratic vermin she took to the altar, the priest, the witnesses, or anyone else who allowed this catastrophe of a marriage to take place, Rob could not guess and had given up trying to understand.

Upon learning of this marriage the previous year, Rob spent a month in the comforting embrace of a gin bottle, then got down to the familiar business of attempting to wriggle out of this mess. He wanted to inherit a dukedom about as much as he wished to further his acquaintance with the hangman. He had gone directly to the godforsaken church in Boulogne where this lunatic marriage had taken place, only to find a parish populated by the most intractably honest and dull citizens he could have conjured up in his worst nightmares. Nobody there was in the least bribable, and perhaps Rob's charm didn't translate into French, because when he attempted to steal the parish register, the townspeople did not prove to be terribly understanding about the matter. On the whole, he preferred English prisons.

This left him with few options. London was filled to the very brim with people who would identify him as his mother's son and who would prove depressingly glad to see a title and fortune inflicted on him.

After dedicating one's life to creating mischief for his betters, Rob would be the worst kind of hypocrite if he found a place among that very group he had spent years robbing, cheating, and otherwise tormenting. It would be sadly unmotivating for the criminal classes to discover that their figurehead was one of the enemies. It would have the effect of a reverse Agincourt speech. The entire city would lay down their arms—or lockpicks, daggers, and coin clippers—and become honest citizens. It would end with decent young troublemakers becoming ardent monarchists and Rob simply couldn't let that happen. He had to be responsible, for the children if nothing else.

This left him with blackmail. If he couldn't erase all evidence of his mother's marriage, he could persuade his mother's husband—now the Duke of Clare, may the pox take him—to pay Rob handsomely to keep his secret. The duke, after all, had a son—Percy, Lord Holland, the worst sort of coxcomb—who the world thought was legitimate; surely the duke would pay through the nose to ensure his son's inheritance and protect his family from scandal, not to mention prevent infamous commoners from moving up in the world. This would be a happy arrangement for everybody concerned.

Rob supposed he could go to the duke in the manner of a beneficent fairy godmother and simply offer to forget what his mother had told him, but—given what he knew of the Duke of Clare—this would likely result in his prompt murder. Besides, he hated the Duke of Clare even more than any run-of-the-mill aristocrat and was rather looking forward to emptying the duke's purse and putting its contents to good use.

It was a good plan. A few anonymous letters, an appropriately mysterious location where he would collect his payment, and he'd go on his merry way.

But then he saw the duke's new wife: much too young for him, with disapproving black eyebrows and an obviously pregnant belly.

And so he did what anyone would do, or at least anyone with a long-standing habit of making terrible choices—he addressed his correspondence to the lady herself. She deserved to know the truth about the man she believed to be her husband. She deserved to choose whether to present him with information that might make him extremely difficult to live with. If the duke were as bad as Rob suspected, then he didn't like to think about what might become of a woman who found herself in possession of such a dangerous secret. He didn't like to think about what might become of a child who was revealed to be illegitimate. Perhaps it would be in everybody's best interest to get this business settled without the duke ever finding out. Surely, the duchess could raise a bit of money on her own.

He wrote the letter. "Dear Madam," he began—polite, but not ingratiating—"As much as one hates to be the bearer of bad news, I regret to inform you . . ." It should have ended with that letter, and indeed would have done if he had been halfway reasonable. But among all the acts of which Rob had rightly and wrongly been accused, nobody had ever accused him of making reasonable choices in matters of the heart.

And yet, nearly three months later, he still thought it was a sufficiently good plan until he tasted the laudanum in his beer and recognized the woman across the table.

October 1751
Ten Weeks Before the Incident

Dear Madam,

As much as one hates to be the bearer of bad news, I regret to inform you that the man you believe to be your husband contracted a valid marriage in 1725 to a woman who still lives. This marriage was duly recorded in the parish register of the Église du Sacré-Couer, Boulogne-sur-Mer, France. I have myself seen both the parish record and the woman. You will, of course, note that this renders invalid not only his marriage to you, but also his marriage to Lord Holland's mother.

It would give me no joy to expose these facts to the world, and I might venture to guess that you are much of the same mind. If you present me with five hundred pounds by the first of January, I will take this secret with me to the grave.

I can be reached via letter at the Lamb and Flag in Hackney. Kindly address correspondence to John Smith.

Your obedient servant,
X

Dear Sir,

How droll it is that you expect me to simply take your word for it that this woman, who if you are to be believed is the rightful Duchess of Clare, still lives. Even supposing that this purported marriage ever took place, you cannot possibly expect me to give you five hundred pounds with no evidence except what may or may not be written in a parish register somewhere in France. You must be one of those gentlemen who is unaccustomed to having his statements challenged, and as such belong to the most sadly overrepresented specimen of humanity.

You may be interested to know that Dante placed blackmailers in the eighth circle of hell, where they were thrown into boiling pits of tar and guarded by demons armed with grappling claws (or possibly hooks; I am not in the mood for accurate translation).

Your mortal enemy,
Marian, Duchess of Clare

⤬

Dear Madam,

Believe me that I would gladly present you with any evidence you could possibly desire if not for the fact that the other parties in this case require privacy. The woman in question has no desire

whatsoever to have her name bandied about town as the lawful wife
of the Duke of Clare, a man she delights in being rid of. I'm afraid I
cannot and will not give you any information about her.

Naturally, it is your right to refuse to take me at my word. I
can't say that I'd be overeager to put much stock in what a blackmailer says, myself. But whatever the case, I will present this information in as public a venue as I can dream up on the first of
January—unless, that is, you pay me five hundred pounds.

I have no idea who Dante is or what you are going on about in re:
circles but you may feel free to enlighten me.

Your obedient servant,

X

P.S. How bold of you to assume that I'm a gentleman.

P.P.S. Address correspondence to Jebediah Chisholm, care of The
Seven Stars in Putney.

⟡

Dear Sir,

Regrettably, I must concede that you are correct about the
parish register. Its contents have been verified, as has the
duke's signature. You are surely clever enough to understand that this means we also know the name of his bride
and are presently looking for Louise Thierry.

I will gladly educate you regarding Dante and any other

poets of the Italian vernacular who strike your fancy. My fee is five hundred pounds, payable immediately.

> Your mortal enemy,
> Marian, Duchess of Clare

P.S. I refuse to believe that you are a woman. There is something inexpressibly masculine about expecting to be believed.

∫

Dear Madam,

Indeed, I confess that I am a man but must refute all charges of being a gentleman. As for my being in the habit of getting my own way, I'm afraid you can't expect me to admit to any such thing.

You say that you have confirmed the contents of the parish registry. As you have not left London, this must mean you have taken somebody into your confidence. I am glad to know that at least you aren't alone in your predicament.

Considering the circumstances, I have put a guard on Madame Thierry.

> Your obedient servant,
> X

P.S. Aloysius Crowley, The Three Tuns, Soho

Dear Sir,

You have put a guard on Madame Thierry? Am I to understand that you believe I wish to harm her? What a vulgar assumption, and quite unwarranted by any of our correspondence. I hardly think myself less a sinner than any of my neighbors, but I've never committed a violent act in my life and have no wish to start now, either with my own hands or by proxy. When we find Madame Thierry, I only wish to confirm that she is who she says she is, and then—perhaps—purchase her silence. It seems unfair for you to be the only one who profits from this sad state of affairs.

As for the rest of your letter, I fear that I do not have words to convey the extent to which I am unimpressed by this show of condescension. You are pleased to know that I am not alone in my predicament, are you? Has it somehow slipped your mind that you placed me in this predicament? Has that escaped your attention? You do not strike me as an especially stupid person, but we both know what kind of judge of character I am.

Your enemy,
Marian, Duchess of Clare (for lack of anything better to call myself)

Dear Madam,

Let's not mince words. It was the duke who placed you in this predicament. I simply let you know about it. Naturally, you're cross
with me, and probably think even less of me for seeking to profit
off your troubles. But don't mistake me for the agent of your
misfortune.

I realize that I expressed myself poorly. I often do, if it comes to
that. What I meant to convey was that when one is in trouble, it is
good to have friends to rely on, or at least to confide in. Due entirely
to my own idiocy, I find myself rather alone, and I wouldn't wish
that on you or on anyone else.

The guard remains on Madame Thierry, not because I mistrust
you, but because one can never predict what unfortunate actions
will seem inevitable in the heat of the moment. This, I'm afraid, I
know from experience.

Your obedient servant,

X

P.S. Francine Delaney, The Red Lion near Covent Garden

⁓

Dear Sir,

May I humbly suggest being less of an idiot and doing
whatever it takes to make amends with your friends? Or

perhaps find some new ones? You are clearly terrible at being alone (I am excellent at it; I will give you lessons for
the reasonable fee of five hundred pounds).

I see that you're adopting a woman's name this time.
Does this mean you will collect your post in women's clothing? How intriguing.

MH

~

Dear Madam,

I avail myself of all manner of disguise. I have been a beggar, a
priest, and a sailor, and that's just in the past week.

You, of course, already know this because you've had a man following me about. I did wonder why you were so willing to write to
me. I'm not particularly experienced in blackmail but I don't believe
a sustained correspondence to be customary. Imagine my dismay
when I realized that someone has lain in wait for me to collect my
letters at the designated taverns and alehouses and then attempted
to follow me.

Naturally, my first thought was that you meant to do away
with me. This, I'm given to understand, *is* customary in blackmail
proceedings. But for various reasons that I won't bore you with, I
can't be too bothered by murder attempts. Much to my surprise,
though, nobody has laid a finger on me, which leads me to believe
that you only wish to discover my identity. I welcome your efforts
as they enlighten what would otherwise be a tedious business; it will,

however, take more than the bumbling attempts of an amateur to discover me.

Your obedient servant,

X

Elspeth Buchanan, The King's Arms, Piccadilly

∽

Dear Sir,

Goodness. Well, that certainly puts me in my place. And here I thought I was being rather clever with my letter writing ruse. Blundering amateur, indeed. I can't remember the last time I received such a set down. Or is it a compliment, given the implication that I'm not a terribly accomplished criminal?

MH

∽

Dear Madam,

I hope this missive finds you in good health and the best of spirits. Your present circumstances are of a sort that must be uniquely trying, even without the added hardship of blackmail. Given the nature of our previous correspondence, it is unlikely that you'll put much faith in what I say, dear lady, but please believe me when I say that I would much prefer never to have come into the knowledge that has formed the basis of our communications.

If I am to be frank—and, really, to whom can one be frank if not the person whose fortune and reputation one holds ransom—I would much prefer you give me the five hundred pounds and let me disappear into the night. I assure you it will be my life's work to keep your secrets. Surely, you will protest that I ought to keep your secret out of the goodness of my heart; the trouble is that my heart isn't in the least good. I am, to the core, a mercenary creature.

Please consider this letter a statement of my good faith promise to uphold my end of our bargain; while I am a rotten sort of fellow, I am not a dishonest one. I anxiously await your reply by the usual means.

Your obedient servant,

X

P.S. Andrew Marvell, The Swan, Ludgate Hill

⁓

Dear Sir,

The two glasses of wine I had with dinner must be my excuse for what I'm about to write, but . . . are you well? The tenor of your last letter makes me doubt it. Furthermore, to go from writing me nearly every second day to leaving a week between letters strikes me as very odd indeed. I assure you that I care not one whit about your well-being, so do not mistake my query for solicitude; I'm merely disconcerted by the sudden absence of a man who holds my fate in the palm of his hand. If you'll permit some (un)friendly advice, I suggest that you avail yourself of your friends at the earliest opportunity.

I will explain this to you as if you were an infant or a small dog, and I will only do so once, so please dedicate all your powers of comprehension to attending to my words. You seem to be under the impression that by keeping what you persist in calling my secret, my life will return to its previous state. However, you have exposed the father of my child as a liar and a cheat. You cannot possibly expect me to return to a parody of matrimony with a man who is not my husband. Do you imagine that I will bear him more children? I am three and twenty. What am I to do for the remainder of my life?

When I agreed to marry the duke, I made a bargain, which he did not uphold. He's thrown my life and that of my dearest friend into utter disarray and confusion, and even if you kept your secret, it would only push that confusion onto future generations. Furthermore, you are not the only person in possession of the information that you hold over my head. What you're asking me to do is to pay five hundred pounds for scant peace of mind and the dubious privilege of living as the wife of a man who has done wrong to me and to all the people I care for in this world.

MH

∽

Dear Marian,

When you put it that way, it makes this project of mine seem almost tawdry. My feelings might get hurt. In all sincerity, here is the problem: I will not keep the Duke of Clare's secret for free.

Regarding your first paragraph, you will perhaps not be surprised to learn that I managed to bollocks up all my friendships due to the small matter of having let them all believe I died a year ago. In my defense, it seemed a perfectly reasonable thing to do at the time. Now, however, I'm rather at a loss for how to explain my continued existence without incurring their wrath.

Your obedient servant,
X

P.S. Aphra Behn, The Dolphin, near the Temple Stairs

∽

You utter madman,

What is wrong with you? I mean that sincerely. Tell them you're alive, you lunatic. Of course they will be cross with you, but what kind of coward must you be to fear their anger when the alternative is their grief, not to mention your own? Do you realize how very spoiled you sound, speaking of friends, in the plural, no less, and wondering whether you can cast them aside because their entirely justified anger would inconvenience you?

Regarding your unwillingness to keep the Duke of Clare's secret for free, permit me to point out that you expect Lord Holland and I to pay for the privilege of keeping that same secret. I have neither any enthusiasm for a lifetime of deception, nor the temperament to sustain hope that the truth of our situation will remain concealed. And for this you ask five hundred pounds? You cannot possibly have thought this through.

M

P.S. This makes two letters in a row that I'm to leave for dead poets and playwrights. Have you run out of silly names to make me say aloud to unsuspecting publicans?

&

Dear Marian,

I hardly know where to begin with my worries.

First, are you delivering these letters yourself? If so, stop at once. Send a boy. Good Lord. The idea of you traipsing about in some of the quarters where I've been receiving my mail is giving me palpitations.

Second, you mention my aliases, which makes me wonder if you're saving these letters. Again, stop at once. Burn them.

> Yours in utter horror,
> R

P.S. Araminta Cleghorn, The Swan, near St. James's, a very respectable and safe part of town

ᔕ

Dear R,

Naturally I save your letters. I press them with posies between the pages of my favorite volume of poetry. Or perhaps I sleep with them beneath my pillow.

Of course I burn them, you thoroughgoing halfwit. What kind of fool do you take me for?

As for the rest, don't worry about my safety. Trust that I have the matter well in hand. I've become quite adept at climbing down the trellis and distracting the guard dogs. It's been years since I turned my hand at learning something new, and this business at least has the advantage of occupying my full faculties.

> M

ᔕ

Dear Marian,

I'm choosing to believe that you aren't serious about climbing out of windows. Perhaps you mean to give me a heart attack and thus rid yourself of me. If so, excellent work; I'll certainly have expired by dawn.

Now I need to know in what volume of poetry you would save my letters, if you had a mind to do such a harebrained thing. A week ago I would have guessed Pope, based on the sheer orderliness of his verse. But now that I know about your penchant for danger, I hardly know what to think.

Yours,
R

P.S. Christopher Marlowe, The Star, Westminster

Dear R,

I'm in some difficulties imagining what it must be like to be the sort of person who receives, much less saves, love letters. Ill-tempered women of middling looks seldom are the recipients of tender feelings; this is not a complaint, as my experience with men is such that I'd be perfectly happy to live out the rest of my days inspiring no feelings whatsoever, tender or otherwise, in any member of that sex.

At one point I might have said Donne, but I find the *Aeneid* more suitable to my present state.

M

❧

Dear Marian,

Dryden's translation? And is this an indication that your present state is violent and harassed by the gods?

I regret to inform you that ill-tempered women, regardless of looks, are as catnip to some men. The fact that you do not know this alarms me.

Yours,
R

P.S. Anna Gentry, The Angel, Islington

❧

Dear R,

The original Latin, and emphatically yes.

There's something infinitely comforting in reading about the misadventures of people who have managed to ruin their lives even more comprehensively than one has done oneself. Naturally, I'm speaking of Dido, whose principal problem is

Aeneas but whose secondary problem is a stunning lack of perspective. When she fails to fortify the walls of Carthage (it's been a while, so please forgive my poor memory) in favor of dallying with Aeneas I want to shake her; things, of course, only get worse from there.

M

Dear Marian,

I can't believe I'm about to write a defense of Aeneas and Dido, and that entirely based on seeing Purcell's opera some years ago and a copy of Dryden's translation that I skimmed this evening. First, you really can't fault Dido for neglecting her duties in favor of Aeneas when she was quite literally *made to do so* by the gods. She didn't stand a chance. You can see her poor mind start to go, which seems like precisely what would become of anyone who was pushed around by no fewer than three gods.

This is probably a regrettable example of my modern sensibilities failing to grasp the nuances of the classical mind, but honestly I do not give a fig and feel nothing but compassion for all the poor fools in all those tiresome epics.

Furthermore, I take issue with your statement that you ruined your life. One, it isn't ruined. Two, you didn't do anything wrong.

Yours in ignorance,

R

P.S. Samuel McAllister, The George and Dragon, near Billingsgate Fish Market

〜

Dear R,

Forgive me, but I'll be the judge as to whether my own life is ruined. Rest assured I'm not going to throw myself on any funeral pyres, though.

I believe it's a total of five gods who conspire to bedevil poor Dido, and when you think of it like that, it's most unfair that Dante has her in hell (albeit one of the outermost circles) for her lust. If she were to be punished for anything, it ought to be poor management of Carthage's building projects.

Have you reconciled with your friends? It's probably terribly indelicate of me to allude to things I learn in the course of following you about, but I have seen you lingering in the vicinity of a certain coffeehouse even though that establishment is closed for the night. You look very sad, and sometimes you even forget to keep to the darkest shadows, which I can only interpret as a sign of great distress and distraction, as you ordinarily have no trouble at all evading me. Screw your courage to the sticking place (whatever that means). Just get it over with. Go inside.

M

◦⟡◦

Dear Marian,

I took your advice. I was slapped, scolded, and otherwise abused but I think they're more or less at peace with my being, as you once put it, an utter lunatic. For reasons that are too complicated to put on paper, I can't give them the reason for my deception. But, as fate would have it, they seem to understand that for me to have done what I did, I must have had a compelling cause. I'm relieved that they seem more pleased by my existence than dismayed by my dishonesty.

Now it's my turn to be indelicate. Trust me that I'd have been done away with years ago if I wasn't able to keep track of when I am and am not in the shadows; if you can see me, it's because I'm letting you see me. You didn't think I'd let you wander about town without being on hand to offer you aid in the event you came to grief, did you?

R

P.S. Theodore Pike, The Saracen's Head, near Smithfield Market

◦⟡◦

Dear R,

Of course they're glad you're alive. I hope you don't need me to point out that this is what makes them your friends.

As for the rest of your letter, I won't even do you the courtesy of a response. Perhaps tonight I'll sneak up on you and steal your hat.

Yours,
Marian

∽

Dearest Marian,

May I suggest that tonight, instead of stealing my hat, you talk to me? It's come to my attention that our social spheres overlap somewhat, and also that we are each in possession of information that might do the other some good.

If that doesn't suit, we could meet in daylight, if you can contrive it.

Your obedient servant,
R

P.S. Adam Clark, The Bull and Bush, Kensington

Chapter 1

*A*s soon as the man passed out—very anticlimactically, Marian was disappointed to note, just like falling asleep—Marian pulled the silk cord from her pocket and set to work binding his wrists. Things were going remarkably well, for once; perhaps she was finally reaping the benefits of meticulous planning. Downstairs in the decidedly seedy public house that the man was wont to frequent, she had slipped the laudanum in his drink and then lured him upstairs before he showed signs of being the worse for wear. When she suggested a hand of cards, he had very obligingly collapsed before she had even finished dealing them out.

"He didn't even finish his beer," Dinah observed when she entered the hired room, bolting the door behind her. "How much did you put in there?"

"It was the same amount you gave me to take after Eliza was born." Marian had measured it out very carefully, making sure not to include a drop more or a drop less. The goal, after all, was only to knock the man out long enough to bind him. Marian did not fancy herself a murderer.

Dinah frowned skeptically and nudged the man with the toe of her boot.

Marian finished tying the knot and got to her feet. "Come, you can kick him all you like later on, but first let's get him into bed."

"Why?"

"I beg your pardon?"

"Why don't we just leave him there?"

They both looked at the recumbent form of the blackmailer. His wrists were secured, and he looked comfortable enough, not that Marian particularly cared about whether the swine was comfortable, even if he was bound to wake up mightily sore after spending the night on the cold, bare floor.

"He needs to be in the bed so I can tie him to the bedposts," Marian decided.

Dinah shrugged a sort of pro forma acquiescence. Marian supposed that she was not paying Dinah nearly enough to pretend that anything happening in this room made sense or was a good idea. Marian had parted company with good ideas some while ago. The very next day Percy was going to hold up his father's carriage in order to steal a book the duke—which was to say Percy's father, of course—would pay handsomely to have returned to him. This, they hoped, would give Percy, Marian, and Marian's daughter enough to live on. A year ago, Marian would have been appalled by the recklessness of this scheme, but a year ago Marian hadn't been worn down by a run of catastrophes. A year ago Marian hadn't known what it meant to be desperate.

Right now, her principal concern was making sure that Rob was *hors de combat* during tomorrow's hold up. Percy's highwayman friend trusted Rob, but probably a lot of people who ought to know better trusted Rob.

With his wrists bound together, it was impossible to get a purchase on his arms. He kept flopping about like a rag doll—except a rag doll who was considerably larger than either of the women.

"You need to untie the knot," Dinah said.

"I don't want to. If he wakes up, he'll kill us."

"He's not going to kill us. You're worth five hundred pounds to him."

That was about as comforting a thought as she was likely to have in these circumstances. "All right," Marian said, and knelt to untie the knot. "Quick, now." They each grabbed an arm and hauled him across the room, the heels of his boots dragging on the bare wood floor. As soon as he was on the bed, Marian tied one of his wrists to the bedpost and breathed a sigh of relief. She took another cord from her pocket—she had come prepared with enough cords to tie up a squid—and set to work on the other arm.

Only when he was secured did she let herself look at him. The scant light in the shabby room came from a branch of candles that sat on the card table beside two abandoned hands of Mariage and a pair of pewter tankards containing ale laced with laudanum. She retrieved the candle branch and held it over the man's unconscious form. She had seen him before, of course, but only from a distance and under cover of night, and she had been more concerned with following his movements than in studying his features.

He had reddish hair, which he wore unpowdered and in a queue. He was about her own age, give or take a year or two. There was a scar bisecting one eyebrow, and another on his cheek. Stubble grew in faint and ruddy along his jaw.

Disconcertingly, a bridge of freckles crossed his nose and then scattered all over the rest of his face. She felt certain that blackmailers shouldn't have freckles. It seemed a decidedly unvillainous characteristic. Then again, she supposed she didn't much look like a kidnapper or poisoner; she had always thought her profile sadly lacking in panache.

She moved to put the candles back on the table, but Dinah stayed her, clamping a hand on Marian's wrist. Marian watched in some chagrin as Dinah cast what appeared to be an appreciative eye over the blackmailer.

Marian snatched her hand away, plunging the recumbent figure into shadows. "You'll have plenty of time to admire him when you check on him throughout the day."

"Unless there's a baby," Dinah said, because she had a life outside aiding and abetting felonies, alas.

"I'll come back as soon as I can." With any luck, by then she and Percy would have what they needed from the duke and wouldn't need to worry about the blackmailer anymore. All she needed to do was ensure that when Percy held up the duke's carriage, this man was far away and therefore couldn't interfere. He was precisely the sort of man who did interfere, who made an absolute sacrament of sticking his nose where it didn't belong, and she couldn't afford any of that. Tomorrow night she would let him go and never have to think about him again.

She didn't know why, after a year of relentlessly dismal luck, she thought things could possibly start to go her way now.

Chapter 2

*R*ob knew he had been drugged before he was quite conscious. He was hardly inexperienced with opium; God knew he had had enough of it poured down his throat before having bones shoved back into place or wounds sewn shut to know how it made his mouth dry, his thoughts clouded.

Then he remembered who had drugged him, and his eyes flew open. Only then did he realize that his wrists were tied and that he was alone.

Rob didn't much care for being restrained. He supposed few people did, but he had spent enough time imprisoned to have an especially dim view of the practice. He was decidedly against it and would make sure Marian had a piece of his mind when she got back. If she got back.

Of course she would come back. She couldn't mean to let him rot alone in a tiny room. If she wanted to murder him she would have done precisely that; she was not a woman who did things by halves or who balked at taking decisive action. This was a comforting thought. Besides, he could hear people in the street below; he could always scream, he supposed.

Or he could—he tugged one of his wrists—yes, he could. These weren't proper ropes and they certainly weren't shackles. They were scarcely stronger than hair ribbons and conveniently silky. His neck was predictably stiff but he was able to turn his head far enough to the side to see what he was doing. Yes, if he moved his thumb, and . . . all right, that hurt quite a bit, and a broken finger wasn't going to do him any good right now. He took a deep breath and forced himself to ignore his rising panic and instead work slowly.

With a great deal of fidgeting, he managed to get his index finger and thumb onto the knot, and from there it was simply a matter of time before he was able to loosen it. He shut his eyes so he wouldn't sense the nearness of the walls or imagine that they were drawing closer and worked by touch alone. And then, just like that, he had his hand out.

He was absolutely going to tell Marian that the next time she saw fit to attempt any abductions, she must first practice her knots. And she was never ever again to use what appeared to be the sash to a dressing gown, for heaven's sake. She had done remarkably well, though, for an amateur. He hadn't recognized her until he had downed enough laudanum to put him out for half the night.

His head still felt full of cotton wool, but he had the uneasy sense that something was wrong—something other than having been kidnapped and held prisoner, that was. He untied his other wrist and shook out his hands, then got shakily to his feet. He felt at his hip for his dagger, only to find that it was missing. That was sensible; he should have expected nothing less of Marian. He reached into his boot and found that the smaller dagger he hid in the lining was still present and accounted for. That was convenient for him, but clearly Marian needed to be educated in the art of concealed weaponry.

Then, his heart in his throat, he traced a finger along the inner lining of his coat, felt the familiar crinkle of papers, and breathed a sigh of relief.

Judging by the light that made its way through the grimy windowpane, it was already midmorning, which meant—dammit to hell. Today was the day of the robbery. He ought to already be at the inn in Oxfordshire, making sure the duke's outriders were appropriately liquored up and their pistols conveniently missing. Now it would be too late to get there in time, and Kit would think Rob had left him high and dry.

He rapidly went through what he knew, willing the laudanum haze to clear from his mind. The duke's son—the one who had, until about a month ago, believed himself to be the duke's legitimate heir—had enlisted the help of Rob's oldest friend, Kit, in holding up his father's carriage. Rob had no idea what the devil the fellow thought he was going to get in this robbery, and he certainly didn't know how the Duke of bloody Clare's son had got his hands on Kit's name as someone who might commit highway robbery for hire.

He also didn't know what had possessed Kit to (1) agree to this madness and (2) fall in love with the man. Rob was the one who fell in love indiscriminately; Kit was the one who told him he was an idiot and grimly patted his shoulder when things fell apart. Rob was entirely unsure how to operate now that the boot was on the other foot.

Rob had agreed to help with the robbery but decided not to tell Kit his own relation to the Duke of Clare or that he had been engaged in a bit of light blackmail.

But now Rob regretted his silence. If Marian had decided to put Rob out of commission for the robbery—and there could be no other explanation for her actions—that meant that she knew not only that he was blackmailing her, but that he was Kit's partner in crime. And so she had, apparently, done what she had to in order to make sure Kit had to go through with the robbery without Rob's help. That was not good. It almost made him mistrustful of her motives.

There would be time later on to think about that. Right now he had to get out before Marian returned.

Chapter 3

There had been a time when Marian would have described herself as an intelligent woman, or at least not an idiot. Or, if an idiot, certainly not the most benighted fool in the kingdom. Now she was quite certain that even the greatest simpleton in all the world could not have bungled things to the extent that she had done. She was coming to believe that she had an unprecedented talent for catastrophe, a rare and legendary gift.

When she and her daughter found themselves destitute and friendless, perhaps Marian could earn her living by penning her memoirs, a cautionary tale for young ladies who might think themselves clever enough to solve all their family's problems through the simple expedient of marrying up in the world. *Marriage: Far More Trouble Than You Might Think* would be the title of her treatise. Although, even that probably wouldn't be of much use to anybody, as she had to believe that marrying bigamous dukes was not a problem that afflicted too many women. At least, she hoped it wasn't, because she wouldn't wish it on her worst enemy. Not that she knew who her worst enemy was anymore—at this point one could people a village with contenders to that title.

No, that was inaccurate, and even in desperate times one must resist the urge to resort to self-deception: her worst enemy was the duke, second was herself, and third was her blackmailer.

Now, that was a fortifying thought, and one she would be sure to include in her next letter. "Dear Sir, Under ordinary circumstances you might congratulate yourself on having achieved the rank of my chief enemy, but as things stand, you're only third on the list, quite possibly lower if we consider the rightful claims of my eldest brother and several members of Parliament."

She absently flicked some of the dried blood off the sleeve of her traveling costume and abruptly remembered that there would be no more letters. The robbery had been—she glanced at the body beside her—not a success. Instead of stealing a book of secrets from the duke and holding it ransom for enough money that she and Percy wouldn't have to live as paupers, she had killed the duke, or near enough so as not to matter. The man was still breathing, but he was also still bleeding, and as the carriage raced along the London road, he was doing rather more of the latter and less of the former. By morning, Percy would be the new duke.

Except—no. Percy would not be the duke. The plan had been to expose the duke's bigamy to the world; that had been the worst punishment they had been able to devise and had the added benefit of freeing both Percy and Marian from his control. The fact of the duke's bigamy would transform Percy into a worthless illegitimate son and Marian into a former mistress. And it would transform the son of a harlot into the duke's heir, but Marian didn't care about that poor fool; what mattered was that she and Percy would be rid of the duke. But if the duke was dead, Marian didn't know where that left them.

Marian's mind wasn't working very well at all, it seemed. She was not thinking, but she was also not feeling, which seemed like a fair enough exchange. Doubtless it was the shock. She could still hear the pistol shots, both of them—first the one the duke aimed at Percy, and then the one she aimed at the duke. Percy had been hit, but only in the leg, and not so badly he couldn't walk. She couldn't think about that. There was nothing she could do about Percy, other than make sure nobody ever knew he had anything to do with the duke's injury. Which, of course, he hadn't. It had been entirely Marian's doing.

The blood had soaked through her left sleeve and a fair amount of spatter covered the left side of her bodice, and, presumably, her face. She was vaguely aware that she was uncomfortable, but the discomfort of her body seemed to be taking place many miles away and possibly to somebody else.

Somehow, they were already at the fringes of London. Marian must have spent most of the journey from Oxfordshire in a stupor. That, and the horses were traveling at a breakneck pace to get the dying duke back to town, where he could be attended by his physician. If he lived that long, that was.

"The duke was shot by brigands," Marian announced to the butler when the carriage arrived at Clare House. "Call for his physician at once. No, I'm unharmed." She repeated it again to the housekeeper, and then, once the men were attempting to get the duke out of the carriage and the rest of the household milled about, trying to look as if they weren't gawking, Marian slipped around the back of the house, grabbed an old cloak off a peg in the stables, and took off through the darkened streets.

She did not fancy being hanged as a murderer. However certain she was that nobody had seen her use the pistol, there was always a chance that she would be exposed. And if she were hanged, she'd be of no use to Eliza, Percy, or her father, none of whom were capable of sensibly arranging their lives without her. Eliza was an infant; Marian's father was elderly and infirm; and Percy, however reasonable she once thought him, had fallen in love with a highwayman and therefore plainly had taken leave of his faculties, the poor man.

She would have to hide until she knew whether she was suspected of murder and then, if necessary, flee to the Continent. How she would arrange everybody's affairs from—Venice, perhaps, as her Italian was more than passable and Percy had spoken highly of the climate—she did not yet know, but these were problems she could solve when she wasn't quite so consumed with the pressing need to get the blood off her person.

There was also something else she had to do: she had left a man tied to a bed, and she needed to make sure he was . . . *well* might not be entirely accurate. But if Dinah had been called away or something had happened to prevent her from checking on him, then he might be left there indefinitely, and Marian wasn't going to be responsible for a man starving to death. Being responsible for one death a day was quite sufficiently iniquitous.

In breeches and sensible boots, it was a fifteen-minute walk to the room she had hired to keep the blackmailer. In a traveling gown and dainty ankle boots, it took far longer. She was out of breath, more from nerves than exertion, when she climbed the final set of stairs, but her hands were almost steady when she removed the key from above the door frame and turned it in the lock.

The room was empty and dark and the window stood wide open. It took a moment for her eyes to adjust to the shadows and another moment still for her thoughts to catch up to her eyes. The bed was empty. The man was gone.

Well, it hardly mattered now, did it. She had only wanted to ensure that he was out of the way and didn't jeopardize the robbery, but the robbery had already gone about as badly as it could have done. Good riddance, then. One less thing to worry about.

Marian tried to rummage through the buzzing chaos in her mind and figure out what to do. She was covered in blood, standing in a room she had hired for the express purpose of imprisoning a man, and she didn't know what to do next. Well, whatever she did, she couldn't do it in the dark, so she took the tinderbox from the chimneypiece and got to work. Her fingers were stiff, possibly with cold, possibly with whatever was making her brain not work, and only after what felt like an hour did she manage to light the splint.

She took the letters from inside her cloak and set them on the grate, then touched the splint to them. They must have dried, or perhaps blood was more flammable than Marian had supposed, because they readily caught on fire. She prodded them with the splint until they were reduced to ash, troubled by the sense that she was bidding a last goodbye to the woman who had received those letters and who had responded to them in what had almost been a spirit of amusement, heaven help her.

With the candles lit, she could see the empty bed, the cords she had used to bind the man's wrists now dangling ineffectively from the bedposts. So, she had bungled the knots. It figured that she hadn't even managed to get that much right.

Her thoughts were interrupted by a sound at the window. She spun around to see a man climbing in, one long leg after the other.

It appeared that she was going to get murdered now, which was a fitting end to a miserable day. She ought to cry out, but she couldn't even do that much. The only sound she managed to produce was a sharp inhalation. Not that screaming would have done much good—this was the sort of street where nobody paid much attention to the odd bout of hollering.

Then the intruder rose to his full height. When the candlelight struck his face she saw that it was the blackmailer.

And she was . . . relieved? Probably a clear sign that she wasn't thinking straight.

"What are you doing?" she asked, struggling to understand the picture before her. If he had freed himself, then why had he come back?

"I'm afraid I had to step out," the blackmailer said, dusting off his breeches. "I had to feed the dog."

"You don't have a dog," Marian said, latching onto the only part of his statement that made any sense. "I've been tailing you for weeks. You live in a hired room in an alarming neighborhood filled with writers. You don't even have a spare pair of boots, let alone a dog."

"The cat, then," he said, waving a breezy hand.

Then her thoughts belatedly supplied the obvious reason for his return. "If you've come back in order to kill me, may I ask that you get it over with? It's been a tedious day."

"That wasn't the plan at all." Only then did he raise his eyes and look at her. "Not to be overly forward, but may I ask whose blood you're covered in? It doesn't appear to be yours, what with how you aren't dead yet. Chiefly, I'm interested in whether it belongs to Kit."

"It's the duke's blood, and it's on my gown, rather than in his veins, because I shot him." Saying it aloud made her feel that she was watching herself from a great height, as if the events of this day and this night were happening to some other unfortunate person.

"Ah," he said, as if she had merely remarked on the weather.

"Unfasten this, will you?" She turned her back on him, which was not a wise idea, tactically, but all her cleverness had resulted in nothing but disaster, so perhaps she'd just settle for flailing ineptitude. Besides, if she didn't get this blood-soaked gown off, she thought she might go raving mad.

She heard his footsteps approach her, then felt a light pressure at her waist. She flinched. "Only looking for your laces," he said mildly. "And there we go."

She felt him untie the tapes at her waist with deftness that suggested a fair bit of practice, but without taking any liberties or even letting his hands linger. The stiffening fabric released itself from her body and she held back a sigh of relief. She stepped out of the skirt and pulled the bodice over her head. They'd need to be burned. She glanced down at her petticoats and sighed. So would they. Her corset, too. Just as well. She took it all off and threw it into a pile, leaving her in nothing but an only moderately bloody shift.

Dimly, she was aware that she was stripping in front of a strange man, but she'd have stripped onstage in an opera house, she'd have stripped in a cathedral in the middle of Sunday services, if it meant getting out of those clothes.

In a small trunk at the foot of the bed, she kept breeches, a shirt, and a full complement of everything she had worn to tail the blackmailer night after night during these past weeks. It had seemed a reasonable precaution, keeping a change of clothes handy, just in case. And for once on this terrible day, her forethought was rewarded, because now she had a clean shirt, and nothing had ever looked as good to her as that piece of linen did at that moment.

"You don't want to put that on," said the man. He was now sitting at the table, lazily shuffling the deck of cards she had dealt the previous night before he succumbed to the laudanum. He did not appear to be watching Marian at all. "Trust me. First, get the blood off. And while you're at it, make sure that none of it is coming from you. Sometimes you don't realize you've hurt yourself until much later, and then you'll have ruined another shirt."

Marian experienced a rush of mad relief at the idea that she might be in the presence of someone who knew what to do when one had murdered one's husband. Because Marian was at a loss, and she didn't much care for being at a loss. She was not the sort of person who sailed through life without a plan, and even though all her plans had resulted in disaster didn't mean she was suddenly averse to the idea of planning ahead, as long as she wasn't the one doing the planning. If this man had the first idea of what to do, she'd take it.

There was an ewer of water on the washstand, but no cloth. She was going to have to rummage through her filthy clothes for a scrap of linen that was clean enough to wash herself, but she doubted there were three square inches of unbloodied fabric in that entire mess.

The man held out a kerchief, almost absently, still not looking up from his cards.

She took it and used it to clean herself as best as she could without a looking glass. Every swipe of the smooth linen against her skin was a relief, as if by scrubbing hard enough she might make it so this day had never happened.

Chapter 4

*R*ob had spent the evening watching the coffeehouse. The plan had been for Kit to return there after the robbery, but instead of Kit, the hired scout returned alone and in an obviously flustered state.

Before that, Rob hadn't borne Marian any ill will. He had been ready to let bygones be bygones. He blackmailed her; she kidnapped him. The slate was clean.

But if she had kidnapped him in order to do something that harmed Kit, all bets were off. So he had gone back to that ghastly little room with the aim of lying in wait.

And now, well, Rob knew what it looked like when a person was in shock. He had been there often enough for it to be as familiar as home. The only tried and true method of dealing with shock was time: you had to let it run its course, and then your mind settled over its new and troubling set of facts like a clean sheet draped over a body.

This woman—covered in blood but still straight-backed and acid-tongued—was the same person who had written him all those letters. All his abominable instincts told him to get her a blanket and some tea. But first he had to take advantage of the way the shock had loosened her tongue and see what information he could extract from her.

"Is your plan to have Kit hang for the duke's murder?" Rob asked when Marian had finished washing and had on a layer of clothing.

He wasn't expecting an honest answer but he also wasn't expecting her to look at him as if highly disappointed to discover how very stupid he was. "If you think I have a plan right now, you've badly misread this situation. I didn't mean for the duke to be shot either by me or anybody else. My plan was for him to live and to give me money. Now that he's dead, he can't very well do that, can he? At the moment, all I want is for neither Percy nor myself to hang for it. And I'd rather your idiot friend not be hanged, either, as that would make Percy cross."

Well. That all aligned nicely with Rob's own interests, if she were being honest, which was very much an open question. "Did anyone see you shoot the duke?"

"No," she said, but with a thread of doubt in her voice. "We were inside the carriage, so nobody ought to have been able to see, but I can't be certain. I told everyone—the coachman and the outriders and so forth—that the highwayman shot the duke, and I think they believed me. I also told them that the duke shot the highwayman, and I think they believed that, too, but that's no credit to me, as it's only the truth."

Rob took a moment to untangle this. "Who did the duke shoot?"

"Percy. It was only his leg, and he was able to walk afterward. I must say, one does not enjoy seeing one's friends shot, however minor the injury."

Rob could not disagree. If Lord Holland had been hurt, that would explain both Kit's failure to return to London and the scout's flustered state. "The duke shot Lord Holland first, and then you shot the duke?"

"Precisely."

So far, she was answering questions rather more coherently than he might have expected. Most people found that being recently doused in blood was not compatible with retaining one's faculties. "Did the duke keep two pistols?" She wouldn't have had the opportunity to reload the pistol.

She hesitated at that. "I used Percy's pistol. I took it from his hand and shot the duke with it."

"Where is it now?"

She gestured at the pile of dirty clothes. "In my pocket, somewhere in there."

Now, that was very good. It wouldn't do for a strange pistol to be found in the carriage. He reached into his coat and produced a flask, which he offered to her. She looked like she could use a drink.

She looked skeptically at the flask, which was mighty rich. He took a drink himself, made an expression that he hoped conveyed that *he,* at least, didn't go about poisoning people, and again offered it to her. This time she drank, wincing at what he could only assume was the unfamiliar taste of gin.

"What will you do now?" he asked.

"My—" She narrowed her eyes, as if suddenly realizing who she was talking to. "What business is it of yours?"

He could have told her that everything she did was his business until he knew that Kit wasn't in danger. Instead he shrugged. "Call me a Good Samaritan."

She made a noise that told him precisely what she thought of that suggestion. "I mean to go to my father's house in Kent."

He knew that her father was the Earl of Eynsham. Perhaps she thought that her father would be able to protect her from arrest. "It makes far more sense for you to go home, play the grieving widow, and repeat your tale about the highwayman to anyone who asks. Fleeing only looks suspicious."

Her gaze shifted from withering to glacial. He was impressed. "This is none of your concern," she said, crisply enunciating each syllable.

He tried a different tack, because he felt it was his duty to discourage this harebrained scheme. "Haven't you got a daughter? She's nothing but a baby. Who's looking after her while you gallivant up and down the London road?"

If the look she gave him a moment earlier was cold, the one she gave him now was outright pestilential. It took some doing to summon up that level of sneery contempt while wearing shabby breeches and an untucked shirt, but Marian managed it. "I hardly need you to remind me of my responsibilities." She unpinned her hair and shook it out, then set about plaiting it. It fell like black silk over her shoulder. Rob looked away. "I'll need to take you with me, of course," she went on.

He raised his eyebrows. "Is that so?"

"I can't just leave you here, free to stir up whatever trouble strikes your fancy."

"Now, what trouble could I possibly stir up?" he asked, mainly to see if her glare could get even more severe.

"You've been blackmailing me," she said with exaggerated patience. "Now you have even more to blackmail me about. Not to mention, this would be an extremely inconvenient time for the invalidity of my marriage to become public knowledge."

He considered pointing out that this made no sense. It was hardly worth his trouble to blackmail her if she were on the gallows. Surely she was clever enough to have figured that out.

But if she wanted to take him with her, he hardly objected—he had no intention of letting her out of his sight until he had satisfied himself that she wasn't going to do anything to bring Kit's name into this disaster. Going along with her to Kent would be much easier than attempting to follow her. And besides, she needed someone with an intact set of wits to accompany her because hers were plainly in shambles.

There was also the fact that he longed to follow her about like a dog on a lead, just for the pleasure of finally being near her after months of thinking about her, but this was a trifling matter.

"What's in it for me?" he asked, because not to ask would be suspicious.

"I have little to offer."

"Now, that's a lie. I daresay your father's house is filled to the rafters with things you could offer me. But that's not what I want from you." As he watched, her back stiffened and he realized his error. "No, not that, for Christ's sake. What a very boring thing to negotiate for." Now she looked offended and he almost laughed. "What I want is for the duke's legitimate heir not to inherit."

She raised an eyebrow. "You know him?"

"He isn't the sort of man who ought to be a duke." That wasn't even a lie: Rob was indeed not the sort of man who ought to be a duke, primarily because he didn't think dukes ought to exist.

"I'll forbear from pointing out that if you were so worried about this man inheriting, you could have left well enough alone and simply not blackmailed me. You could have kept the duke's bigamy to yourself."

He ground his teeth. "It was complicated."

"As far as my ability to ensure that Percy inherits, don't you think I would have done so already if that were in my power? Do you think I'd have resorted to highway robbery and poisoning and kidnapping, not to mention a fair bit of larceny, if I had any other recourse?"

"You *have* been busy," he murmured, thinking of what a waste it was that in all the thousands of love poems written across the ages, nobody had ever thought to catalogue their beloved's proficiency in crime. "In any event, I don't care in the least whether Lord Holland inherits. I don't care who inherits, in fact, as long as it isn't the duke's heir by his legal wife."

She looked at him thoughtfully. "I could try."

He held out his hand and she stared at it for the space of a few heartbeats before reaching out. He expected her hand to be cool, but it was almost hot to the touch. He shook it as he would the hand of anyone with whom he had made a bargain, then let it drop.

"It'll be too late to get a stagecoach," Rob observed, stretching his legs out. She looked sharply at him. So, she had thought he'd demand more from her. "Don't act so surprised," he said. "You've already killed one man today. I don't wish to be the second."

He heard her suck in a breath. "He was alive when I left him at Clare House."

"Well, you'd better hope he dies before he can tell anyone who shot him. That, in case you hadn't noticed, would be a good reason for you to stay in London."

She looked aghast. "Are you suggesting I—"

"I'm suggesting that it would be prudent to finish what you started." He felt honor bound to at least point this out. "Barring that, either we wait until dawn for a coach, or we hire horses and leave now. Can you ride?"

Another icy look came his way. "Yes, I can ride."

"Can you ride fast? Not sidesaddle."

"I can ride fast astride *and* sidesaddle."

The next time he found himself inside a church, he would light a candle for the patron saint of thieves and vagabonds, whoever that busy fellow might be, because he had not been looking forward to spending any time at all in a cramped coach. "And you have the money to hire horses, I hope. I'm not particularly keen on funding my own abduction."

"Of course I do," she said. She retrieved a coin purse from the pile of garments on the floor and tucked it into her pocket. He followed it with his eyes. It was always good to know where the money was.

"Excellent, then," he said, getting to his feet and folding his newspaper. He watched as she ransacked a chest of drawers that he had hardly noticed.

"I need to leave a note for my friend, to let her know what happened."

"Christ, no. Don't leave it here. If you absolutely must, you can write a note at the first inn we pass and send it in the post."

"I'm not leaving a signed confession, you ridiculous man. I'm letting her know that I'm alive and so are you, so she doesn't spend the next week worrying about getting arrested for murder. I feel keenly the unpleasantness of that position."

"Have it your way." He rummaged through his haversack until he turned up a scrap of paper and a pencil. She scribbled something on the paper and tossed it on the bed.

He picked it up, of course, ignoring anything he might be tempted to feel at the sight of that familiar handwriting. *Both of us are well. Change of plans.* No signature, no initial. He put it back where he had found it. "Now, gather up your clothes and the pistol."

She picked up a cloak but nudged the remainder of the pile with her boot. "I don't need any of that. We can leave it behind."

"The point, my dear lady, is to leave as little evidence as possible connecting you with this place. Your story is going to be that you were in a state of extreme shock after your husband was viciously struck down by brigands, and in that vulnerable state you sought the protection and comfort of your father. You've never been to this place and neither have I."

She looked at him for a moment and seemed on the verge of arguing. Then she nodded and stooped to gather her clothes in a bundle.

"The pistol as well," he said. "Actually, give the pistol to me."

"I'm not giving you a weapon," she scoffed.

"Marian, darling," he said. "Don't be daft." He opened his coat. He wasn't sure whether she'd be able to see his own pistol in the dark but trusted that the candlelight at least illuminated the hilts of his knives. Her eyes went wide.

"Naturally," she said. "You needed to equip yourself to walk your dog."

"I thought we decided it was a cat. Now, give me the pistol. Unless you somehow managed to reload it, it won't do you any good anyway. You said it was Lord Holland's?"

She handed him the pistol with obvious reluctance. He made sure it wasn't loaded and tucked it into the waistband of his breeches.

"After you," he said, opening the door into the stairwell, and watched her sail out, the hood of her cloak up over her head, not sparing the room a backward glance over her shoulder.

Chapter 5

*D*uring her previous nighttime forays into the streets of London, Marian had primarily relied on stealth and shadow to keep safe.

Tonight, this man attempted neither. He walked briskly down the middle of the street, boot heels clicking on cobblestone, his cape flying behind him. Marian was tall, but he was taller, and she had to strain to keep pace with him.

They proceeded south and east, passing through narrow lanes lined with crooked houses out into wide avenues boasting great guildhalls, and then back again to narrow passages. The rank smell of the river met her nose, and when she looked around she was surprised to find that she knew where she was. Before her stood the monument to the Great Fire and beyond it the clock tower of St. Magnus. This was a part of town Marian knew only from having tailed the man who now led her, but it seemed that she had learned it well enough.

When London Bridge came into view, the man barely broke stride as he stooped to pick up what appeared to be a brick. She supposed that she ought to worry that she was about to be bludgeoned and summarily cast into the river, but he would hardly need a brick to do away with her when he was armed to the teeth with weapons that were more suited to the purpose. Come to that, he wouldn't need any weapons at all if he simply pushed her into the Thames.

She decided that at some point in the distant, unimaginable future she would think about why she was worried about none of those things. For now, she crossed the bridge.

There was only one roadway along the bridge, hemmed in by looming houses. For all it was the middle of the night, it was far from quiet—there was the steady hum of the river below and muffled nighttime sounds from the buildings that surrounded them: a hissing cat, a crying baby, not to mention the usual rustling and scurrying that came from all darkened corners of London.

At the sound of the baby she clenched her teeth. There was no sense in thinking about it. Eliza had a nice warm house and people to look after her. Marian's feelings on the subject were of no consequence. What mattered was that Eliza was safe. In a few days, Marian would ensure that her father was safe, as well. She ought to have checked in on him months ago, but during her confinement she had been in no state to go so far as the dining room, let alone Canterbury. Surely, the housekeeper or nurse would have written if the earl's condition had worsened. She couldn't quite imagine what worse would look like: a year ago, he was unable to remember the names of most people around him, or whether he was at Chiltern Hall or Little Hinton. That was why, when she needed to get her father away from the gaze of her eldest brother, Richard, who boasted that he would send their father off to an institution at the slightest provocation, Marian seized on Little Hinton, the house where her father had spent the first fifty years of his life, as the solution to their problems. She ought to have asked her other brother, Marcus, to check on their father, but Marcus had been busy both with his own affairs and with investigating the duke's bigamy. And, really, did it always have to fall to her to tell people what they ought to be doing?

When they reached the drawbridge, the man held out his hand. For a moment she thought that he was offering comfort or understanding or something equally impertinent and irrelevant. But he only wanted the bundle of bloody clothing she carried under her cloak. When she handed it to him, he did something with the brick, swiftly knotting the remains of her petticoat around it, then dropped the parcel into the churning river below. She resisted the urge to watch the bundle fall. Somehow, she trusted that it would reach the water, rather than landing on one of the great island-like starlings that supported the bridge's many arches. She had the distinct sense that this was not the first time this man had dropped something off this bridge, and also that he could be relied upon to dispose of incriminating evidence.

Despite the roadway being closed in by houses and shielded from the worst of the wind, it was colder on the bridge than it had been on solid ground. The cold distracted her from the thoughts that had begun to pound at her mind like a bill collector at the door. She had killed a man, or near enough to it so as not to matter. And it hadn't been in self-defense. It hadn't even been in Percy's defense, at least not in any kind of sense that would matter to a judge. She didn't even know if it mattered in a moral sense, or an ethical sense, or whatever standard she was supposed to apply to her conscience.

Whatever it was, she probably ought to feel something about it. Remorse would seem to be the bare minimum, and some sorrow or anger wouldn't go amiss. But all of her emotions had deserted her, leaving her brain a scrubbed-out husk. On the one hand, this was tremendously convenient, as she doubted that any emotion her mind might see fit to generate presently would be one she enjoyed very much. On the other hand, the sensation was rather like standing up only to discover that her feet had gone numb.

On the south side of the river, they passed one church and then another. So many churches. She tried to remember the song Eliza's nursery maid sang to her, cheerfully listing out churches and ending, improbably, with a beheading. Or perhaps not so improbably—the main thrust of childrearing seemed to be to keep children from the gallows, and with good reason; she had a doting and indulgent parent and easily hoodwinked governesses and look what had become of her. The path to sin and ruination was much shorter than she might have guessed.

The man looked back at her and she realized she had been humming the song about church bells. She stopped.

"There's no use dwelling on it," he said, turning a corner. "It's never an easy feeling, when you know you've sent a man out of the world. I'd tell you that it gets easier, but it doesn't."

"That's not—you don't know what you're talking about." She

supposed she ought to be more alarmed by the fact that he had just confessed to killing more than one person, but she no longer felt capable of alarm.

"I wish I didn't, sweetheart, but I'm a storehouse of information on the topic."

She sniffed and carried on following him through a neighborhood that seemed to consist entirely of taverns, graveyards, and still more churches.

"I don't know your name," she said. "If we mean to travel together, I need to know what to call you."

For the first time since the drawbridge, he halted. "You know my name," he said, turning toward her. "You've tailed me for how long now?"

"A few weeks," she admitted.

"And obviously you figured out that I'm friends with Kit."

"I think you have a very high opinion of yourself to imagine that news of your celebrity precedes you," she said, even though of course he was correct. She had seen him come and go from Mr. Webb's coffeehouse at all hours. From that fact and Dinah's gossip and the contents of his letters, she had identified him as the confederate of Mr. Webb who had evidently returned from the dead, a man everyone simply referred to as Rob.

She knew those facts and a good many besides, but she still didn't know his surname. "We haven't been introduced. I don't know what to call you."

"In my circles, being an accessory to a murder counts as a proper introduction." And then he shook his head and carried on walking. "Rob," he said, not looking back at her.

"Rob," she repeated. It was an unwanted intimacy, and she felt guilty shaping her mouth around the syllable. She would prefer to call him *sir*, as she had addressed him in her letters, but she couldn't think about those letters, because then she'd have to think about what had happened when the duke had found them, and then—

Besides, she could hardly call him sir while he—of all the vulgarity—called her darling and sweetheart. "Surely you have a surname."

"Brooks," he said with a faint frown, as if answering a question so personal that Marian ought to be ashamed of herself.

She would call him Mr. Brooks, then, however little he liked it. But when she tried to think of him as Mr. Brooks, it felt absurd. It didn't fit him in the least. It was like when people referred to Eliza as Lady Elizabeth, even though she wore nappies and spent most of the day with her thumb in her mouth. It was no good. In her mind, she would have to think of him as Rob, and she held him fully responsible for not being a person one could think of in a sensible way.

Rob stopped before a collection of buildings that looked and smelled like stables and rapped on the door, even though it had to be well past midnight. The door was answered by a boy who was still rubbing sleep from his eyes.

"Go fetch your da," Rob said, giving the boy a halfpenny. They stood in the meager shelter of the doorway while waiting for the boy or his father to return. They were so close together that she had nowhere to look if she didn't want to look at Rob, his features so near that they could be understood only separately:

the straight line of his nose, the perpetually amused curve of his mouth, the freckles that concentrated on the bridge of his nose before scattering everywhere. She closed her eyes.

The sound of heavy footsteps was followed by the appearance of a man who was hastily shoving the tails of his shirt into breeches. He carried a lantern, which he held up to examine Rob's face. "It's you," he said. "Figures. Come on, then." He led the way to the stableyard. "Been a while."

"Would you believe me if I told you I had little need for horses this past year?"

The stable keeper snorted. "We all reckoned you were in prison."

"Come now, that was only for a little while. And it was in France, so it hardly counts."

"Also heard you were dead."

"What are things coming to when you can't even believe gossip."

"What'll you need, then? Two horses?"

"Yes, for a week, I'd say. They need to be sturdy."

The stable keeper opened a stall door, revealing a chestnut gelding. "Bertie'll do for you," he told Rob. "And for your friend . . ." He eyed Marian up and down. She knew he was trying to figure out what she weighed, an entirely sensible means of suiting rider to horse, but still her skin crawled. He opened another door, a few stalls down. Inside was a bay mare. "Gwen. Short for Guinevere." When Rob raised an eyebrow, the man shrugged sheepishly. "I let the girls name her," he added by way of explanation.

Then the man asked for a sum so princely that Marian decided that in her next life she ought to run a stable. Perhaps that was what she should have done a little over a year ago when faced with the problem of an estate in ruins and a father whose mind seemed to occasionally take its leave. She could have turned Chiltern Hall into a stable and hired out the horses, and thereby avoided marrying and murdering any dukes whatsoever.

Without making any attempt to bargain, Rob withdrew his coin purse and put the requisite number of coins into the stableman's palm, adding another for good measure—and, Marian supposed, silence.

"Give the girls my love," Rob said.

"Come back soon and give it to them yourself," the man grumbled as he returned indoors, but he seemed, if anything, pleased to have seen Rob, pleased to have been dragged from his bed and into what could only be trouble.

The boy who had answered the door returned, carrying a lantern and a parcel. "Da said to give you these," he said, following his words with a yawn. Rob thanked the lad with a wink and another halfpenny, then took the lantern and parcel.

Marian saddled the mare, aware that Rob's eyes were on her. Likely he didn't believe that she knew how to ride and was waiting for her to make a false step. But she had been saddling her own mounts since she could be trusted not to either fall off a horse or get kicked in the head by one, and a year of inactivity was hardly going to rob her of a lifetime's worth of experience. She adjusted the mare's bridle and set the stirrups at a length that looked suitable, then swung herself into the saddle.

Meanwhile, Rob began whispering to his own horse. Of course he was one of those people who insisted on talking to animals.

Marian preferred to communicate with horses in their own language: she rode them well and not too hard and made sure they were fed and watered. That was what horses cared about; everything else was mere self-indulgence.

She took the opportunity to adjust the folds of her cloak and retrieve her coin purse, removing slightly more than Rob had paid for the horses.

"This is yours," she said, holding out her hand.

He took the coins and counted them, as if Marian meant to cheat him, the insufferable man.

"This is too much," he said.

"I didn't have smaller coins."

"Christ," he muttered. "Of course she doesn't." He dropped the coins into his own money pouch and mounted the horse. "When we get out of the city, you ride close by me, you hear?"

With that, he rode out of the stableyard and Marian was left to follow behind.

Chapter 6

*B*y the time they reached Dartford, a pitiable distance
south of the Thames, Rob decided he'd call this a smash-
ing success if neither of them fell asleep in the saddle. There was
a time when he could have stayed awake and alert for two solid
days and then been fresh as a daisy after a few hours of sleep. But
that was long in the past—before a string of injuries and misadventures, and when he was closer to fifteen than thirty. Now he
was increasingly drawn to the charms of a soft mattress and clean
sheets, and wasn't that a depressing thought.

"Where exactly in Kent are you going?" he asked.

"Little Hinton," Marian said. "It's near Canterbury."

Rob sighed and inwardly cursed Kent for being inconveniently
large. Of course Marian wouldn't need to go somewhere easy
to reach, like Blackheath or Sevenoaks—nothing about her was
ever easy. Canterbury would mean at least two days in the saddle.
But it would also mean that she was close enough to the sea to
get to France without much fuss, if that was what things came
to. He wondered if she had thought of that, and decided that it

was highly unlikely that Marian, however addled, hadn't thought of everything.

He started to flag before the first rays of dawn pinkened the sky. They really had to keep riding until it was full daylight, because by then any inn they stopped at would be busy enough that two strangers would pass unnoticed.

Until they knew whether Marian was suspected of the duke's murder, they needed to keep their heads down and avoid the more well-traveled roads. Glancing at Marian, he decided that nobody with any brains at all would see the unkempt, disheveled person beside him and think they were looking at the Duchess of Clare. The moon was full and the night was cloudless, so he could see her profile clearly. She sat straight in the saddle, and she plainly hadn't been lying about knowing how to ride. She didn't ride like someone who was only used to the manicured paths of Hyde Park: he saw her looking out for rabbit holes and roots, as if it were second nature.

A strange melody drifted to him on the breeze and he frowned. This was maybe the fourth time he had heard it that night, and now he was beyond frustrated that he couldn't identify it. "What are you humming?" he asked.

She drew herself up straight, and he was surprised to see that her back could go any straighter than it already had been. "I apologize," she said, managing to make it sound nothing like an apology at all. "I don't mean to annoy you."

"It was a question, not a complaint. What is it? I can't place it."

"Oh. It's the song about the churches."

That didn't help in the least. "Sing me a line."

"I'll do nothing of the sort," she snapped, as if he had asked her to take all her clothes off. In fact, she had done exactly that a few hours earlier, without so much as asking him to turn his back or look away. He had kept his eyes averted anyway, in a fit of modesty on his own part that he didn't quite know what to think of.

"We can stop up ahead by that stile and have a bite to eat but only if you'll sing a line for me." He had been about to suggest that they rest the horses anyway, but she didn't need to know that.

She pressed her lips together into what might have been the snootiest expression he had ever seen in twenty-five years on this planet, and then sighed. "Fine," she said, in a tone that made it clear she was humoring him and was far above things like food and rest and human weakness. "When I am rich, ring the bells of Fleet Ditch," she sang.

He frowned. She had been humming off key, and her singing voice was even further from the mark, but he'd know that rhyme anywhere. "You mean—" He cleared his throat. "When I am rich, ring the bells of Shoreditch."

"No, I mean Fleet Ditch."

"That makes no sense. Fleet Ditch isn't even a—for Christ's sake, it's Shoreditch, because that's where the rich merchants live."

"I've never heard of it," she said, dismissing rhyme, merchants, and possibly all of East London.

Of course she hadn't heard of Shoreditch, though. She was raised in the country—riding horses, by the looks of things.

"I'd like to know where an earl's daughter learned 'Oranges and Lemons.'"

There came that pinched expression again. "One of the maids in my daughter's nursery sings it to her. And she says Fleet Ditch."

Something happened to her voice when she said *my daughter,* as if a cold wind had just blown in. "Where is she from?"

"I beg your pardon."

What a trick it was to be able to say *I beg your pardon* in a way that meant *fuck off and die,* and to look serene and saintly while saying it. "The maid," he clarified.

"London."

"I gathered as much, but where in London?"

She sniffed. "I haven't the faintest notion."

They arrived at the stile and dismounted. She was moving stiffly; it had been a while since she had been on horseback, he guessed. Without needing to be told, she led her horse to a stream that ran alongside the road. Definitely country born and bred, then. He took his horse and followed her.

"Fleet Ditch is nothing more than a sewer," he said. He felt better, as if he had won a very important point.

"I can't possibly express to you how little I care."

With a reckless little thrill, he realized that this was the caustic, acerbic woman who had written him all those letters. She had disappeared for a few hours under the weight of shock, but that tart little reply was familiar in a way that plucked at something in his heart.

And, really, his heart needed to shut up about it. There was a time and a place for that silly business and now was not it. He had got a bit carried away with the letters, that was all, and perhaps let himself become overfond of a person he knew only as words on a sheet of costly paper. His hand went automatically to the parcel in his coat.

After the horses had drunk their fill, he tied both bridles to the stile and sat on the wall. After a moment, Marian followed. He unwrapped the bundle of food, revealing a loaf of brown bread and a wedge of cheese. He broke the bread in half and held out both portions for Marian to take her pick.

She reached out with an ungloved hand. Her fingers had to be stiff with cold. Hell, she had to be chilled to the bone, but she wasn't even shivering. Even Rob was feeling it, and he had more experience and more meat on his bones. He had never seen her up close until tonight, but from across the street, when she was all trussed up in a bodice and skirts, it always looked like there was more of her.

"When was the last time you ate?" he asked. She was eating with a speed that Rob knew from experience meant the kind of hunger that gnawed at your bones.

She hesitated for a long, troubling minute. "Breakfast," she finally said, sounding utterly unconvincing.

Nearly a full day, then, if not more. And she hadn't said a word about it. He cut the cheese into four pieces and offered her three.

"I'll take only what's mine," she said, and took two pieces.

As far as life philosophies went, that was a piss poor one, but he decided to spare her his thoughts on the topic since she had had a trying day and was half frozen, thoroughly starved, and probably still a little bit mad with shock. He unscrewed the cap of his flask and held it out to her. "We don't have anything to drink except gin, unless you want to take your chances with that stream."

She waved away the flask and mounted her horse. He slid off the fence, dusting his trousers and rearranging his cuffs and in general taking his time about it, and out of the corner of his eye watched Marian pretend not to be steaming with impatience. The fact that she could manage irritation at a time when most people would have drowned in panic was a testament to her backbone. And the fact that Rob was ready to rhapsodize over such a thing as *backbone* was a testament to his own besottedness. He was fully disgusted with himself.

Luck was truly on their side, because as the first hints of dawn appeared in the sky, there was a sharp increase in the number of conveyances on the road: carts carrying homespun and candles and great piles of potatoes. It had to be market day in Sevenoaks. He had hoped that they'd run into a market today, but to find one first thing was more than he could have asked for. The inns would be too full for anyone to pay much attention to them and they'd be able to pick up a change of clothes. They might even catch wind of any news from London about the Duke of Clare, his attackers, and whether Marian was wanted for his murder.

"Tuck your plait into your shirt," he said. He wasn't worried about her being recognized as the possibly fugitive Duchess of Clare, but rather that she would stand out as a woman dressed in breeches. If she was going to blend into a crowd, she needed either a tricorn hat or a skirt, so as to make the pendulum swing decisively one way or the other.

"You tuck your own plait into your shirt," she retorted.

"Your plait clearly belongs to a woman. It reaches your waist," he said. "And it's as thick as a mooring line." Horrified, he realized that his tone was one of breathless fascination. "I don't know how you stuff it all under those wigs you lot wear."

"If you hand me one of those daggers, I'll cut it off."

"Like hell you will. You'll ruin the blade."

She gave him a look that could have frozen the gin in his flask and withered the crops in the field, if it hadn't been December and the landscape already quite barren. But she tucked her hair into her shirt nonetheless, acting extremely put upon. He removed his hat and held it out to her.

"No thank you," she said tartly.

"It's not a present, darling. It's a disguise, until we can get you a better one."

She sighed and took the hat, as if it were a tremendous burden to her. He tipped the brim over her forehead at a rakish angle.

When they reached the town, they first stopped at an inn. Inns on market day mornings were never at their best. The atmosphere was one of businesslike efficiency, which Rob disliked on principle. Nobody lingered over a pint or warmed their feet by the fire. There was no singing, no laughter, hardly even any conversation beyond essential questions and answers. Dismal. It was always better later on, when people had a bit of time on their hands and a word to spare for a fellow traveler, when stories were swapped across battered oak tables and bellies were full of supper and ale. Some of the happiest hours of his life had been spent in such a way, generally with Kit, and the memory made him

feel both wistful and somehow homesick, in the way that happy
memories too often did.

Once the horses were being seen to, they made their way
through the crowd into the taproom. There was an empty table
in one of the corners, and maybe they spotted it at the same time,
or maybe they both realized that a dark corner was just what they
needed, but they both headed toward it. Rob made for the seat
that would put his back to the wall, but Marian's hand clasped
the chair back before he could sit down.

"Ah, no," Rob said, making what he felt was a reasonably gallant gesture at the other chair.

"Ah, yes," Marian said, making what Rob was amused to realize was an even more gallant gesture.

"I need to be able to see the room," Rob said.

"Why?"

The truth was that, as a rule, he liked to keep his back to the
wall. He wanted to know whether he was about to be confronted
with thief takers or magistrates or any other old acquaintances
he'd prefer never to meet again in this lifetime. Or, for that matter, acquaintances he'd be happy to see—one never knew. "Because we're trying to avoid anyone recognizing you."

She looked at him for a long moment, then sat in the seat that
put her back to the room. So, perhaps she didn't want to quarrel with him at every opportunity. He was more than willing to
quarrel with her, both because she was quite good at it—it was
always wise to encourage excellence—and because it seemed to
distract her from all the bad things that no doubt were churning
around in her mind. Whenever he looked at her, she was either

scowling at him or she appeared lost in a miserable reverie, and he much preferred the scowl.

When the barmaid brought over a couple of pints of ale, they both drained their tankards in a single go.

"The next time I flee from home under cover of night, I'm bringing a skin of ale," Marian said, and good Lord, that was almost a joke. He knew she was capable of humor, of course, and had a sheaf of letters tucked into the lining of his coat to prove it. But to hear it came as more of a relief than he had anticipated and he had to make sure he wasn't smiling broadly at her like the fool that he was.

"Next time you'll know better," he said consolingly. "But you brought your coin purse, which makes up for a multitude of sins. It would have been a right pain in the arse if I had to steal a pair of horses."

"Could you have?" she asked, sounding genuinely curious.

"Could I have, she asks," Rob scoffed. "I could and I have."

"Felicitations," she said.

"To crime," he said, after the barmaid brought them a fresh pair of pints and bowls of stew. "Because sometimes it needs to be done."

She looked at him for a long moment, then raised her glass.

Chapter 7

$\mathcal{M}$arian disapproved entirely of markets: they were noisy and crowded, with people and livestock alike milling about without any apparent pattern.

Rob sighed and took Marian by the elbow, towing her along. The crowds seemed to part for him, which was both predictable and annoying. She had noticed the way he winked at the barmaids and joked around with the ostlers. He smiled at strangers and tossed coins to naughty boys who were almost certainly up to no good and shouldn't be encouraged.

The unfortunate fact of the matter was that Rob was charming. She ought to have guessed as much from his letters. He was one of those people who managed to convince the world that it ought to rejoice in his mere existence.

Marian was ill-disposed to charming men. She didn't trust anyone who could use their words and their wits to bend the minds of the people around them. They got away with too much. The duke was one of those men, for all he seldom bothered to use his charm on Marian after they were married. He had charmed her senseless while he was courting her, and she was mortified to recall how badly taken in she had been.

She had believed him to be in love with her. She believed she was getting the better end of the bargain because he was infatuated with her. He had said—he had said all manner of silly things, and he had said them charmingly, and she had believed him. She might not have reciprocated the sentiment, but she knew the value of marrying a man who held one dear. She had been naive and foolish, too eager to believe what he said because she so badly needed what he offered.

She must have stopped walking at some point, because she was standing in front of a stall piled with unfortunate, lumpen gourds, and Rob was a few steps ahead, tugging her along, his fingers firm and solid around her wrist

"Right," he said. "Of course. Having another one, are you?" Before she could protest, he slid his fingers from her wrist to her hand. She could feel his calluses against the soft skin of her palm. "Damn it, your hands are cold," he muttered. "All right. Come on, now. I know it's bad, but you'll feel better after you get some sleep."

Rob made his way along the rows of stalls as if he visited this market every week. He seemed to know exactly what he wanted and where to find it, and within an hour had purchased a large leather satchel, a basket, half a dozen apples, a wedge of cheese, a cake of soap, a comb, and a razor. And with every purchase, he dazzled the person behind the stall, whether a buxom young matron or an elderly man with no teeth. She wanted to tell him that these farmers or merchants or whatever they were simply wanted to sell their wares and collect his coins, that they didn't want his smiles or his friendly chatter. But they did seem to want his smiles and his chatter—Marian knew what forced smiles looked like and she certainly knew what reluctant conversation sounded like, and these were neither. It was infuriating, really.

"Gown or breeches?" Rob asked as they left the central thoroughfare behind and approached a handful of stalls on the outskirts of the market.

"I beg your pardon?"

"Which do you plan to wear? Or do you plan to alternate? It's of no importance to me, except that we both need a change of clothes and I'd like to know what to look for."

"Breeches," she said without hesitation, because while she could ride in a skirt—she could probably ride in court dress, complete with panniers, if it came down to it—she didn't wish to. She had spent years hacking about the countryside in her brother's outgrown riding clothes, not wanting to incur the expense of a new riding habit that she would surely ruin on the first muddy day.

Without comment, he purchased a pair of shirts that looked new, a hat that decidedly did not, some gloves, and a pair of buckskins. She hoped the buckskins were for her, because the breeches she had on now were Percy's, and since they were Percy's, they were made of some ridiculous fine fabric that would not withstand much longer in the saddle.

It occurred to her that she could buy her own buckskins, if need be. "Are those for me?" she asked, gesturing to the buckskins, which now lay folded inside the basket.

"Yes. Do you not care for them? We have another fifty or so miles to go, and I thought you could do with something sturdier." He gestured at his own breeches, which were indeed buckskins, and were also nicely fitted over muscular thighs in a way she preferred not to contemplate.

"Thank you," she said tightly. "They'll do."

"Are you going to bleed?"

She blinked up at him. "I'm uninjured. We established that last night."

"Your monthlies. Will you be getting them in the next week? If so, we'll need to buy cloths."

She refused to blush. This man had seen her half naked and was presently abetting her flight from the law. The existence of her courses was surely no cause for embarrassment, especially since he did not seem in the least embarrassed and she refused to be outdone. "No," she said. She had finished bleeding a few days ago, thank the holy mother and all the saints. She had thus far not needed the herbs Dinah had given her and which remained tucked inside the ticking of her mattress.

By now it was nearly noon and she had been awake for at least thirty hours, to say nothing of how poor her sleep had been the night before the robbery. The two pints of ale she thirstily drank at the inn must have been stronger than she was accustomed to, because she was all but swaying on her feet. The only thing keeping her awake was her nerves.

"We'll take a room at an inn in the next town," Rob said, as if reading her mind. "Now that we have baggage like respectable people, the innkeeper won't throw us out on our ears."

"I could ride until nightfall," she lied, and then wanted to kick herself, because she was becoming increasingly aware that every muscle in her body ached. It was infuriating that she was so defeated by something as simple as riding a horse, something that had been as easy as breathing before months of illness and convalescence.

Rob was right that she needed to rest, but she didn't like how he seemed to anticipate her needs and then act on them. She was dimly aware that what she was objecting to was simply basic consideration, but it had been a long day. It had been a long year, during which one of the few lessons she had learned was never to let anyone know that you needed anything. Need was only weakness by another name. And if someone could give you what you needed, they could just as easily take it away.

"Bully for you," Rob said. "But I'm tired and the horses need to rest. We'll stop at the next town, start again at first light tomorrow, and with any luck make it past Maidstone by tomorrow night."

"Have it your way," she said.

"Thank you, darling," he said casually. The endearment made her skin feel hot, even though she knew it was too facetious to mean anything. He seemed to have found his way around titles and honorifics by simply reverting to the most appallingly impertinent mode of addressing her.

When they had been writing one another almost daily, she hadn't tried to imagine what he looked like. There were certain facts one could glean from a person's letters—class, education, intelligence, and even age, for example—but looks weren't among them. Now she was seeing him in full daylight and had to admit that he was reasonably attractive, as far as men went. He was pleasant to look at, in a slightly weather-beaten sort of way. His voice was pleasant, too, a rough but lazy drawl that wavered between what she took to be an ironic impersonation of an upper-class accent and something that sounded almost like the real thing. Plainly, he had some education; she had guessed that much from his letters. He ought to be in a respectable trade, not doing . . . whatever this was.

They made their way through the crowds and back to the inn, fetched their horses, and rode in near silence until they reached the next village. At the first inn they saw, Rob smiled winningly and leaned across the counter and no doubt spilled all manner of foolishness into the ear of the innkeeper's wife, and a moment later they were standing in a tidy little room that contained a bed, a washstand, and a fire.

She was very tired and her thoughts took a moment to catch up with her eyes. There was only one room, and only one bed.

"I assumed you'd prefer not to let me out of your sight," Rob said, evidently guessing her train of thought, "hostages traditionally not being afforded much in the way of freedom."

"Ha!" she scoffed. "I pity anyone who attempts to kidnap you." For several hours, she hadn't even thought about why he was there, why he was breaking bread with her, why he was shepherding her through the market and supplying her with clean clothes. Fatigue had a way of dulling the intellect, she supposed, but also she had simply accepted his companionship as right and natural. All those weeks of letters had tricked her into a familiarity that was purely imaginary. "You wouldn't be here unless you wanted to be," she said, realizing the truth of her words as soon as she spoke them.

"How unobliging of you. I was hungering for a new experience and I'd never been kidnapped before," Rob said, shrugging out of his coat and flinging it onto the back of a chair. "Or perhaps I can't get enough of your company."

"You are a tedious flirt." She spotted a folding screen propped in a corner and set it up so that it would shield her from view. The previous night, she had stripped naked right in front of him and he hadn't paid her the least bit of attention. She remembered him handing her a handkerchief without even looking up from his cards. She didn't know if this was due to tact on his part or simply because he was so used to being confronted with nudity that it had ceased to be interesting.

She didn't entirely like either explanation.

"May I have one of the new shirts?" she asked. "I plan to bathe." He handed her one of the shirts without comment.

With enormous relief, she stripped out of her dirty clothes. When they reached Little Hinton, she would burn it all. The water in the ewer was lukewarm, which was at least better than ice cold, and she set about using the flannel to scrub her face.

"Do you want soap?" Rob asked. He was on the other side of the screen, but less than an arm's length away.

She did want soap. Badly. "Yes," she said, adding a grudging "please." She stuck her hand out from behind the screen and he dropped the cake of soap into it.

It was not very nice soap, smelling faintly of lye and crumbling as she tried to use it. As she washed, she heard movement on the other side of the screen. The thud of one boot hitting the floor, then the other. The rustling of fabric, the slide of leather over skin. Rob was undressing—of course he was; they were both planning to sleep. She tried not to think about it. She was getting very good at not thinking about things, but she was going to have to get even better if she meant to spend another two days in Rob's company.

After she dried herself on the sheet of linen that hung beside the washstand, she pulled the shirt over her head. It hung past her hips, of course, but without a waistcoat it gaped in the front. She tried not to think about that, too.

Rob was already in bed, decently covered by the sheet and, thank heavens, wearing a shirt. He was on his stomach, with his arms pillowed under his head, facing the wall. She drew the curtains, casting the room into near darkness, then climbed into bed.

Chapter 8

Rob had every intention of sleeping for as long as his body would let him, but his mind had other ideas.

Thus far, he had done a decent job of pushing away any less polite thoughts he might have about Marian, but as soon as he recalled that she was half naked next to him in bed, all hope was lost. He just wasn't going to let himself think about Marian and nakedness in the same sentence, because while he was usually all for complicating things with that sort of thought and indeed that sort of action, he didn't think matters could rightly get more complicated than they already were with Marian. Attempting to dally with someone who had shot their spouse the previous day, and who—whether they realized it or not—depended on him for a safe journey perhaps merited a stronger word than *complicated*.

So he lay in bed, trying sedulously not to think complicating thoughts, which went about as well as it ever did. It might have gone better if he hadn't been so bad at sitting in cold, dark rooms. Cold, dark rooms that he wasn't supposed to leave. The walls began to creep in on him and the windows seemed to grow bars. He started to think that maybe the door wouldn't open if he tried the handle, and that maybe if he stood, he'd find manacles on his wrists and—

He leapt out of bed, his heart racing. For no reason, of course. He was free and safe and all the other things a person could wish to be. Completely free, and mildly insane, apparently. This was nothing new, though, even if it had got a bit more dramatic in the last year.

He slid into his clothes, dressing as quietly as he could. It was already dark, but there was noise coming from downstairs, which meant—if this inn were like other country inns—it wasn't yet past ten. There would still be people in the taproom, and if he was lucky there would still be supper on offer.

Marian didn't stir as Rob threw on his coat and made his way toward the door, nor when he stumbled over one of the boots she had strewn in the middle of the floor, nor even when he tripped over the other one and let loose a volley of hissed profanity. He paused with his hand on the door latch, looking at her over his shoulder. Her mouth was half open and she had one arm flung out to the side, dangling off the bed, and it was the least dignified he had seen her, which—considering that he had also seen her standing in her shift, covered in blood—was really saying something. She looked her age, which he knew was only twenty-two or so, not so much younger than himself. He could imagine that she really was the same person who had written him all those letters—arch, wry, and a little silly. He was reminded, inconveniently, of how much he liked her.

Well, he liked a lot of people. He'd probably find some more people to like downstairs, most of whom had neither married nor

shot a single duke, nor embroiled Rob's best friend in a scheme
that could have killed him. And with that cheering thought, he
shut the door firmly behind him and made his way down to the
taproom, which was indeed filled with people. The place smelled
of tobacco, woodsmoke, and hops, and it gleamed with firelight
glinting off the pewter dishes that lined the walls. It was warm,
comfortably loud, and cheerful. Rob felt about eighty percent
happier just walking into the room.

He settled himself in front of the fire, where a pair of fat spaniels promptly approached him with their tails wagging, acting
like nobody had ever fed them in their lives. He scratched them
behind the ears, which always gave a man an innocent look. Nobody could possibly be up to much of anything when they were
making a fuss over a dog.

Then he insinuated himself into the nearest conversation at
hand, in which two women and a man discussed a blowfly in-
festation of plague-like proportions on one of the women's sheep
farms the previous summer. Rob had never raised a sheep in his
life and only seldom came closer to one than as muttonchops or
a new coat. But when the older of the two women turned to him
for support of her policy of shearing the poor, afflicted sheep and
then putting them in a separate paddock, he knew enough to
agree. She was old, and likely wouldn't have any sheep at all if she
didn't know how to keep them.

"It's the only way," he said sagely, and just like that he had
three new friends. Five, if you counted the spaniels, to whom he
fed bits of the ham and bread the barmaid brought to the table.

Six, if you counted the wide-eyed infant, who was passed around the table like a jug of ale. Rob became the receptacle of a great deal of blowfly-related wisdom and advice, as well as instructions regarding prayers, herbal concoctions, and vaguely witchy practices all designed to thwart the blowfly's rapacious tendencies. After a quarter of an hour, he had developed a deep and abiding respect for the blowfly.

When the conversation took an unfortunate turn in the direction of maggots—a turn he really should have foreseen as the natural outcome of the blowfly—he gently steered it to topics that were less likely to interfere with his enjoyment of his supper. The younger of the women was evidently the infant's mother, and Rob proceeded to say all the usual things one said about babies—he had never in all his years seen a baby so fat and pink, and surely that was a gleam of intelligence in his eyes, and wasn't he the very spit of his father—and soon found himself holding the infant in question, who had been presented to him in the manner of a great treat being offered. And Rob did like babies as much as he liked people of any age, so it actually was a bit of a treat.

When his new companions asked him what his business was in that part of Kent, he said that he was passing through on his way to Canterbury. It turned out that the younger of the women came from Maidstone, which he was certain to pass through, and had a great deal to say about which inns were worth stopping at and which were to be avoided at all costs. Rob got a pencil and paper from the innkeeper and dutifully wrote down everything the woman said, up to and including her request that he tell the proprietress of the Seven Stars in Maidstone that Nellie and the baby sent their love.

There, he told himself, folding the paper and tucking it into his pocket when his companions left the table and repaired to their beds. He was simply a sociable fellow. The past year had taken him away from all his friends, so he had latched onto Marian's letters as the next best thing to friendship. It didn't signify in the least. Any notion that he was fond of her—or, worse, trusted her—was an illusion brought about by his loneliness and confusion. He would bring her to her father's house, because he had told her he would, and because she was clearly in no state to be left alone. But he would leave her in the bosom of her family or possibly stowed away on a fishing boat headed for Calais, and then return to London and be done with her.

He was feeling very pleased with himself for having resolved that problem to his satisfaction when he looked toward the stairs and saw a figure leaning against the wall, half covered by shadows. He didn't have a clear view of her face, but he did recognize those breeches, which he had bought that very morning. He kicked out one of the empty chairs at his table and raised an eyebrow in her direction. She hesitated, then made her way across the room.

As she approached, he noticed that she had tucked her braid into her coat as he had suggested that morning. She looked unremarkable, like any apprentice or young man, only more drawn and wearier. Anyone's gaze would pass her right over, which was good, exactly what they needed.

Why, then, did he never want to look away? It had to be because he had thought about her so much but seen her only a few times. She was pale, both naturally and with the added pallor of hunger and exhaustion. With that complexion, one expected blue eyes or maybe gray, but hers were dark to the point that they were nearly black. Her eyebrows were of a blackness that matched her hair, arching across her forehead in a way that he couldn't help but find vaguely villainous. She might have looked severe, but the effect was ruined by her nose, which tipped up in a very silly fashion, and her chin, which was pointy enough to make her face heart-shaped.

Nobody would call her pretty, and handsome also seemed to miss the mark. He had seen her done up in powder and silks and knew that she was certainly very striking in that state. She was interesting-looking, but he couldn't tell if this was because of her face or his feelings.

"Mr. Lawson," he said, addressing her by the name she was traveling under.

"I thought you left," she said reproachfully, ignoring the chair he had kicked out and instead sitting across from him. "You mustn't do that."

Her back was straight and she managed to look down her nose at him in an imperious manner that, much as he hated to acknowledge it, made him perk up like a dog hearing the sound of his name. He braced a forearm on the table and leaned in so his words would reach only her ears. "I have bad news for you, kitten—"

She abruptly sat back. "Kitten! I think not."

"Darling," he continued smoothly, "I come and go as I please, understand? I know you've had a rough go of it and have precious little reason to trust anyone, least of all me, but I haven't the slightest intention of sitting around in dark little rooms, not for your convenience or anybody else's."

She sniffed. "You gave me a fright, that's all. I didn't know how I was meant to get to Little Hinton on my own."

"Come, now. You're going to tell me that after traipsing about London—and some of the seedier bits of London, at that—at all hours of the night, and after contriving to poison your enemies' drinks—"

"One enemy! If you can even call yourself that. And it was only laudanum! You make me sound like a Medici!"

"If the shoe fits, love."

"Medicis, one has to imagine, navigated their way out of difficulties with much more style and cunning than I managed."

"You managed just fine," Rob said. "It might not have turned out precisely as you hoped—"

"It certainly didn't," she said with feeling.

"—but when you needed to pull the trigger, you did it."

She narrowed her eyes at him. "You know nothing of what happened that day."

"I trust that you had your reasons and did what needed to be done." Rob heard the words as they left his mouth and was deeply annoyed to discover that they were the truth. He was here only because he trusted her, much as he might like to pretend otherwise. He was an even bigger fool than he had supposed.

"Do you?" she asked, one black eyebrow arched, and he feared that she had realized exactly what he had. He suppressed the urge to look away, to hide his face.

The worst part was that she didn't trust him in return—she had woken in the dark and suspected that he had left her. She thought he might have his own motives, some sense of self-preservation. Christ. The knowledge that she was as much of a fool as he was might at least have been some consolation.

Instead she looked at him as if she could see right through him, as if her gaze was a sharp knife that exposed everything he was. Then her eyes flickered from his face to his plate. He had saved a portion of bread and ham with the aim of wrapping it in a napkin and bringing it to the room for her to eat when she woke. Instead, he slid it across the table to her now.

She pushed it back. "That's yours."

"I'm giving it to you."

"I'm not taking your charity. I have my own money, and I already owe you for what you bought at the market."

If she thought he was in the business of giving charity to earls' daughters, she could guess again. "I'll look away," he offered, turning his attention to one of the spaniels, who had come over to rest her chin on his thigh, having evidently guessed that food was being given away and presenting herself as a worthy candidate. "And you can take it. You can spirit it away. It'll be very cunning of you."

"I want to pay for my food, not steal it, you daft man."

"But who's to say this food was mine to begin with?"

"You bought it," she said slowly, as if it was dawning on her that she was dealing with a lunatic. "I can call the innkeeper over if you'd like him to explain this to you."

It occurred to him that perhaps he could make his point with a different example. "Forget about the food. Let's think about something else. A pistol, let's say." He tapped his chin. "Now why would you take a pistol that doesn't belong to you."

She sighed loudly and gazed at the ceiling, as if for strength. He suppressed a smile.

"Oh, I know!" he went on, again leaning close and lowering his voice so as not to be overheard. "Perhaps you needed it to shoot your—"

She threw up her hands. "Yes, yes, if you're trying to very cleverly point out that I'm hardly a pillar of virtue, then I already know that. Don't be tedious. I just want to pay for my own food."

"Did you bring your coin purse downstairs?"

She glared at him. "No."

"In that case we return to our lesson on ethical thievery. Let's abandon the pistol—"

"First we abandoned the bread and ham, and then we abandoned the pistol, and I'm about to abandon my patience."

"Let's say you stole my horse," he went on, ignoring her, "but I bought the horse using money I stole from somebody else. Who does the horse belong to?"

"Do your friends find this as boring as I do? I wonder."

"The horse doesn't belong to anyone."

"Give me that pistol I stole two examples ago so I can shoot myself and make this end."

"It's not loaded," he said repressively. "You never stole any shot. You're lucky to have me around if you don't even understand how pistols work."

She stared at him. "You are ridiculous. I let my life get thrown into an uproar by a ridiculous man. How lowering. Villains are supposed to be serious."

"I, a villain?" He put his hand to his heart. "You wound me."

"I wish I wounded you," she grumbled.

"Eat," he said.

With the air of a woman much put upon, she ate, and he very definitely did not grin as he watched her.

Chapter 9

The path they took the next morning ran more or less parallel to the Canterbury road. It was little more than a footpath, just barely wide enough for two horses.

"The lads in the stable said it's the old Pilgrims' Way to Canterbury," Rob said. "From Winchester, I suppose."

Marian sniffed but couldn't help but be amused. Of course Rob believed that sort of tale. "There are footpaths everywhere, and one imagines most of them were made by drovers bringing livestock to market. It seems unnecessarily quaint to bring pilgrims into it."

Rob sighed, and Marian felt churlish for having spoiled his fun. She nudged her horse and rode ahead.

At midday, they stopped at an inn. Within five minutes of their entering the taproom, Rob was telling the innkeeper's wife that some woman named Nellie from Wrotham Heath sent her love and that the baby was growing fat and healthy.

"I haven't seen her in a twelvemonth," said the woman, who was plump and quite pretty. She had a dimple in her cheek and Rob smiled at her like she was a butter pudding just for him. Marian disliked her on principle.

"She's been busy with the baby and the farm," Rob said, as if he were this Nellie's oldest confidante.

It was absurd. And Marian couldn't figure out why he did it, other than being an unrepentant flirt, of course. She might have thought he was angling to get a free supper, but instead he overpaid at every opportunity. She was left to conclude that he simply liked talking to people. She was exhausted just watching him. She was exhausted just thinking about it.

But she had talked to Rob for at least an hour straight that morning and at no point had it been tedious. Whenever she thought the conversation was about to careen into one of the many prickly briar patches that littered her mind, it instead changed course. And that, she was forced to acknowledge, was because Rob made it change course. This meant that he was likely learning the entire landscape of her being, just by feeling out the brambles and thorns. She did not enjoy the realization that her boundaries were being tested, as if she were an old fence. Soon enough he'd know where all the weak and dangerous bits were.

"Is your beer sour?" Rob asked, looking at her from across the table. "Mine's all right. Better than all right, even."

"It's perfectly fine."

"You were frowning."

"No I wasn't," she lied. "My face is just like this."

"I've seen you smile."

"An oversight on my part. It won't happen again."

He grinned at that, and she quickly brought the tankard to her lips to hide any smile of her own that might want to force its way out.

"How old is your daughter?" he asked, and Marian froze with her tankard halfway to her mouth.

"Four months," Marian said. This wasn't the first time Rob had asked about Eliza, but until now she had deflected, and each time he backed off. He was being so cautious with her, and it made her feel exposed. But it also made her feel—well, it had been a long time since anyone had been careful with her, and she didn't know exactly how it made her feel. "She'll be five months on the Epiphany," she added.

"Where is she?" Rob's voice was balanced between casual and cautious.

"She's in London. I couldn't very well take her with me on horseback in the dead of winter." *I didn't abandon her,* she wanted to protest. "If anything happens to me, or if I need to leave the country, Percy will look after her. He adores her." Marian often wished she could be half as natural and affectionate around the baby as Percy was. "And I gave the nursery maid five pounds to take Eliza to my brother Marcus if there's any trouble from the duke." And some doing it had taken to get her hands on that much money when the duke refused to give her any pin money. There had been weeks of sneaking teaspoons and other bits and bobs from every house she set foot in.

"Fleet Ditch?"

"I beg your pardon?"

"The nursery maid who for some perverse reason sees fit to sing the rhyme with Fleet Ditch in place of Shoreditch."

"Precisely."

He leaned close. "Where did you shoot him?"

This seemed like an abrupt change of topic, but Marian put two fingers to the center of her chest and tapped.

Rob nodded. "If he survived, he won't be in any shape to harm the child."

Marian had been telling herself as much, but it was reassuring to hear it from someone with more experience of wounds. She gave him a tight nod of acknowledgment.

"Does she look like you?"

What an odd question. "She looks like Percy, but as bald as an egg."

He smiled at that.

Marian realized she had eaten all her stew while hardly tasting it. It had been like this at all her meals since leaving London. The last time she had this kind of appetite she had been thirteen and letting her hems down what seemed like every fortnight.

Rob absently slid a slice of bread onto her plate while looking at something over her shoulder, frowning intently.

"Those men," he said, in something very close to a growl. "They're bothering Mrs. Denny."

"Mrs. Denny?"

"The innkeeper's wife. No, don't turn around. One of them pinched her and the other made a rude comment. Mr. Denny is in the stables because one of the ostlers has mumps."

"Men," Marian said. She knew which group of men Rob was referring to, because they were speaking twice as loud as anyone else.

"Precisely," Rob agreed grimly, and got to his feet. "Don't move."

Marian disregarded this order, of course, immediately moving into the seat that Rob had vacated, which gave her a clear view. At a table in the center of the room sat a group of men about her own age or a bit older. They were dressed as gentlemen might in order to ride to hounds, but instead of making themselves useful outside, they were sitting in a warm inn drinking themselves silly. Their boots and coats were all new, London made, and costly.

For a moment she was certain that Rob was about to give the men a stern talking to. She suppressed a groan. Surely he ought to know by now that this would only make things worse for the woman they were bothering. Indeed, Mrs. Denny was eying Rob with a weary trepidation. She likely knew how to handle herself, it being her bread and butter to cope with men who were in their cups.

But Rob didn't speak to the men at all. Instead he walked between Mrs. Denny and the table of rude men and then tripped over his own feet.

"A thousand pardons," he said, all affability. Attempting to recover his balance, he somehow hooked one of his boots around the leg of a chair and sent the man who had been occupying it tumbling to the floor. When he reached out a hand to help the fallen man to his feet, he elbowed another man in the eye.

If she hadn't seen how Rob usually moved, with a lazy grace and unconscious ease, she might have thought he was simply being clumsy. She narrowed her eyes. What followed was a flurry of apologies and back pats. Any bystander might have been under the impression that these men were Rob's newest friends.

Out of the corner of her eye, she saw Mrs. Denny disappear and return a moment later with a man who appeared to be the innkeeper. Rob, it seemed, had seen the same thing because he extricated himself from the tangle of limbs at the gentlemen's table, this time doing no more damage than letting his forearm collide with one of the men's noses, and returned to Marian.

"Time to leave?" she murmured, already getting to her feet.

He retrieved his purse from his pocket, dropped a frankly egregious quantity of coins onto the table, and headed for the door.

"Not a word," he said to her when they stepped into the cold, bright winter day.

She remained silent until they were saddled and well along the path leading out of the village.

"I've narrowed it down," she said. "Either you put poison into their drinks—"

"And you'd know about that."

"Low-lying fruit, Rob. If not poison, which I doubt because that would look very bad for Mrs. Denny's kitchen, then you picked their pockets, and in broad daylight, too." She sighed and frowned at him. "They'll figure out later on what happened."

"They'd better. But by then we'll be well on our way."

"You'll find yourself in a world of trouble on your way back to London."

"I'll take different roads."

"I hope you got enough to make the risk worthwhile."

"I hardly counted it," Rob said. "There wasn't time."

"Count it now."

"Mercenary," he murmured, but he dug into his pockets and

began sifting through an assortment of coinage. "One pound, eight shillings, thruppence."

She tried not to look impressed. "You ought to deduct the four shillings you left your Mrs. Denny."

"It seemed only fair to share with her."

"Indeed," she sniffed. "You defended her honor very ably. She's lucky to have such a champion." That made him laugh, for some reason. She ignored him. "She would have been perfectly willing to flirt with you without your having made such a spectacle."

"Marian," he said, a horrible knowing quality to his voice, "are you jealous?"

"Ha! What on earth could I be jealous of? I don't want you to flirt with me."

"I flirt with you incessantly."

"You flirt with old ladies and inanimate objects."

He laughed again, and she made the mistake of looking at him. He needed to put that smile away before he did some mischief with it. She had to change the subject immediately. "You're surprisingly good at stealing things. I usually imagine pickpockets as small children, but you're . . ." She realized she had no dignified way of ending that sentence. "Large."

"So we've moved on to personal remarks, have we?" he murmured in a tone that was indeed flirtatious, and in order to avoid seeing what his face was doing, she turned her head as if to admire the brown and scraggy winter fields. "I was little and scrawny when I started, and simply kept my hand in the game since then."

"But you're educated. You're literate."

"Are you under the impression that all people who turn to crime are illiterate? Because if so, I'll be sure to send for a looking glass at tonight's inn."

"No," she said patiently, gritting her teeth, "I'm wondering when you had time to pick pockets if you were in school."

"My adoptive parents sent me to school, but then they died, and then Kit's family died, and neither of us were terribly pleased about it, so we decided to steal things from rich people. Or, really, I decided that. Kit was all set to burn down Cheveril Castle with the duke still inside, but I convinced him that I'd starve and die a miserable death if he were hanged for arson."

It sounded like there were a thousand stories buried between those glib lines. There was loyalty and grief and a long friendship, and she wished she knew more about all of it. She found that she wanted to hear all the stories that Rob had to tell. "So you became highwaymen as a safer alternative?"

"It seemed a better use of our talents. It made perfect sense when I was fifteen."

"Have you ever been caught?"

She was evidently being hilarious again, because he let out a loud shout of a laugh. "Have I been caught? Marian," he said, looking at her with an expression she couldn't quite decipher. "Yes, darling, I've been caught."

"Doesn't that make you want to stop?" The mere prospect of being discovered as the duke's murderer made her nearly frantic with worry, which was why she was refusing to let herself think about it.

"Not in the least. It makes me want to figure out ways to avoid being caught."

"Wait," she said, remembering something he had said a moment earlier, when she had been too busy not looking at his profile to quite pay attention to his words. "Mr. Webb was ready to burn down Cheveril Castle? What did the duke have to do with anything?"

Now he was staring at her. "You don't know? You didn't know about Kit's history with the duke when you and Lord Holland tried to hire him to hold up the duke's carriage?"

"No," Marian said, her heart now beating nervously. "Why should I have?"

"How did you get his name?"

"Dinah got it for me."

"And who is Dinah?"

"My midwife. She asked a friend of hers, a woman she says knows everything about everybody." Marian did not know what she expected, but Rob letting loose a torrent of laughter mixed with profanity was not it.

"When they say it's a small world, they really aren't exaggerating," he said, and then trotted off ahead of her without another word.

Chapter 10

$\mathcal{H}$is mother? His mother, of all people, had identified Kit as a highwayman? And Rob even knew who this mid-wife was—a fair-haired woman in her forties who looked after the girls who worked for his mother. Why his mother had seen fit to confide in her was a mystery to him. They were absolutely going to have words when he returned home.

Unfortunately, those words would probably consist of his mother reminding him that for over a year he let her believe he was dead and that he had absolutely no moral high ground to reproach her. And then he'd apologize. Again.

"If you ever contemplate letting your friends and family believe that you're dead, Marian, let me tell you that it's not as good an idea as you might think."

"I'll bear that in mind," she said. He could hear the smile in her voice and didn't dare turn his head in case he chased it away.

The sun was beginning to set, casting long shadows on the path before them and stripping the countryside of what little color it had. "Would you mind walking the horses for a while?" he asked.

By way of an answer, she dismounted. He noticed that she

came to walk between the horses and so he did the same. The path was narrow and their shoulders almost touched.

"So," she said in the tone people use right before they're about to say something better left unsaid. "Are you and Mr. Webb very good friends?"

He huffed out a short laugh and saw the air cloud before his face. "I hope so. He seems to have forgiven me."

"That isn't what I meant. I watched you stare at his coffee-house night after night before you got up the courage to go inside, and I know that you slept there every night afterward until we left London."

Rob tried to determine what, exactly, she was getting at. "Kit and I grew up together. He's my oldest and best friend."

"Is that all he is?"

"All? Good God, isn't it enough?" Kit had been the one constant in his life, the one thing he could depend on. And Rob was altogether too conscious of having nearly thrown that away.

"Are you always this dense? I'm asking if you and Mr. Webb are lovers. Or if you're in love with him or he with you. How infuriating that you make me spell it out when I hoped to be discreet."

Well, Rob supposed, it stood to reason that any friend of Lord Holland's would have to be broad-minded in that regard. "Ah, no. None of those things. Are you trying to figure out whether Kit is spoken for?"

"Now why would I want to do that."

"Lord Holland has nothing to worry about in that quarter, either from me or from anyone else."

"I can't imagine what Percy has to do with this," she said lightly, in the way people did when the truth couldn't be spoken aloud, so an unconvincing lie was a serviceable second best.

"I think we can both imagine precisely what Lord Holland has to do with it, more's the pity. Kit's a lovely man, you know."

"So is Percy—well, no, Percy is a good many things, but not lovely. He's the most loyal person I've ever known. He would do anything for the people he cares about. He's also clever and funny, and the past few months have been hard on him."

As far as Rob could tell, Lord Holland was an extravagant popinjay who had never been burdened by a single thought for another human being in his entire life, but he was willing to concede that he might be biased against anyone who put Kit in harm's way. "Whereas they've been a balmy springtime day for you?"

"Percy had expectations. I never did. If I can get my father sorted, then I'm no worse off now than I was a year ago. There's Eliza to think of, but she'll never know that she's missed out on being a fine lady."

Rob truly did not know what to say to any of this. The daughter of an earl had no expectations? A woman who thought herself the wife of a duke had lost nothing? "You spent a year living as the wife of a man who cannot have been a good husband."

"There is that," she said, as if he had pointed out that there were clouds in the sky or that her horse had thrown a shoe. "But it doesn't affect my future."

"He took you to bed on false pretenses," Rob said, his face suddenly hot. He thought of his mother, and he thought of the things his mother had told him about the duke. "And got you with child on false pretenses. That's . . ." He fumbled for a word, but there wasn't one quite equal to the task. "Not right," he finally settled on.

"It's in the past," she said, her tone a little hard around the edges, "and now I'm rid of him." She was silent for a moment, presumably recalling the exact manner in which she had rid herself of him.

For a few minutes, the only sound was the horses' hooves on the dirt path and the wind rustling through a nearby stand of trees.

"What will you do with your takings?" Marian eventually asked. "One pound, eight shillings, and thruppence."

"A bath and a fire at tonight's inn," Rob said promptly, because the colder it got, the more he thought about that fire, "and then, if we're being honest, the rest will go to the first beggar with a sad story I encounter on the way back to London. Kit used to have to take charge of my coin purse."

"Well, I'll do no such thing. You and your largesse are entirely on your own. I will beg use of your bathwater, though."

They were making their way along the Kentish downs, now, and the wind that whipped through the hills was as harsh and cold as if it came straight off the sea beyond.

She stopped walking. "Come here," she said, and took his hands, rubbing them between her own. Then, still holding his hands, she bent her head and breathed on them. "Why on earth don't you have gloves on," she muttered. He stayed perfectly still, afraid that if he moved she'd notice that she was holding his hands. "Do you want my cloak? It's very warm."

He looked at her to see if she was teasing him, but her expression was serious. She was—Christ, she was *worried* for him. The notion made his cheeks heat, made him want to look away. "No thank you," he said, because the idea of her cloak around his shoulders made him feel both pleased and ashamed in a way he didn't quite know what to make of. He extracted his hands from her grip as gently as possible, but she immediately stepped back as if rebuked.

"It's too cold to linger," she said. "Besides, your horse has a stone in his hoof and the sooner we get it out, the better. Haven't you noticed?"

Before he could say that he had not noticed, and how on earth had she when the horse was behaving perfectly normally, she had already remounted her horse and was racing ahead of him, her cloak whipping behind her.

They rode until they reached a small whitewashed inn, the sun already sinking beneath the horizon behind them.

"Is this all right?" she asked, out of breath.

"Perfect."

As they handed the horses off to the ostlers, Rob took a look around the innyard. It was busier than he thought a rural inn ought to be on a winter's night. This was no coaching inn. And, indeed, there were no coaches in the stableyard and hardly any horses. Instead, most of the activity seemed to come from half a dozen children running between the stables and the kitchens.

"You'll catch your death!" cried an aproned woman from the door. "Get back in here!" The children paid this no heed.

"Confounded kittens," grumbled the ostler.

"Heaven help me," said Marian under her breath.

"What?"

"Your eyes literally lit up. I've only read about that in books. I've never seen it happen."

"They did not," he protested, but they probably had. He was actually pretty excited about the prospect of seeing kittens.

She shook her head but smiled at him. It was a real smile, one that showed her teeth. He was very much afraid that his face was doing all kinds of obvious and horrible things right now, even worse than when he heard about the kittens.

"Give me the satchel and I'll get a room and order a hot meal," she said.

This was the first time she had offered to do this, instead preferring to linger discreetly in the background while Rob made arrangements. Her disguise wasn't foolproof, but she was covered in a layer of dust from the road and he didn't think anyone catching a glimpse of her in the firelight would jump to the conclusion that she was any woman, let alone the Duchess of Clare. "Thank you."

"Enjoy your kittens," she called over her shoulder as she strode across the innyard. "And make sure that hoof is tended to."

She spoke both parts of that sentence with an equal degree of brisk authority, as if everything from Rob's amusements to the horse's welfare fell under the shelter of her command. He watched her hold the door open for a pair of girls who scurried toward the stables and for a moment wanted to call her back in order to—well, he wasn't quite sure what, except that he wasn't ready to see her go. He doubted that he'd ever be ready to see her go, not when they reached her father's house, nor after whatever came next.

Chapter 11

This is rank duplicity," Rob announced when he walked into the room and saw that the bath was set up and that Marian had already used it. He sat on the edge of the bed and began to tug off his boots. "You lured me away with kittens and then took advantage of my absence to get the first bath."

She was now fully dressed and wrapped in the bed quilt while she combed her hair out. "That's about the lay of the land, yes. There's another kettle boiling on the fire, so you'll have no cause to complain about cold water." It was the best bath she had ever taken. She would probably die from whatever chill she caught from going to bed with wet hair, but it would be worth it. "How were your kittens? Were they good?"

"Have there ever been bad kittens?" He dropped his coat onto the back of the chair and began unbuttoning his waistcoat. "No, there have not."

"I don't know how you harden your heart enough to do crimes, Rob."

"Darling, when I steal from someone, it's my good deed for the day."

The endearment felt different coming from him when he was in the process of pulling his shirt over his head. She probably ought to look away, but she didn't. And now she knew that his chest was covered in hair a shade darker than the hair on his head. Worse, she imagined what it would feel like to touch. He had one large scar on his shoulder, and she wondered if he had smaller scars on his arms and chest as he did his face and hands. He was too far away to tell.

There had been a time when Marian hadn't been quite so indifferent to the charms of men; there had been a time when she and Percy had waxed rhapsodic about things like forearms and chins and chest hair. A year of marriage to the duke had diminished any enthusiasm she might once have had for a handsome man.

Rob cleared his throat and looked at her pointedly. She hastily averted her eyes. "Don't look away on my account, pet."

Her mouth was dry. "*Pet?* I think not."

"Have it your way, darling." He hooked his thumbs into the top of his buckskins, as if contemplating whether to take them off.

"If you didn't flirt with everyone and everything, I might take you seriously, and then where would you be? You ought to watch your mouth."

"I flirt with you incessantly. I've been flirting with you for months. I think I've moved past flirting and onto something else altogether, and if you haven't noticed, then you haven't been paying any attention at all."

Her heart sped up. "What's that supposed to mean?"

He looked at her intently for a long moment. "It means just say the word, love."

For a minute she felt like she was balanced on the edge of a precipice. All she had to do, he said, was say the word. And then what?

She was free to say yes; her marriage to the duke had left her with no vows worth honoring, not only because of the duke's bigamy, but because of his unapologetic indifference to her life. He had insisted on attempting to get her with child, even after the physicians told him what that might mean for her; Marian could not consider that she was bound to any such man.

In a youth that seemed to have ended an eternity ago, Marian wouldn't have hesitated. She had been surrounded by people who didn't hesitate over such matters, namely Percy and Marcus, who had spent their school holidays bedding one another in addition to every other like-minded gentleman in Oxfordshire. Marian refused to accept that a different rule applied to herself, and so there had been an instructive but underwhelming afternoon with her dancing master and a much less underwhelming summer with the solicitor's sister.

Her life might have been easier if she had followed everybody else's rules instead of the rules that felt just and right in her own mind. But if she had been that sort of person, she would have balked at pulling the trigger, and she didn't know what would have become of Eliza, of Percy, of herself, if she hadn't done so.

No, Marian could guess what her own fate would have been. Dinah's herbs weren't perfect—she had said so herself. Eventually Marian would again fall pregnant, and this time the incessant sickness that had nearly starved her during her past confinement might take her life. Dinah had been uncharacteristically grave about the likelihood of her illness recurring; even the duke's physicians had agreed.

She realized that Rob was still looking at her.

"Bathe, Mr. Brooks. *Behind* the screen, thank you." She resumed combing her hair but saw out of the corner of her eye that Rob had ducked behind the screen. A moment later she heard the sound of water being poured into the tub.

"Earlier, you called me Rob."

"Nonsense." She probably had, though. She had been thinking of him as Rob for days, now.

She heard small splashing sounds as he, presumably, lowered himself into the tub. A hazy and incomplete picture of Rob bathing formed in her mind. She was very annoyed with herself, both for having thought of such a thing and also for not having enough information to present a complete image.

"Do you know what I wish we had?" Rob asked.

"I feel certain that I'm about to find out." She braced herself for something lewd.

"A book. Any book. Even a bad book would do. I like to read before I fall asleep."

"What do you consider a bad book?" she asked before she could think about whether she was relieved or disappointed that he had not, after all, suggested something lewd.

"Philosophy," he said promptly. "I can't abide it. I read one sentence of Locke or Hobbes and by the end I can't remember where it started. I like novels."

"You would like novels."

"I do. Even the bad ones. Even the ones that trade in the most mawkish sentiment." He paused. "Especially those, even. Why, what book would you have?"

She couldn't remember the last time she had read anything for pleasure, but that was too pitiful to admit. "If you want a book so badly, why not steal one?"

"If you find me a villainous bookseller, I'll rob them blind."

"Yes, of course, how silly of me to forget that you're the arbiter of who gets to keep their property and who doesn't, and of who gets punished and who doesn't."

"Do you know anybody better suited?" he asked. "If you say anything about the law, I'll cry from frustration, I really will. Even though I'm bored senseless by Locke and Hobbes, I do know the principles. We were all living in horrible caves and hitting one another with sticks and then we stopped because we agreed to have laws instead. I just don't particularly care."

She opened her mouth to protest but found that she couldn't.

"I think we're still in the cave, hitting one another with sticks," Rob went on. "I know that I broke the law when I stole from those arseholes at the tavern this afternoon. But how is what I did any different from putting poor men into debtors' prison? What I did is comparatively gentle. A targeted tax on rich men who behave badly. It's very civilized, actually."

She remembered all the odds and ends she had pilfered that autumn from houses where she had been an invited guest. Those people hadn't done anything to warrant having their belongings taken, but she had become increasingly fearful of the duke, and the duke had become increasingly suspicious of her and tight with his purse strings. She wanted to give the nursery maid a sum to take Eliza away to a place of safety, if it came to that. Stealing had been wrong, but Marian had done it anyway because it needed to be done, just as she had shot the duke because there had been no court she could have appealed to, no law she could have relied on.

"Have I shocked you?" Rob asked from behind the screen.

"You'll have to try harder than that if you want to shock me," Marian said, glad to have her thoughts dragged back to the present, even if the present consisted of Rob emerging from behind the screen with a linen sheet wrapped around his waist.

He gave her an odd look and then rummaged through his satchel for a shirt. "I don't want to shock you in the least bit, Marian."

She didn't like his tone of voice. It was soft and patient, and he spoke as if Marian ought to be aware of things of which she decidedly was not. "I'll leave you to get dressed. Our supper is probably waiting for us downstairs."

She had to wait only a few minutes in the parlor before Rob joined her, smelling of soap, his hair curling damply around his collar. They ate mutton stew and potatoes while Rob kept up a steady stream of inconsequential chatter, which was typical. What wasn't typical, though, was that he spoke solely with her— not with the people at the neighboring table and only as much as politeness dictated to the girl who brought their supper. She didn't know if he was doing this to make a point, or even if she wanted him to be doing so.

"Do you want more?"

She looked up from where she had been using the tines of her

fork to trace patterns in the gravy that was left at the bottom of
her bowl. She had eaten all her stew and potatoes, and then one
of Rob's potatoes that he slid onto her plate. She had also had two
pints of beer. "I'm not hungry."

"I think you're always hungry," he observed casually. "You eat
so quickly it hardly hits the sides."

She felt her cheeks heat. "How uncouth of me."

"Far from it. I'm only asking because I'm wondering when the
last time was that you ate your fill."

"This afternoon. You were there."

He frowned. "Before leaving London, I meant."

She hadn't the slightest idea. She had been rather preoccupied,
as Rob well knew. "I had things on my mind."

"Was he not feeding you?" He said this while bringing his cup
of beer to his mouth, so casually that she had to repeat his words
in her mind.

She put her fork down. "You're asking whether he starved me.
No, he didn't. He never harmed me in any of the ways you're
likely thinking of."

"Marian," he said, sad and reproachful, and she wanted to
slap him.

"I can't have you thinking that the duke behaved like the villain in one of those novels you like so much. He didn't starve me
or beat me or chain me up."

"Because those are the only ways a person can be harmed, of
course."

Marian knew perfectly well that she had been harmed and she
didn't need Rob to agree. Except—she didn't want Rob to think

that her killing the duke was justified for reasons that existed only in Rob's head. But she couldn't tell him the real reasons, not without telling him far, far too much. Marian was used to her morals not matching those of everyone around her, but she didn't want Rob to discover the truth and then decide that Marian had done something awful. She didn't think she could stand that.

"You're not listening to a word I say." She pushed her chair back, its legs scraping unpleasantly across the floor, then got to her feet. And once she had done that, she had no choice but to walk out of the room. There was nowhere to go, of course, which only made her feel even more of a fool. She cursed herself for not asking for separate rooms.

Instead she went where she had always gone when she needed to escape, apologizing to the stableboys who probably wanted to huddle over the brazier rather than keep an eye on a stranger. There were a good half dozen horses. She saw Gwen, who had to be sick to death of the sight of her, so she kept her distance. Breathing in the familiar scent of hay and horses and saddle soap, she leaned against one of the posts and closed her eyes.

And that was where Rob found her some half an hour later. He made a great big noisy fuss upon entering the stable, presumably to warn her of his presence and give her time to either flee or resign herself.

"It took you longer than I'd have thought," she said, not bothering to open her eyes. "What did you do, check under every bed in the inn?"

"We're not all as skilled as you at tracking people in the dead of night." He leaned on the post beside her, close enough that the fabric of their sleeves rubbed together, but no closer. "I'm sorry I didn't listen to you. All I meant to say was that I trust you had sufficient reason to do what you did."

Marian sighed and wished she believed him. "You're so eager to trust people."

"I—what—" he sputtered.

"You lost all your friends last year. I think you don't know how to even exist without being surrounded by people you love and trust. You've convinced yourself that I'm one of them. That's why you wrote me back even when you must have known I was using your letters to follow you. You don't know how to be alone."

He was silent, but his body remained tense, and she knew she had hit a nerve. She told herself that she shouldn't mind being a convenient way for Rob to fill an emptiness. She was used to being useful.

Chapter 12

*R*ob could not go to bed without visiting the kittens one last time, and Marian must have been in a conciliatory mood because she went with him, going so far as to sit on the clean straw and allow one of the bolder kittens to paw at the sleeve of her coat.

Rob sat beside her and produced his flask, holding it out to Marian. To his surprise, she took it.

"It seems like a night for hard spirits," she explained, after drinking and passing it back to him.

"Because of the cold?"

"Because we're both maudlin."

Rob wanted to tell her to speak for herself, but she was right. He took a long drink of gin, wincing. A few good meals with decent ale or wine and now gin tasted like bile laced with arsenic.

"I'm homesick," he said. "Not for a home—I haven't had one of those in a long time. But for the way things used to be. I've made a mess of everything and I can't go back."

She nodded but didn't ask him to explain. Likely she didn't

need to; between the contents of his letters and what she had seen while following him, she already knew the state of things.

"You love him very much, your Mr. Webb."

"Not in the way you mean. Well, if I had known that he fancied men, then perhaps I'd have felt differently and made a fool of myself, but I—Christ, even though we weren't like that, we were together."

She held out her hand for the flask and he gave it to her. "There are different manners of being together," she said after drinking.

Rob took the flask back and drank. "I've killed for him and I'd do it again," he said. The gin was getting to his head, because he had never talked about this to anyone.

"Likewise," she said tightly. That was the first she had said about her reasons for killing the duke and Rob knew better than to press for more. Instead he handed her the flask.

"You know, my letters weren't only bait so that I could follow you," she said some minutes later.

His heart thudded in his chest. "Oh?"

"You weren't an entirely unengaging correspondent."

"I'm staggered by the praise."

"And you were one of only two people I could speak to about my predicament," she said.

"The other was Lord Holland?"

"Percy, yes. As I said, Marcus knew as well, but we sent him all over Britain and France to wheedle his way into the confidence of the duke's old cronies to see if they recalled anything about this Elsie Terry or Louise Thierry. I could hardly go to him and weep on his shoulder."

Rob didn't quite know where to start with that statement. He wanted to linger over the idea that she considered her caustic letters to have been the equivalent of crying on someone's shoulder. And then he wanted to know all about how she had persuaded her brother—who was, by all reports, mild mannered to a fault—to engage in nothing less than espionage with a frankly terrifying cast of characters. But there was also the fact that she had apparently learned his mother's real name. If she knew that much, it was only a matter of time before she found out that he was Elsie Terry's son. The longer he put off telling her, the greater a betrayal it would be when she learned the truth.

But right now they were on the edge of what felt to Rob like something terribly fragile and terribly important, proof that they really had become friends over the course of all those letters. He didn't want to spoil it.

They drank until the flask was empty and the kittens had tired of playing with their boots and fallen asleep in a fluffy heap. Then they made their way inside and up the stairs, occasionally leaning against one another when the room began to spin.

Once the door was shut, Marian flung herself across the bed. "I've never been this inebriated. This is why they warn against gin."

"It's an efficient means to an end," he agreed, lying beside her.

"What odds would you give me that I get my boots off before falling asleep?"

The incongruity of Marian, who usually spoke like somebody's persnickety grandmother, now adopting the argot of a bookmaker, made Rob laugh. He rolled over to bury his face in the pillow. "Four to one. But I know you too well to bet against you, even when you're as drunk as a lord," he said when he had collected himself.

She sat up and promptly fell off the bed.

"The mattress was right *there* a minute ago," she said, regarding the floor in some bewilderment.

"Get back up here," he said, extending his hand. "You're in shark-infested waters and this is the only raft." She let out a sound that might have been a laugh—he wouldn't know, as he had never heard her laugh and hardly even seen her smile. She grabbed his hand and hauled herself up, then he tugged her onto the bed. She landed on top of him, which hadn't been his goal but wasn't something he was going to complain about either. When his hands came to rest on her hips, she looked down at him with a slightly unfocused gaze.

So far, he had avoided touching her unnecessarily, primarily because not everyone found touch comforting, but also he was afraid that all it would take would be a squeeze of her fingers and he'd tumble from admiring her to adoring her, or from adoring her to whatever was even worse. But by now he knew that if she didn't want him to touch her, she'd move her hand away, and if he didn't want to fall in love with her, he was already fucked.

He was lost, and he had been from about the first time she sent him a scathing letter—what kind of person did that to a man who held her future in the palm of his hand?—and followed it up with trivia about that Italian fellow and his peculiarly organized version of hell. The die was cast long before she showed up in that little room, covered in blood. And now, after two days together, his fate was sealed.

He reminded himself that this was the Duchess of Clare, that anything he started with her would only end in heartbreak. But he had never paid much attention to warnings.

"You were a terrible blackmailer," she said, poking him in the sternum. As she had been using both hands to prop herself up, this gesture caused her to fall fully onto his chest.

"It was a humbling experience," he agreed.

"Given another fortnight, I could have worn you down. I'd have had you paying me a few pounds just for the favor of praying for your soul." Her words were muffled, both by the alcohol and the fact that she was speaking the words directly into the fabric of his shirt. "You didn't even seem to be having any fun at all. This afternoon, when you stole from those dreadful young men, you enjoyed yourself. So why did you blackmail me?"

"It was the principle of the thing, darling. When I came into possession of a secret like that, I had to use it to wrangle money from the duke."

"But you didn't go after the duke. You went after me."

"It would have been worse to go behind your back," he countered, aware that this likely did not make any sense to her, seeing as it no longer made much sense to him, either. "I regret it. I regret a good many things, but that's near the top of the list."

"I don't regret it. I needed to know the truth, and following you did get me some exercise."

"Some exercise," he repeated faintly.

"And I've never been much use at making friends in the ordinary way, so that was a pleasant surprise."

"Making friends."

She raised her head, seemingly with great effort, and scowled at him. "Do you mean to repeat everything I say?"

"I beg your pardon."

"Quite," she said imperiously. "I still think you were a lunatic to respond to my letters."

"Everybody who loves me says that. Truly, you should hear my mother and Kit on the topic of my lunacy. Besides, maybe I was after a bit of exercise and some new friends, too."

"Not some new friends. One new friend. Just me. You and me."

"You and me, Marian."

She studied him, a little bleary-eyed but warm and intent. "Your eyes are pretty," she said, and Rob felt a flush spread from his chest to his neck to the tips of his ears.

"Pretty," he repeated.

"Like honey. Or brandy, maybe. Or cinnamon."

"Those are all good things," he said idiotically. But, really, he had always just thought his eyes were brown.

She nodded very seriously. "And you have a lot of freckles."

"They're all over me," he said and then froze, as if he hadn't been half naked in front of her just a few hours earlier. Her eyes were wide now, as if she had the same thought.

Then she reached up and tucked a strand of hair behind his ear.

"Marian," he said, barely managing to get the word out. "What is happening right now?"

She cast him a faintly disappointed look, and good Christ that should not have gone straight to his prick. "You said that all I had to do was say the word."

"Oh God," he said. "Have you always been this brave?"

She sniffed. "Obviously."

With that, she rested her head on his chest and went to sleep.

Chapter 13

When Marian woke, two things struck her with equal urgency. First, her head was filled with knives and rocks. Second, her head was currently on Rob's chest.

She remembered the previous night with rather more clarity than she would have liked, or even thought possible given the volume of gin she had consumed.

"Are you finally awake?" Rob asked, his voice a raw rumble that she could feel as much as hear. "Thought you might have died."

"Ha ha," she managed, and the sound of her own voice was enough to give the knives and rocks in her skull a good shake. She winced into the fabric of Rob's shirt, aware that she probably ought to extricate herself, but as that would involve moving, it was presently out of the question. It would also involve Rob removing his arm, which was a heavy band around her waist. "Maybe I did die, and this is the hell I so richly deserve."

"Hell seems unlikely, darling, because I'm entirely comfortable, even if you did wake me with your snoring."

The injustice of this was enough to make her raise her head. "I do not snore."

"Oh really. So all those sounds must have come from some other person who spent the night burrowed into my clothes like a vole. Or perhaps I dreamed I was on a pig farm."

She reached for a pillow and smacked him in the head with it. "Slanderer."

"You snored the previous night as well. You snore like a man twice your age and twice your size. It's impressive, really."

She hauled herself out of bed. One advantage to falling asleep in her clothes was that now she didn't have to get dressed, which was excellent news as she didn't think she was equal to so much as putting on a pair of breeches in her current state.

"You'll feel better after a cup of tea," Rob said.

"I know," she said, peeved. "This isn't the first time I've had too much to drink."

She made her way to the window. The glass was frosted over, so she unlatched the window and threw it open, letting in a gust of icy wind.

"What in hell?" Rob grumbled.

"Checking the weather." The first rays of sun had barely made it over the horizon, but she could tell that overnight a hard frost had settled over the valley that their path would take them through. It was not a sensible day for any kind of travel, least of all on horseback, and certainly not while hungover, but it would take only a few hours to reach Little Hinton. "There isn't any snow on the ground, at least," she said.

An hour and several cups of tea later, they were on their mounts. The countryside was hushed and still, the sky a field of gray that almost concealed the rising sun. The horses' hooves crunched along the frozen turf and Marian winced in sympathy. She nudged Gwen into a canter, but when she looked over her shoulder, Rob was several lengths behind.

"Why are you dawdling?"

"I'm doing no such thing," Rob said.

"You are." She brought her horse to a stop to let him catch up. "Is your horse injured? Are you injured?" She doubted that the paltry matter of a hangover would be enough to slow him down.

"Nothing of the sort."

Marian might have believed him if she hadn't spent the past two days noticing what it looked like when he was lying—a widening of the eyes, a tendency to blink. Then she noticed that his cloak wriggled in a manner that cloaks decidedly should not. She stared at him. "Tell me you don't have a kitten under there."

"I don't have a kitten," Rob protested. "They're much too young to be taken from their mother, Marian. What kind of monster do you take me for?"

She sighed. "Show it to me."

"It's not a kitten."

"You and it are both going into the river unless you show me."

He sighed and pulled back a corner of his cloak. The animal within extended a paw and took a swipe at his jaw, which he just narrowly ducked away from.

"You deserved that," Marian observed. "What *is* that thing?"

Rob looked down at the creature and Marian followed his gaze. Indeed, it was not a kitten. It was the ugliest cat she had ever seen. It was missing an ear and most of its tail and had a general air of defeat and hardship.

"While I was admiring the kittens, I noticed this poor unfortunate fellow skulking about in the shadows. He's skin and bones, as you can see for yourself. It looks like he found himself on the wrong side of one of the barn cats. I don't think he's much of a mouser." The cat gave a great squawk and wriggled in Rob's arms. "Cats are supposed to like horses. He's spent his whole life in a stable, for Christ's sake. Why can't he settle?"

"I daresay he hasn't spent much time on horseback," Marian observed dryly. "Give him to me."

Rob hesitated. "He's quite violent, as you've seen."

She held out her hands. "Give him over," she said, in the tone of voice she had noticed made him go quiet.

She promptly wrapped the animal snugly in her cloak and then tucked it under her arm as if it were a loaf of bread. As boys, both Marcus and Percy had been softhearted fools, forever attempting to rescue wounded animals, but lacking the stomach to deal with such matters as blood and bone. Marian had learned quickly how to spirit those poor creatures to safety.

"If I get fleas, it's your fault," she called out, cantering off. "It's for your own good," she told the cat a mile or so later. "Nobody expects you to understand this, and you have every right to be displeased with him for kidnapping you, but he couldn't leave you to starve."

"You know I can hear you," Rob pointed out.

"*And* he's rude," she told the cat.

"How come you talk to the cat but never the horses?"

She looked at him as if he were a lost cause. "Because horses don't speak English."

"And cats do?" he asked.

Instead of answering, she nudged Gwen into a gallop.

The day warmed a little as the sun rose higher, which Marian would have found promising if the improved weather hadn't also brought with it some ominous-looking clouds. Before long, she could almost taste the incoming rain.

"How much farther to your father's house?" Rob asked.

"An hour, at most."

The storm was closer than that, though. They both looked at the darkening sky.

"There's a barn up ahead." Rob pointed to a stone building not far from the path. Marian wanted to protest, and perhaps Rob could tell, because he forestalled her arguments. "There are two horses, a cat, and a man who would rather not get drenched," he said. "Let's go to the barn, and you can figure out some other way to be stoic about the elements later on."

She shot him a glare, but her heart wasn't in it, and they rode off in the direction of the barn.

The first raindrops fell, and before long the drizzle became a steady patter of rain. With no warning, a clap of thunder banged overhead, and Marian's horse startled and began to rear up. Marian immediately bent low over the mare's neck and held on with her thighs. This wasn't the first time a horse had reared on her and she doubted it would be the last. For what felt like minutes but was likely no more than the space of a few heartbeats, the horse danced about, frantic and mad, before finally settling on all fours.

"Well then," Marian said, a bit out of breath. "Just when we were about to get bored. Thank you, Gwen." Then she turned to Rob, who was staring at her. "Shall we?" she asked.

"You should have dismounted," Rob said.

"She would have bolted, and I'm not losing a horse that isn't mine. Besides, think how frightened she would have been, all alone and cold and hungry in a part of the country she doesn't know."

"Jesus Christ," he muttered.

Marian looked at the bundle of cat that she still held under her arm. "As for you, don't even think about complaining."

"You kept hold of the bloody cat?"

"Tell me, Rob. How would the situation have been improved by dropping him?"

Rob shook his head and cantered off ahead of her.

When they reached the barn, they found it empty. In the roof was a hole so large that they had to put the horses on one end and then confine themselves to another corner, the cat in a dejected bundle at their feet.

It was only natural, she supposed, that they leaned into one another's space. It didn't have to mean anything other than that they were both cold and didn't have much room. They had spent the night even closer.

"Marian," he said, looking down at her with an expression that was far too earnest.

"Don't be stupid," she said, not hoping that he'd listen. "If you mean to kiss me, just do it. There's no need for all this." Had he not noticed her behavior the previous night?

He snorted, but his expression was no less fond. "I'm gone on you."

She refrained from rolling her eyes. "You just think you are because you're used to being surrounded by friends and now I'm all you have."

"Bollocks."

She was right, of course, but she had never seen the point of arguing with men when they got emotional. "Very well, then," she said. "You're gone on me. I can't imagine what you hope to achieve by saying so."

This was evidently yet another instance of her being inadvertently hilarious, because he laughed. But his laugh was soft and—heaven help the poor man—it was terribly fond and tender. He brought a hand up to her jaw.

"I'll let you puzzle that one out on your own, Marian."

For a moment they stood like that, barely a hair's breadth between them, and Marian let herself believe that nothing mattered except the little space in the world that their two bodies took up together.

She leaned forward, closing the small gap between them. It had been so long since she'd kissed anyone, and for a moment she hesitated, not sure which way to tilt her head. Rob paused as she did and she knew that he always would, that he'd let her take the lead, that he'd never take more than she gave. A rush of warm and soft feelings threatened to engulf her, but she was made of sterner stuff than Rob, so she ignored all that silliness and kissed him.

He tasted like the sugary tea they had imbibed by the bucketful that morning. His lips were a little chapped as they moved against hers, and the hand that skimmed under her coat to land on her waist was cold through the fabric of her shirt. He was careful, but not tentative.

As they kissed, heat gathered in her, and she was hit by a rush of relief that she still had this—that after everything, she could still want someone.

Then a chunk of the roof fell in and they both swore. He grabbed his bag, she grabbed the cat, and they were in their saddles without a word being exchanged, as if they had done this a thousand times and as if they were going to do it a thousand more.

Chapter 14

Rob shielded his eyes from the rain and looked at the view before him. The path, which had been steadily but gently climbing all morning, took a turn and suddenly they had an open view of the countryside for miles around. It was a study in drab browns and grays: barren fields, leafless trees, and even a sky that was dark and dull with heavy rainclouds. He had the vaguely embarrassed sensation of being an unexpected visitor, of seeing a person in old clothes and without their hair done. The landscape probably looked better at any other time of year—dressed in the green of summer or even blanketed in snow.

He realized he had brought his horse to a stop and Marian had followed suit. "It probably looked much nicer a few months ago," he said, as if he had to apologize on the land's behalf.

"The countryside is exhausting to look at in the summer," she said, wiping raindrops from her face with the sleeve of her coat, "with every flower and tree competing for one's attention. And it looks precisely the way one expects it to, with sheep dotting every hill and every branch heaving with leaves. It's already achieved whatever it's going to achieve."

"I don't follow."

"In the winter, you can imagine that the land could become anything. In the summer, all that's left is for winter to come."

Rob had never heard anyone express anything of the sort and didn't know what to say, or even to think, beyond reflecting that if anyone were to enjoy an uninterrupted view of mud and dirt it would have to be Marian.

A few minutes later, Rob could make out the faintest suggestion of a roofline through the rainfall. It was about time. He was no stranger to discomfort—he and Kit had spent a winter living rough, and prison was cold and wet on the best of days—but the past hour ranked among the most unpleasantly damp of his life. He wanted nothing more than to strip his clothes and roast before a fire. Marian hardly seemed to notice the cold, but Rob knew better.

He held up a hand to shield his eyes from the rain so he could get a look at the place. He didn't know what he was expecting, but this certainly wasn't it. Marian's father was the Earl of Eynsham, and the natural habitat of an earl was a ridiculous stone palace with great silly windows that let out all the heat. Or perhaps one of those aggressively symmetrical manors whose columned porticoes gaped like the mouth of a whale. Rob was pretty sure a house with more than four bedrooms couldn't help but look sinister.

But this house was about one step removed from a cottage. All it needed was a thatched roof and some chickens pecking at the dirt and the picture would be complete.

Marian rode straight to a tiny stable at the back of the house and dismounted her horse in a single easy movement. "Netley!" she called. Rob realized he had never before heard her raise her voice, but one had to nearly shout to be heard over the rain. "We'll have to tend to the horses ourselves," she said.

Inside the stable, though, they were greeted by a man the approximate age of God himself, bearded and grizzled and pointing a rifle at Rob's chest.

"Netley!" Marian called happily. "Oh dear, you don't recognize me in these clothes. It's Lady Marian."

The man stepped closer, taking in her attire with narrowed eyes, but lowering his weapon. "Is that so?"

"Yes," she laughed. "I've ridden all the way from London."

"Daft thing to do, my lady."

"Wasn't it? This is Mr. Brooks."

Netley looked critically at Rob. "He's not the one you married."

"Mr. Brooks made sure I didn't get into too much trouble on the way here."

Netley glanced at Rob and muttered something that sounded like *had your work cut out for you, then.*

"Thank you, Netley. You'll see that the horses are looked after, won't you? They've had a rough few days." Then Marian strode across the muddy stretch of dirt that stood between the stable and the house. Rob followed, his boots squelching in the mud.

She pushed open a door at the rear of the house and soon Rob found himself standing in a snug kitchen whose warmth almost made him sob with relief. But Marian didn't so much as pause in front of the hearth. "Hester!" she called, crossing the kitchen and passing through another door. "Hester!" she repeated.

Rob opened his mouth to suggest that they divest themselves of their sodden cloaks and boots, but before he could say anything, Marian shoved the cat at him and strode farther into the house.

They were now in a small entry hall that was almost entirely filled by a staircase. At the top of those stairs appeared a woman in a plain gray dress and a crisp white apron. "Lady Marian!" she cried and made her careful way down the stairs. Marian went up to greet her halfway. "Lady—Your Grace, rather," the woman who was presumably Hester repeated, holding Marian at arm's length and looking at her. She appeared even older than Netley, her face deeply creased and her hair so white it hardly contrasted with her cap. "But you're soaked through, dear. You'll catch a—"

"How's my father?"

Hester hesitated for a moment, and Rob saw Marian's face fall. "Not well, I'm afraid," Hester said, accepting Marian's proffered arm as they descended the stairs. "He'll be glad to see you. And thank goodness you're in breeches. How clever of you to think of that. He doesn't know any time has passed, bless him, and Nurse and I have stopped trying to set him right. We've been telling him you're out for a ride, God forgive us, but it felt cruel to tell him every day that you're gone. He always took it so poorly."

"You've done the best you can," Marian said firmly, a hint of steel in her jaw. "Hester, this is Mr. Brooks. He brought me here from town."

Rob gave the old lady as decent a bow as he could manage while sopping wet and holding a discontented cat. The cat mewled in protest.

While Marian disappeared upstairs, Rob let himself be bustled into the kitchen, where the elderly servant brought him a clean shirt and Rob set about drying both himself and the cat while attempting to salvage his coat. The boots, he feared, would not be long for this world. He reached inside his coat and felt for the packet of letters; they were damp around the edges but might be saved if he laid them out to dry. As for the cat, he crouched by the fire, glaring at Rob with murder in his eyes.

When Rob had got himself as dry as he could without stripping naked, he looked around the kitchen. It was small and square, not so different from the kitchen in the cottage where he had grown up. He decided to make himself useful and brew a pot of tea. Four plain cups hung on hooks over a dresser and a commonplace earthenware teapot sat nearby. On the shelves sat an assortment of vessels and cannisters.

But the sugar cannister was nearly empty and the tea caddy had only an inch or so of leaves at the bottom. He glanced around the room and noticed what he should have seen right away—there was no sign of a kitchen maid, much less a cook. On the hearth was a single pot instead of meat on a spit or the array of dishes he would expect in a grand kitchen.

He scraped a small portion of the remaining tea leaves into the teapot. So it was that Marian found him some time later, carefully pouring weak tea into a pair of cups.

She looked like a drowned rat, with her dark hair plastered against her head. Her lips were pale with cold and her face blotchy with patches of red. But there was the stubborn set of her jaw, the uncompromising slant of her eyebrows, the flinty hardness that sometimes flashed in her eyes. He saw those details, and with them he saw the whole of Marian, and he never wanted to look away.

He handed her the cup because that was all he could do. "I take it your father isn't well." He had put together enough from what Hester had said to have a pretty good idea of what was wrong with the earl.

"He didn't recognize me."

"I'm sorry."

She wrapped her hands around the teacup. "It's worse than last year. I knew he wouldn't recover. The physicians all said he would only worsen. But I thought—well, I was stupid."

"You were hopeful."

"As I said."

He wanted to take her hand, but instead he sipped his tea. "Why is your father here and not at Chiltern Hall?"

She gave him a level look. "We lived here when I was a child, before my father inherited. He was a younger son, and nobody ever expected him to inherit, least of all himself. That's immaterial. In any event, when his wits began to leave him, his mind often drifted back to those days. A little over a year ago, when he began to become lost in the grounds and ask after my mother, I thought he'd do better here, in the house that he still seemed to think was his home." She took a sip of her tea and grimaced, presumably because it was both weak and unsweetened. "Clearly it didn't work. I ought to stop being surprised when my plans come to nothing but disaster."

There was more to it than that, obviously. There seemed to be no servants in the house besides the old lady, Netley, and a nurse. The woodpile was down to the last few logs and the kitchen had only the plainest food. How was it that the Duchess of Clare was unable to keep her father in grander style?

From the wrinkle between her eyebrows as her gaze flicked between the weak tea and the contents of the kitchen, he guessed that she was similarly puzzled. He realized that for the first time, he was seeing her worried. She hadn't been worried when they fled from London, nor when that blasted horse nearly threw her. But now she was distressed.

If he were in his right mind, this shouldn't matter to him. He had accomplished what he set out to do: he had delivered her to safety and ensured that she didn't throw Kit to the wolves. Now he could leave her here and return to whatever was left of his life. When he returned to London, he could write her a letter informing her whether she was wanted for the duke's murder.

But he already knew that he wasn't going to do any of that. This sense he had that her troubles were somehow his troubles was dangerous; he knew that. But Rob had never been deterred by danger.

Chapter 15

$\mathcal{M}$ arian made her way through the house. The furniture was mismatched, all the walls needed painting, and every room was half the size of its counterpart at Chiltern Hall. The chimneys on the east side of the house smoked badly, there were signs of a leak in the roof over Hester's bedchamber, and every window rattled in its frame and let in great drafts of air.

In the bedroom that she was to use, she peeled off her wet clothing and began dressing in the clothes Hester left for her. They were Hester's own clothes, and Hester was about twice her size and six inches shorter, but Marian was only happy to get out of her sodden buckskins. She hung her wet clothes before the weakly sputtering fire. She would need to do something about this predicament immediately; she couldn't bear to think of her father in a cold house.

"Hester," Marian said when the old woman arrived in the bedroom, carrying a stack of bed linens, "where are the other servants?" Marian sent more than enough to cover the wages of a pair of maids.

"Forgive me, Your Grace, but you asked us not to write unless it was urgent."

Marian took one side of the sheet and helped drape it over the mattress. She had indeed asked Hester not to write, believing that the fewer people who knew where her father was, the better. "Whatever it is, you ought to tell me now."

"I had to let the maids go. Sir John Fanshawe raised the rents this past quarter."

"I see," Marian said faintly. A chill passed over her, and it wasn't entirely from the cold. "He must have raised it by quite a bit if the sum I sent didn't cover it."

Hester twisted her hands in her apron. "He knows the Duke of Clare has deep pockets. And . . . well. He said something about how you'd prefer for Lord Richard not to know about the decline in the earl's health."

Of course that would be it. Of course this Sir John would be friends with her eldest brother. One of the reasons Marian had moved her father clear across the country was that Richard had begun to drop hints about their father being safer in a place where he could be looked after, a nice private institution where he could be kept under lock and key—and where the estate would be safe from any of their father's caprices. Marian had understood what he meant: a lunatic asylum.

Marian had already taken steps to ensure that the earl couldn't touch any more of his capital, but she could hardly tell her brother that she had been forging their father's signature for years. Besides, the damage was already done—the money was gone, the estate having long since dwindled to the acres around Chiltern Hall and a handful of investments that Marian kept out of her father's reach. Locking the earl up would do nothing to improve the estate's fortunes. Richard was living—quite comfortably, at that—off his wife's fortune, and if the remnants of the estate were left untouched, it would recover in time for Richard's son to have something to inherit. But she knew from experience that there was no reasoning with Richard; he was one of those men who greeted all attempts at argument with vitriolic disagreement, simply on principle.

So Marian married the duke, the duke paid off Marian's father's debts, and Marian moved her father across the country to a place where he would be out of Richard's sight and, she hoped, out of Richard's mind.

But now this Sir John Fanshawe, some man she knew only from the handful of letters in which she had arranged to hire this house, thought he could threaten Marian's father's safety simply to line his pockets. She didn't know if Richard would care in the least what Sir John had to say about the earl's mind. But it didn't matter. A year of marriage to the duke had taught Marian to take seriously even the idlest of hints made by men who had the power to make good on their threats.

Something wilted inside her at the knowledge that after everything—after murder and bloodshed, after nights spent sneaking around and mornings spent plotting, after nearly losing her life—she was once again captive to the whims of a man who knew her to be powerless against him. She felt hard done by to be blackmailed twice in a single autumn. She felt hard done by in general, truth be told.

What she needed now was to get up and dust herself off. The past year may have been an unbroken string of catastrophes, but she was alive and Eliza was healthy. A year ago nobody would have given her odds on either outcome. Even now, months after Eliza's birth, she sometimes hesitated to eat or drink lest it bring on another bout of sickness; sometimes she would smell peppermint or ginger and forcibly remember the noxious and useless decoctions prescribed by the duke's physicians. Sometimes she woke up gasping, remembering the weeks of headache and inability to fill her lungs, the sense of drowning on dry land.

After Eliza was born, the wet nurse had seen to the baby, who at that point seemed as much a stranger as she had while still in the womb, the only thing they had in common their likely demise. *This is my daughter,* Marian would think to herself, trying to believe it. She would look at Eliza's tiny red face and try to see the child as hers, as family.

When the first blackmail letter came, it somehow made more sense than *daughter* and *mother* and *wife*. Here was a mission, here was a task. It was a rope thrown to a castaway. And there was the man on the other side of the letters—by turns clever and dangerous, a shadow in the night, a person who seemed to see her as who she was. Marian had almost found her way back to the person she believed herself to be.

Well, she had almost done a good number of things, and none of them amounted to the slightest good. She had almost provided for Percy's and Eliza's futures but now the duke was dead and there would be no money from him. She had almost managed to care for her father but instead he was in a shabby little house and the threat of the asylum still hung over his head.

And over her dead body would she allow anyone else to threaten the safety of the people she loved. She simply would not stand for it. She had dealt with worse than Sir John Fanshawe and lived to tell the tale.

Chapter 16

*R*ob was still at the kitchen table, on his second cup of tea, when he made the acquaintance of yet another elderly person, this one even older than the last two. The average age of residents in this house had to be damned near a hundred.

"And who are you?" asked the man. His gray hair was tied in a neat queue and he wore knee breeches and a pair of spectacles with thick lenses. He was, Rob supposed, the butler.

"Robert Brooks." Rob wasn't sure why he felt compelled to use his full name. He didn't have much to do with butlers and had to admit he was a little bit awed. "I brought Marian from London." That made him sound like a coachman—which, he supposed, wasn't far from the mark.

"Marian?" the man asked sharply.

"The Duchess of Clare," Rob said, correcting himself.

Some confusion dissolved from the man's face. "A grand lady. A fine figure of a woman."

That wouldn't be how Rob would describe Marian, but he supposed it wasn't untrue, if one's ideal of womanhood extended to scrappy termagants with acid tongues, which Rob's admittedly did. "Indeed. I made a pot of tea, if you care for some." Rob hoped he wasn't being presumptuous.

"Can't stand the stuff." The butler instead passed through a door and emerged a moment later with a bottle of brandy. "Foul day. Have this instead. Do you a world of good." He splashed a generous quantity into Rob's cup and then another few inches into one of the empty cups. Rob murmured his thanks.

"One of Lucy's gets won a hundred guineas at Newmarket. Richard was a damned fool to sell him. A hundred guineas, I tell you."

"That's quite a sum," Rob agreed.

"I should say so." The man fixed him with dark eyes that must have once been coal black but were now clouded over. He narrowed them and pointed a bony finger at Rob. "Drink your brandy to ward off the chill, young man."

Rob did as he was told. He didn't much care for brandy but the way the butler was looking at him would have got him to drink candle wax.

"No sign of the rain letting up, is there? Probably have to find a bed for the duchess. Eleanor will be beside herself."

Rob didn't know who Eleanor was, but if the pattern held then she would be approaching a hundred and ten. "I believe she's taking Hester's room."

"Dear me, no, can't have that. You'll have to tell Eleanor yourself, because I need to make sure Lucy's dry." He rose to his feet and Rob followed suit, not liking the way the older man wobbled.

"I can check on Lucy myself," Rob offered. There was no way this man was going to make it through the muddy bog that was the expanse of ground between the house and the stable without coming to grief.

"Father!"

Rob turned to see Marian in the kitchen doorway.

"You weren't in your room." Marian approached the old man, reaching for his arm. He took a shaky step backward and lost his footing. Rob caught him, the old man's frame a negligible weight in his arms.

"Your mistress would not like to hear that you've been running about with no shoes or cap," the man told Marian, firmly but not unkindly, as he regained his balance. "I suggest you do something about that before she returns."

"I see," Marian said slowly, her face doing something complicated. "What a very good idea. What if I walk you upstairs first?"

Hester appeared then, red-faced, out of breath, and full of apologies. Pleading and coaxing, she got the man to follow her upstairs.

"Your father," Rob said unnecessarily once they were alone.

Marian began opening and shutting cupboards and drawers, as if performing an inventory, or as if the solution to all her troubles might be found among the ladles. "He's the only one who's unaware of it."

Rob didn't know what to say. He couldn't imagine someone he loved not knowing him. "He's very old," he said.

"He was past fifty when I was born." She opened a door on the wall opposite the hearth and peered in. "Larder. Some butter and cheese. Oh, and a ham. Well, that's the first good news I've had today, and it's a ham."

"He was about to go outside to check on a horse named Lucy."

She stilled with her hand on the door. "Lucy's a stallion back at Chiltern Hall."

"Lucy is a stallion?"

"Short for Lucifer. He was horrible as a two-year-old but Marcus and I doted on him and we got him sorted out. Father thought his name was indecent, so he shortened it to Lucy." She turned to face Rob. "He was going to go outside? Heaven help us. Hester and Nurse left him alone to find clean bedsheets. He has to be watched every minute of the day and night." She pulled at the cuffs of a gray woolen gown that was too short in the sleeves and too wide everywhere else.

"Who is Eleanor?"

"My mother. She died when I was a baby."

Rob wondered how much of the confusion that the elderly experienced had to do with the fact that the people—and animals, apparently—who filled their memories were no longer around, and the insides of their minds no longer matched the world outside.

It occurred to Rob that when the earl spoke of the Duchess of Clare, he had meant Marian's predecessor, Lord Holland's mother. It also occurred to him that he had just had a conversation with an earl. He didn't think he had ever done that before. He certainly hadn't wanted to. Christ, it had been bad enough when Rob had thought him a butler.

And yet now that he thought about it, he could see the old man's resemblance to his daughter. But where she was hard edges and sharpened knives, he seemed gentle, vulnerable almost.

Marian resumed her progress through the kitchen, now opening jars and cannisters and examining their contents. He followed her, leaning back against the shelves she was inspecting. "Oats," she announced, and put the cannister back.

"If you're doing an inventory, would you like me to write things down?"

She was only a few inches away, close enough that when she took down the next cannister, her arm brushed against his shoulder. "I'm not doing an inventory."

"I know."

"Dried currants," she said, peering into an earthenware jar. "Care for some?"

"Why not." He held out his hand, palm up.

She removed a cluster of tiny currants with two fingers and brought it not to his palm but toward his mouth. He stayed perfectly still but so did she, the fruit six inches from his lips, her eyes a little wide and her jaw firmly set. He bent his head and took the fruit, letting his lips remain on her fingertips only for a moment before pulling away.

"The landlord has raised the rent," she said. "To far more than what we agreed on. It's plain extortion, with a little blackmail thrown in just for fun. I can't ask Richard for help, because he'd like nothing more than to have our father sent to some genteel version of Bedlam, which is why Father needs to be here rather than anywhere near Richard. I could write Percy or Marcus and ask them to come up with the balance, but Marcus is impossible to find in addition to never having any money, and as for Percy, he has troubles of his own."

Rob wanted to sift through this information about asylums and extortion, but decided to focus on what was apparently Marian's most pressing concern. "Who pays for the running of this household?"

"My father's estate is depleted, but not so badly that he can't afford to live in a shabby little house with a couple of elderly retainers."

Sometimes Marian didn't even bother to pitch her voice in a way that made her lies believable. He took it as a compliment. "That's not an answer."

She looked at him as if deciding whether to tell him the truth. "I do. I pay for it. A few years ago, I won a bit of money at Newmarket. Not a lot, mind you. But enough, and the duke never knew about it, so it was safe."

"Why not use your father's own income?"

"Because it's all tied up. When Father's mind began to slip, many of his decisions were not very wise. And even in my grandfather's time, there were years of bad investments. Much of the estate was either sold or mortgaged." She frowned. "The debts were terrible."

He heard the past tense there. He had been wondering for months what had possessed her to marry the duke, and he supposed that now he had an answer. "The duke?"

"He paid off my father's debts when we married." She let out a bitter laugh. "I really thought that would be an end to it. I am *not* going to let Sir John Fanshawe steal from my father."

"Naturally," he agreed. "I didn't for a minute think you would. You've dealt with worse men than Sir John Fanshawe, whoever he is."

"Precisely," Marian agreed.

"I wonder if you'll shoot him or poison him," he mused.

"Certainly not, Rob, be practical." She was almost smiling. "Unless his heir is more fair-minded, killing the man would do me no good at all."

She had said his name only a handful of times, and he wanted to clutch each instance in his fist like a lucky penny. "So you plan to make off with all his silver," he said.

"I'm going to talk to him," she said repressively.

"Ah, so he's a reasonable, charitably minded fellow?"

She gave him a withering look. "Doubtful. But I can't move directly to more straightforward means without first giving him a chance." The cautious optimism slid off her face and was replaced with something grim. "However, I can't present myself in his drawing room until I know whether I'm wanted for murder."

Rob started calculating how quickly he could get to London and back. "I could do it for you. I could visit his home, possibly have a few choice and terrifying words with him, but more likely help myself to whatever I can fit in my pockets and easily pawn."

She looked like she was considering what he said, but then turned on her heel and began inspecting a wall on the opposite side of the room. When she came to another door, she opened it. "Ah. This is the room Hester said you could have. There's a bed and a chair. I think it'll do for you."

He followed her in. "I'd sleep in the stables and you know it."

"Nonsense." She began to strip the bed and he went to help her, pulling the sheets off one end of the mattress. "I'll bring you clean sheets presently." She was gone before he could protest. He opened his satchel and took out all their shirts and the bar of soap. In the scullery, he filled a bucket with water and dumped the shirts and soap in to soak. He wasn't going to have an eighty-year-old woman do his wash. Worse still, he wasn't going to have Marian do it.

Marian returned, carrying a stack of neatly folded sheets. He intercepted her in the kitchen. "I'll make the bed myself."

"You're a guest."

This was so absurd that he started to laugh.

"Oh good," she said, pushing past him into the bedroom. "You've finally gone round the bend. The signs have always been there."

"Remember when you kidnapped me?" he choked out.

"If that's what this is about, you can feel free to leave." She gestured to the door.

"Oh, be quiet. Want to hear the funniest part? I was kidnapping you, too."

"No you were not. I would have noticed."

Now he had tears in his eyes and he was laughing so hard his stomach hurt. He braced a forearm against a bedpost and rested his head against it. "Marian. If you attempt to make my bed I will riot."

She tossed the linens onto the mattress. "You can sleep on the floor for all I care." Her voice came from so close that he could feel her breath on his neck.

Slowly, he turned to face her. Her jaw was set and she was almost glaring at him, as if daring him to close the gap between them. He stayed still, maybe even pliant, wanting to let her choose whether to do this and also wanting to see exactly what she'd do with him.

"It was a bargain," she said. One of her hands came to rest on his upper arm, almost as if to hold him in place, and he let out a breath he hadn't known he was holding. "We made a bargain."

She bent toward him, slowly and carefully, so their lips brushed, moving her mouth against his as if learning the shape of him. When he put a hand on her hip, she stepped closer, her skirts grazing his legs.

"So we did," he agreed, his lips touching the corner of her mouth. They had made a bargain—and they had done it because when they each were without anyone else to trust, they had trusted one another.

She moved so slowly and deliberately it was as if she were inventing the concept of kissing right there on the spot, as precisely as if she were counting change in the marketplace. He kissed her back with none of those qualities, with nothing but profligacy.

He brought a hand to the nape of her neck. She had put her hair up, and he wanted it. He found the pin and plucked it out, then unrolled the long plait he had been eying for days. He loosened the cord that tied it and twisted his fingers into the mass of heavy black locks, tethering himself to her. Her lips were warm against his own, and her grip on his arm tightened.

She moved even closer, crowding against him, then nudging him backward until he hit the wall. Finally, there was nothing but the hard wall behind him and her warm, insistent presence against his chest.

When she skimmed a thumb over his cheekbone, he heard himself make a sound that was almost pained. No—it was a sound of longing, because that's what he was doing, that's what he had been doing for days and weeks and months, and he hardly knew what to do with himself now that he had Marian in his arms. Here she was, hard angles and unexpected warmth, busy hands and unspoken demands, and it was everything he had tried not to hope for and wanted anyway.

It was happening too fast. He wanted to remember this—the taste of tea on her lips, the jut of her hip under his hand. He wanted to take this moment and press it between the pages of something properly embarrassing. He didn't want this to be consigned to the heap of things he could remember only wistfully. Rob knew that he had a long and varied history of fucking things up, and he didn't want to add Marian to the list. He wanted—he wanted things that wouldn't happen, but try telling that to his heart.

He pulled back and shook his head a little. He kept his hands on her, hoping that she'd understand that he wanted to keep her close—Christ, did he ever—but she stepped back immediately.

"No," he started to protest. "Wait."

She gave a brisk shake of her head, one that he wanted to believe only meant *later*.

Chapter 17

When Hester went off to see whether any of the silver could be spared for the pawn shop, Marian sat at the kitchen table, rested her face in her hands, and sighed. She was exhausted, tired to a degree she hadn't known it was possible to achieve, not only from a lack of sleep but from the monotony of failure. She only looked up when she heard the chair across from hers scrape along the floor.

"Rain's letting up," Rob said. He must have been out to check on the horses. Droplets of water clung to his face and the fabric of his coat. He wore rainwater and mud the way other men wore silk coats, only better, and she *wanted* him. She wanted to take him to bed and make terrible choices. And he wanted her, too, even though the poor idiot had tried to be decent earlier. There had been a bed *right there.*

It had been so long since she'd felt that way, so long since she'd wanted to touch and be touched, that she half feared those desires belonged to someone else, some long gone and much better version of herself. When he'd pulled away, she felt as if she had been dropped into her present self from a great height, and the shock was still with her.

And now he was looking at her as if she were a cake, if cakes were also religious icons, and she was possessed of a mortifying certainty that she was looking at him in precisely the same deranged manner.

It was time to say something bracing, clearly. Time to remind them both of the lay of the land.

"You'll probably want to be off soon, then."

He raised his eyebrows. "Not especially. But I'll need to go anyway. Do you want me to bring her back to you?"

"Bring who?"

"Your daughter." Rob tucked a loose strand of hair behind his ear. Marian thought his cheeks might be a bit red. "Do you want me to bring her back here? With her wet nurse and Fleet Ditch and whoever else she requires."

Marian stared at him. "You would do that?"

"Well, yes." Now his cheeks were decidedly red, as if he were embarrassed to be making the offer.

"It would mean days in a carriage with a fractious infant. She's exceptionally fussy and belligerent," Marian said, a little proudly.

"I'm accustomed to traveling with fussy and belligerent companions," he said softly, too affectionately for Marian to take offense.

It was too cold for a child to make an unnecessary journey, and this house was too small to add a child and a pair of servants for no reason but her own contentment. But the fact that Rob had offered to undertake a journey that would mean at least a week of additional travel, and offered it as if he were tossing a farthing to a crossing sweep, made her feel as if all her clothing were too tight.

"Thank you," she said, "but Eliza ought to stay at Clare House. Percy is forever popping in and out of the nursery. Far more often than I do, in fact. They would miss one another." She looked at him and tried to find any sign of judgment in his face. She almost wished she could find some.

Hester returned to the kitchen. "Mr. Brooks. His lordship asked whether you were staying for supper."

He raised his eyebrows. "I was under the impression that he thought me a coachman."

"It's hard to say what he's thinking, sir."

"He noticed that you're a gentleman," Marian said absently, only realizing what she had said when she saw Rob stiffen across the table. "The way you speak, the way you carry yourself. He'd pay more attention to those things than he would your coat or your boots. Not that there's anything wrong with your coat or boots," she admitted, letting her gaze travel up his body.

"The way I carry myself," Rob repeated, as if she had accused him of untold depravity. "What does that even mean?"

"I'm probably being very snooty. Perhaps everyone in the middle class speaks the way you do. I wouldn't know, I'm afraid."

"Middle class?" he sputtered, fully outraged. "Middle *class*? I—you infernal—you make me sound like a *banker*." He shot her an offended look and stalked away to join the earl in the dining room.

Marian hung back behind the door, surreptitiously watching

her father and Rob share a meal of baked ham and discuss some sentimental novel Marian had never heard of but which Hester had apparently read aloud to the earl.

Surely the stab of envy she felt did her no credit, but she wished she were at the table as well. It was over a year since she had shared a meal with her father, and if she had known on the eve of her wedding that it would be the last time he would know her, then she might have tried harder to make it matter, or at least tried to sear it into her memory. It wouldn't do her any good to dwell on that, though; she should consign that last dinner to her list of regrets, where it would have abundant company.

Well, she could set things right for him now, somehow. She could at least make sure that he lived in comfort. She didn't know what would become of her in the future, but now she could act. She could—she wasn't quite certain what she could do, but Rob didn't seem to have any doubt that she could do it, and he was the expert in criminal enterprises, so she was inclined to trust his judgment.

The fires, however insufficient she had at first deemed them, warmed the kitchen to the point that she longed for the cold, so she took one last look at the men at the dinner table and then grabbed her cloak off a peg by the door, stepped into her boots, and walked outside into the dusk. The rain had dwindled enough that she was able to run across the garden to the stable without soaking her cloak.

Marian did not think that she imagined the alarmed look with which Gwen greeted her. "Don't worry. You'll have all night to rest before you need to leave this nice, warm stall." Netley had covered the horses in blankets, but the stable was warm in the way stables often were when filled with large animals. She checked that they had clean straw to bed down in and more than enough hay and water.

She wasn't surprised when she heard the stable door open and then snick shut. "How was dinner?" she asked without turning away from Gwen.

"Your father told me all about those circles of hell you once mentioned to me." This was Rob pretending to be ignorant, as if upon receiving that letter he hadn't immediately hunted down a copy of the *Inferno* and then beguiled an Italian into translating it aloud for him. "He also told me that you translated it when you were—"

Marian's hand stilled on Gwen's forehead. "He mentioned me?"

"Bragged about you, actually." Rob came up behind her. "You're proficient in five languages."

Surely, the fact that her father remembered her, at least as a person who might exist somewhere in the world, shouldn't make her chest feel so tight. "He's told me many times that my Greek is simply execrable, so that's a lie." She gripped the top of Gwen's stall door. "Where does he think I am?"

"I don't know. I don't think he knows, either. But he sang your praises until the bottle of wine was empty. He's a lovely man and he adores you."

"Thank you for telling me." It was a kindness, one of too many from Rob. He had done her more kindnesses in the past week than she had performed over the course of her life. He was reckless in his kindness, extravagant to the point of decadence.

Sometimes she thought he didn't realize what he was doing, that it was simply his nature to hand over everything that a person might hold dear without any regard for what havoc such prodigality might wreak on the sensibilities of a reasonable person.

She could feel his body behind hers, not touching, but near enough that she could reach back and touch his hip if she wanted. She could feel her body remembering the shape of his, and she wanted that again, wanted to turn around and feel the muscles of his arms bunch and flex as he held himself still. She wanted him all to herself and felt greedy with wanting him. He had made a sound earlier, a little needy sigh, and she wanted to make him do it again.

"According to your father, Fanshawe collects rare manuscripts," he murmured in her ear. "From what I've heard, there are dealers who specialize in those and don't ask too many questions about where they come from."

Her heart thudded in her chest as she realized what he was doing—not only supplying her with useful intelligence but reminding her that she had the means to take care of the people who were hers to care for.

When she turned to face him, his hands immediately landed on her—one on her waist, one on her elbow, as if he had been waiting. As if he wanted this as much as she did. He certainly talked as if he thought her something special, but that was just a habit he had fallen into, a silly bit of moonshine of the sort that men were wont to indulge in. She let herself press her lips to his and felt his small indrawn breath, the slide of his hand to her lower back, the gratifying race of his heartbeat. As before, he let her be the first to taste his lips, the first to press closer.

It would never do, none of it would. If this kept up, she'd be flat on her back, or up against the wall, her skirts around her waist, and she'd be glad of it. Holding her breath, she turned him so he was facing the closed stable door. It took only the slightest nudge of her hand on his hip, the briefest pause of bemusement, and then he went, as if he had been waiting for her to do precisely that, as if lovers were forever pushing him against things. Perhaps they were, and wasn't that a thought.

He put his hands against the door, palms flat, as she stood on her toes and brought her mouth to the part of his neck right below his ear. He shuddered then, his skin warm and soft under her lips. As she moved her mouth under his jaw, she felt the rasp of stubble. She pressed the length of her body against his.

"Is this all right?" she asked.

He was silent for a moment, then cleared his throat. When he spoke he sounded dazed, barely awake. "Better than all right."

"I want to touch you." Best to get that out in the open, she supposed.

There was another pause, during which she could almost hear him determining whether there had been an unspoken *and not have you touch me back* in her statement. There had been. "I'd like that," he said. "I think I'd like anything you did to me, Marian."

At those last few words, heat began to gather low in her belly and she rocked her hips against him, only once. Then she returned her attention to his neck, and he removed his hands from the door only long enough to loosen his collar and give her access. Now she could push his hair aside and kiss the place where his shoulder met his neck and trace the line of his collarbone with her fingertips. He tasted like rain and salt and cheap soap.

In the ordinary course of things, a man's collarbone held no fascination for her; she would be hard pressed to name a single part of any man that did. But she had watched Rob for days and, however much she might like to deny it, had known him for longer. She knew the outside of his body and the inside of his mind and somehow, under her hands, it all connected. She thought that maybe if she could get her hands all over him, every inch of him, then maybe it would all start to make sense.

She slid one of her hands down the front of his waistcoat, button by button, over his hard chest and the plane of his stomach. She could feel his indrawn breath when she went lower, stilling at the hem.

"Still all right?" He had said that he'd like anything she did but he couldn't know that in advance. Or perhaps he could; she couldn't, though. And while she felt reasonably confident that they were on common ground, she wasn't about to start groping around in a person's underthings without their say so.

"Yes." He swallowed, and she felt it under her lips. "Please."

That *please* was nothing more than a whisper, hardly vocalized at all, and she liked it. She wanted more of it. She dragged her hand lower and felt the hard length of him against her palm. He was fully hard, and only from her pawing ineptly at him and administering a few odd kisses. She liked that, too.

"That can't be comfortable." It was probably very unkind to

tease a man in this state but she was feeling pleased with herself and pleased with him. She smiled against the warmth of his skin.

He made an inarticulate noise that she translated as agreement, tempered by a hesitancy to beg her to do something about it.

She unfastened and opened his breeches just enough, then shoved his shirt out of the way. When she curled her hand around his erection, it was hot in her palm, with enough wetness at the tip that she could glide her fist down its length and back up again. He made a sound that was somewhere between a hiss and a sigh, as if signaling a very gentle and welcome capitulation.

She hadn't done this before, not exactly, but the mechanics seemed straightforward, and even if they hadn't been, his responses were enough of a road map. "Yes," he said. "That. God yes."

Every muscle and sinew in his body was taut and she wished she could see them all but settled for letting her left hand roam across his chest, his hip, anywhere she could reach, while with her other hand she brought him off.

She could probably have made it last a very long time, teasing and stroking until he was flustered and desperate and a little cross, but it was cold and she was feeling charitable, so when he drew in his breath and balled his hands into fists and said "Marian, I'm going to—" she didn't stop.

As he approached his crisis, he folded his arms against the door in front of him and buried his face in the crook of his elbow, turning away from her. His body went even more tense, and he made a noise that sounded like swallowed words.

Then he went lax, sinking against the door with a good deal

of softly muttered profanity, and she went with him, leaning against him.

"Serves me right for not having a handkerchief, if I have to clean us up with a horse blanket," he mumbled, sounding dazed.

She realized what he meant and handed him the kerchief she had wrapped along the neckline of her bodice, and then a moment later she was in his arms, being soundly, if messily, kissed.

"Let me?" he asked. But he didn't do anything, just held her, examining her with a questioning look. "May I return the favor?"

She didn't quite know how to answer that. She wanted his hands on her; she knew how pleasurable a lover's touch could be, but she also knew—she knew other things as well. She supposed there was little damage he could do now, spent as he was. And she was almost certain that he would desist if she told him to. Almost.

That *almost* was enough to stop her. She didn't want to find out that Rob was worse than she hoped. Instead, she would remember how he had felt, what he had sounded like, and put those memories to good use later on, in the privacy and safety of her bedchamber.

"Another time," she said.

Chapter 18

*R*ob had bedded down in a number of peculiar places over the years, but sleeping under the roof of a nobleman after debauching his daughter in the stable was easily at the top of the list. It also sounded like the stuff of a very commonplace erotic fantasy, although not the sort of fantasy Rob ever went in for. To be fair, he didn't think that what he and Marian had done could fairly be called debauchery, unless Marian had been the one debauching him, and now *that* was the sort of fantasy he did go in for.

He climbed into the narrow bed. The room was small and close, with only one little window off in a corner. When the walls began to feel too near, Rob gave up attempting to sleep and went out to sit in the kitchen. The chairs were hard but he managed to arrange himself with his arms folded on the table in front of him and eventually fell asleep.

The night passed in a dreamless haze, and when he woke it was to discover Marian standing beside him. He gingerly sat up, all too aware of muscles that were stiff from sleeping badly and knowing that a day on horseback would hardly improve them. "Did you wake early to see me off?"

"Nonsense. I'm not here to see you off," she said bracingly. "I'm here to bid farewell to Gwen." But she was almost smiling, and the back of her hand brushed his shoulder. "Why are you in the kitchen? Was the bed unacceptable?"

"The bed was grand." He wasn't sure how to explain this, or whether to try. "I don't do so well with small rooms. I . . ." He searched for an explanation that wouldn't make him sound too mad but judged that he and Marian had long since passed the point where a little madness would matter. "They remind me of prison, I suppose. I have a number of complaints about prisons. Chief among them is the fact that one can't leave, but second is the closeness of the space."

She frowned. "If you had said something, I would have found someplace else."

"Saying something would have meant thinking about it, and I don't do so well with that, either, to be honest."

She gave him that penetrating look he was coming to know so well. Then she set about putting the kettle on, and together they made a pot of tea—not talking, just passing things to one another as needed, and Rob had the dizzying realization that he wanted to do this tomorrow, and then the day after.

He already knew that he wanted to keep Marian close, or to keep himself close to Marian, or whatever arrangement allowed him to see her in almost any capacity. This was no more than a variation on a feeling he had experienced many times: there were several people he chose to keep in his life and whose absence would pain him. What was new was the desire to . . . he wasn't sure. Boil water in a drafty kitchen? Prepare hot drinks? Wake too early and potter about in near silence? Some combination of all those things, probably.

It had been a long time since he had wanted a home, and he doubted that was what he wanted now. He had grown up in a proper home: loving parents, hot suppers, a roof over his head, and a cozy bed. When all that had come to an end, there had been a time when he wanted nothing more than to rest his head in the same place for more than a night or two. He had wanted a place to hang his hat, hot meals, and a table to eat them at. But he had been young then, with a lot of growing up left to do, and he had done that growing up out in the open and on the road. The urge to be still, the longing for a place of his own, had been worn out of him until he began to want the precise opposite. And then there had come those unfortunate interludes in prison, which, he reasoned, would make anyone want to keep moving. Too many nights in the same place had a way of making the walls creep closer even in the airiest of rooms.

This little domestic tableau had simply got to his head. That was all. He adored Marian, he had spent a surprisingly pleasant day in this odd house, and his poor brain had tried to do the sums and instead made an error. He'd feel more himself when he was out in the fresh air.

She set the cup of tea before him. "I don't think I'd care for prison," she said, settling into the chair he kicked out for her.

"You don't need to worry about that."

"You'll send word right away?"

He wondered what he had said or done to make her misapprehend his intentions. "Marian, I mean to come back immediately and tell you all about it myself. If the news is bad, I'll have you on a fishing boat instantly. If the news is good, I'll help you deal with Fanshawe." Another possibility occurred to him. "Unless you'd prefer that I stay in London. I don't want to be a bother."

"Ha! You long to be a bother. You would not, however, succeed in this instance."

They held one another's gaze for a long moment, and he had the sense that she knew all his most embarrassing thoughts while keeping her own safely under lock and key. "Good," he said. "Are there any other errands I can dispatch for you while I'm in town?"

She turned her cup in her hands. "I'd like to know that Eliza and Percy are well."

"Do you want me to deliver a message to Holland? He'll want to know that you're well, too, you know."

"I don't know what to say to him."

He nodded. There wasn't much one could say in a letter to a man whose father one has shot, however good one's reasons were. There was nothing Rob could say that Marian didn't already know. If she didn't find her own reasons for shooting the duke sufficient to salve her conscience, then Rob couldn't help with that. Christ, Rob knew better than most that sometimes nothing could salve your conscience. You just had to live with the guilt and find other ways to be the kind of person you wanted to be.

"I think Holland would want to hear from you even if you had killed a score of men."

"Probably. He doesn't know about my father."

"He doesn't?" Rob was too stunned to conceal his surprise.

"He was abroad when Father began to have his funny turns, and when he came back we already had enough to worry about. Besides, he would have thought me a fool for marrying his father to pay my father's debts."

Rob experienced an unexpected and altogether unwanted pang of sympathy for Holland. Imagine, returning home to discover that one's childhood friend has married one's wicked father. "So, if he didn't know why you married the duke, did he imagine that it was a love match?"

She swirled the tea in her cup. "No."

But she had hesitated rather longer than Rob liked. "*Was* it a love match?"

"No," she said, shaking her head. "It wasn't. But I didn't think I was marrying my enemy, either." She gave a humorless laugh. "I thought he loved me. And I thought I could do worse than marry a man who loved me, was willing to pay my father's debts, and didn't require a proper dowry. I thought I'd have my own household and half a dozen children and that it would be like any other marriage that began on practical grounds."

"Is that what you would have chosen?"

She gave him an exasperated look. "Who among us gets to choose?"

He prodded her foot with the toe of his boot. "Humor me."

"Fine. I always supposed I'd marry at some point, but barring that, I thought I'd carry on translating my father's manuscripts and exercising the horses."

That still didn't even begin to answer the question of what she actually wanted. "You wouldn't have wanted a lover?"

"I *had* a lover," she retorted. "More than one, in fact."

He whistled. "Busy lady."

"Not at once, you oaf. Neither were any kind of great passion, you understand. But my most recent arrangement was pleasant. Fun," she added, as if borrowing a word from another language. "She eventually became bored and subsequently fell in love with her sister's governess, with whom she now shares a cottage in Wiltshire." Marian sipped her tea. "And then I got married, so it hardly mattered. She deserved better than someone who only wanted a pleasant arrangement, I suppose."

"I don't know. Sometimes what you want is a bit of fun. However," he added, not wanting to think too hard about why he needed to be so clear on that point, "sometimes you want something else. I mean, I'm never in the same place for too long, which has made it difficult to manage anything lasting, but I . . ." He didn't quite know how to finish that statement without sounding pitiful. "I always think it's going to be lasting when I fall in love."

He looked her dead in the eye so there could be no mistaking his meaning. And she didn't look away. Instead she frowned. "I doubt that. You're too clever to lie to yourself. You probably only hope that it will be lasting." She got to her feet and stepped out of the room. "There," she said when she returned a moment later, waving a sheet of paper in the air to dry. "For Percy."

"I'll see that he gets it," Rob said, folding the paper and tucking it into his coat pocket.

"You know," Marian said, "when you press your lips together like that and look dissatisfied with the world and everyone in it, you remind me of Percy."

"I look nothing like Lord Holland," he said too quickly. According to his mother, he had every reason to look like Lord Holland, and moreover Lord Holland's father, but Rob absolutely refused to consider it. It was one thing to accept that his mother had been married to the miserable bastard but quite another to acknowledge that the man had sired him. Rob had always been quite content to assume that his mother had fallen pregnant by some anonymous and probably horrible man who paid for his mother's favors; it was quite another to imagine that it was that particular horrible man.

It was altogether too much to imagine that Marian had married—or thought she had married—the same man and had a child by him. His mind simply couldn't arrange those facts in a logical manner.

"But you do," Marian went on. "It's the cheekbones, mostly. But the cloud of irritation heightens the likeness."

"You ought to tell your Lord Holland that he resembles me. He'll be furious."

"He will and I shall."

This was probably when Rob ought to tell Marian the truth. For him not to tell her was a serious lie of omission. But he didn't know how to even start, especially since he didn't want to think about it, let alone talk about it. They were alone, so he leaned across the table and kissed her cheek, then scooped up his haver-sack and headed out to the stable.

He saddled and readied the horses. He would be taking both horses back with him, riding them in turns. When he returned to Little Hinton, it would need to be on the stagecoach, which was a dismal prospect but at least it would be fast.

Marian followed him out, the cat at her heels, looking every inch witch and familiar. She made straight for Gwen and stroked the horse's muzzle in an offhand way, as if they had been horse and rider for a decade, rather than the lesser part of a week.

"Don't let him stint on the apples," she advised the mare.

"As if I would ever do such a thing." He looked at her, as if he could burn the image of her into his memory. He had seen her in a silk gown and he had seen her in worn and dirty riding clothes. He had seen her covered in blood. And now he saw her in an ill-fitting borrowed gown with her hair crookedly pinned up. He wanted to see her a thousand more ways. He mounted the horse before he could tell her so. "I'll be back on the fifth night."

"So soon?"

He fully intended to return on the fourth night if he could manage it. "I don't have that much to do in London." They both knew that the real reason was that she would want the news he brought with him. She looked like she wanted to thank him, but instead she reached into her apron pocket and withdrew a pair of gloves. They were the gloves he had bought at the market in Sevenoaks, which somehow had been only a few days ago but felt like the experience of a prior lifetime. He felt like he had always been on roads and in inns and semi-dilapidated houses with Marian, and that everything else was a daydream.

"Yours have seen better days," she said, still holding out the gloves.

He took his own worn gloves off and shoved them in his sack, then put on Marian's. He flicked the brim of his hat and rode off.

Chapter 19

*R*ob was bleary eyed and in none too fine a mood when he arrived at his mother's house. His first stop after returning the horses had been Kit's, but Kit wasn't home and the shop was already closed, so Rob had to go to the trouble of picking the lock and leaving a note, then dragging his exhausted body to his mother's.

"If you'll put me in the blue parlor, I'll keep out of your hair until she has a minute," he told the girl who answered the door. One of the rules governing Rob's time at his mother's establishment was never to refer to her as his mother. She insisted that nobody needed to know she had an adult son. Rob had been born when she was very young, and now she was a little past forty. Precisely how far past forty was a mystery even to Rob.

The girl gave him an appraising glance, then briskly led him not to the blue parlor, but to a storeroom near the coal cellar, having evidently decided that his bedraggled state did not meet the standards of the public parts of the house.

"You smell like horses and look like death," announced his

mother when she swept into the room in a cloud of perfume and silk. "Where have you been?"

"I took the lady into the country."

"The duchess?"

"Technically, she isn't—"

"Don't split hairs with me." She sank onto an overturned crate, arranging her skirts around her. "You took her into the country? Why? Do you simply enjoy vanishing and giving me more gray hair?"

"Because she needed me."

His mother widened her eyes. "It's like that, is it?"

"It's not like anything."

She remained silent, an old and unfairly effective trick.

"I admire her, all right?" he said.

"Don't get her with child. She nearly died the last time and the midwife says she won't make it through another." She pursed her lips. "Not that the duke cared about that, of course."

The sounds of the bustling house disappeared, as if he had stood too near a discharging pistol. His face was hot, and when he met his mother's eyes he knew she could see everything that he was feeling. "I'm not going to get her with child."

"Ha! If I had a penny for every man who said that," his mother said, exasperated. "See that you don't. Dinah's fond of her—"

At the name of the midwife, he remembered that he had a couple of choice words picked out on the topic of his mother's indiscretion. "About Dinah—"

"Well, are you going to marry the duchess? That'll tidy everything up, nice as ninepence. It turns out her marriage to one duke was no good, so she marries another."

He ignored this, because the alternative was a descent into whatever mad world his mother was currently inhabiting. "I came to find out what news there is of the duke."

"He's dead, shot by highwaymen." She looked at him curiously. "You wouldn't happen to know anything about that?"

"I swear on my honor that I was in London that entire day."

"Of course you were. Tied to a bed over a shabby public house near Charing Cross, you were."

He stared at her. "Tell me you didn't arrange for that." He could imagine his mother dropping a hint in Dinah's ear, who in turn passed the suggestion to Marian.

"A happy coincidence," she said with a wave of her hand.

"Wait. You knew I was being held prisoner and you left me there?"

"I thought it might discourage you from blackmailing helpless young women in the future. You always did have to learn your lessons the hard way. Besides, it was a very nice alibi, was it not? You can thank me later. But where was Kit?"

"Kit couldn't hold up a pram these days, let alone a coach and six. I take it the highwayman remains at large?"

"Nobody got a good look at the man, it seems. The duke lingered a couple of days after being shot, which is a marvel I can only explain by the devil looking after his own."

"You should have been a spymaster, Mother."

"Who says I'm not?"

"I'd like to think a spymaster wouldn't share her friends' secrets with midwives."

"Would you, now? What if the midwife were also a friend? What if she herself had a friend in a desperate situation? What if I thought I could bring together a handful of people with a common enemy? An enemy I happen to share. I have a notion that this is precisely what spymasters do." She sighed. "Honestly, you are *so* young, Robert. A veritable baby."

Before he could protest, they were interrupted by the arrival of a maid with a tray of buns and a bottle of wine, and remained silent until the girl left.

"Lord Holland—or I suppose I should say the new Duke of Clare—has been making life very difficult for a good number of solicitors," his mother said. "The duke's body was hardly cold before he started bolloxing up investments and divesting the estate of property."

Rob didn't think any topic could interest him less than the Duke of Clare's investments, but he thought it might interest Marian. "Any other news? How's Kit?" Rob asked.

"He's well." She narrowed her eyes. "Why shouldn't he be?"

"No reason."

His mother sighed. "I don't suppose there's any point in requesting that the next time you vanish, you send a note. Poor Kit can't take the suspense of you flitting in and out of his life. He has delicate nerves."

Rob stored that away to mock Kit about for the rest of their lives. "I was gone less than a week. And I don't think I'll be vanishing again any time soon."

"Is that so? Any particular reason?"

"My advancing years."

"I think you *are* going to marry her."

He rubbed the back of his neck. "Enough of this, Mother."

"It'll be a little odd, what with her daughter being your sister."

"We've been through this. I don't accept that this is even the case."

"That's because you don't spend nearly enough time in front of a looking glass."

"You've said yourself that someone else could have been my father."

"Any number of men could have been, but I was only married to one of them, and the law is what it is, whether you like it or not. You do look like him. There's no explaining that away."

"Don't be tedious." Rob looked like his mother. Reddish hair, tendency to freckle. It was true that his mother was plump and rather short, with a round face and none of the cheekbones that Marian had mentioned, but surely there were many tall, lean men who found their way into his mother's bed in 1725. "Holland seems content to take up his coronet, and I'm more than happy for him to do so."

"To think that you could have spared yourself all the trouble of blackmailing that poor girl."

Rob decided that he would sooner die than let Marian know that anyone had described her as a poor girl. "One more thing. Do you happen to know anything about a Sir John Fanshawe?"

She raised her eyebrows. "I'll find what I can. See me before you leave tomorrow."

"I don't suppose there's a room you might let me have for the night."

"At the end of the corridor on the top floor. Ring for a bath before you even think about getting into bed."

He got to his feet and crossed the room, stopping only to press a kiss onto his mother's head. "Thank you."

He slept for twelve hours, waking only when the morning sun streamed through the uncurtained window. He dressed in a set of clean clothes that he had left behind the last time he stayed at his mother's, then went immediately to Clare House. A falsified delivery at the kitchen door, a pleasant chat with the cook, an entire plate of biscuits, and he had satisfied himself that Eliza was well. He had seen the child with his own eyes, safe in the arms of a neat-looking nursery maid. Seldom had he beheld an infant as comprehensively fat and rosy and whose cheeks deserved so many pinches as this one. He restrained himself and carried on to his next errand.

Before he left for London, Marian had asked an additional favor from him. "Percy already paid for it," she had said, giving him an address. "It's simply a matter of arranging for the portrait to get to him."

He had agreed as a matter of course. He didn't much want to see Holland. In addition to not liking the man, which he had always considered reason enough to avoid a person, he also didn't want to answer any of the questions Holland would undoubtedly have about Marian.

He would do it, though. *Here's your portrait, Marian is well, goodbye.* He could manage that much.

He hadn't expected the portrait to be quite so large, though. Marian and Holland looked out from the canvas, at least as large as life. Marian was done up in silk, her black hair powdered nearly white and her skin a similar shade of alabaster. There was a quantity of rouge in all the usual places. Holland had been done up to much the same effect. Even the baby, in Marian's arms and looking alarmingly like Holland (and alarmingly like the looking glass, it had to be said), was all pink and white.

He tried to tell himself that he didn't like the people in this portrait. They were rich and spoiled, entitled and extravagant. There was a mean little twist to Holland's mouth and something irritated and obstreperous about the set of Marian's jaw. He tried to tell himself that he knew the real Marian and that it wasn't this imperious aristocrat. But he had seen that expression on her face a dozen times and he loved it there.

There was something about seeing her dressed like that, Holland at her side, Cheveril Castle in the background, that made Rob realize exactly what he had done. She was the Duchess of Clare and he had fallen in love with her.

As a rule, he avoided thinking too much about the future and this was no exception; he knew he wanted more of Marian but hadn't considered how to make that happen. They couldn't simply ride about the countryside indefinitely. But now he saw how it would end: Marian would come back to London and live at Clare House with Holland. He couldn't imagine how he'd contrive to see her at all, let alone see as much of her as he'd like.

Wrapped in paper and tied in twine, the canvas was unwieldy, and it took some doing to get it through the streets without both it and Rob getting splattered with mud. The sun had set, which only made the operation more awkward, and Rob was treated to a variety of insults, profanity, and oaths from the people he narrowly avoided bludgeoning with the portrait.

Finally, he reached Kit's coffeehouse. It would have made more sense to bring the blasted canvas to Clare House, but he grit his teeth and decided to do a favor for Kit—and, by extension, Holland. It was obvious that the pair of them were—ugh, there was no word for it but *smitten*. Kit deserved nothing but happiness, even if he did have the poor choice to attach himself to the likes of Holland. Knowing Kit, he might be in need of an excuse to get in touch with the man, and the painting would provide a handy one.

But when he got to Kit's, he saw Kit and Holland stepping out of the coffeehouse, their heads bent together, plainly not in need of any kind of excuse to speak to one another. It would be the work of a minute to cross the street and approach them, deliver the parcel and Marian's note, and take himself off. He could do that.

But he could see Kit's face, could see the way his friend leaned toward Holland, and he couldn't interrupt. It had been a decade since he had seen Kit look openly content. It was as if something inside Kit had uncoiled—a tension that Rob hadn't even known his friend carried. And Holland was no better, looking almost giddy with happiness. It was more than a bit unsettling. Rob didn't know how to cross the street and interrupt them, because then they would stop being happy and start asking questions that he couldn't answer.

In his pocket, he carried Marian's letter for Holland. It could hardly be called a letter, consisting of four words and bearing neither salutation nor signature: "Kiss Eliza for me." It would satisfy Holland that Marian was alive, at least. But it wasn't enough, just like Rob failing to cross the street and talk to Kit wasn't enough. It was all so far from adequate. Kit deserved better. Even that prig Holland probably deserved better. Rob didn't know why he and Marian had in common this prickly inability to let their closest and best friends see the messier parts of themselves.

He stayed in the shadows and waited for them to leave, waited even longer for the shop to close, stamping his feet to ward off the cold. Then he picked the confounded locks for the second time in less than a day, left the painting and Marian's note in plain view, and prepared to leave London once again.

Chapter 20

On the third day after Rob left, it began to snow.

Marian and Netley did their best to keep the cart horse warm in the stable as the snow continued to fall throughout the day, gathering in hillocks and waves across the garden and piling high against the kitchen door. It was the sort of wet and clumpy snow that didn't want to be swept and left sheets of ice in its wake.

Marian tried to reassure herself that Rob wasn't delusional enough to think that this was acceptable traveling weather. He would stop at an inn, flirt with everyone and everything, pet a dog, hold a baby, and wind up spending all his money on rounds of drinks for his new friends. A snowbound inn was probably Rob's idea of a grand time. She really didn't have to worry.

She didn't like to think about why she was worrying in the first place—Rob, after all, had triumphed over greater dangers than inclement weather and had the scars to prove it—so she set about clearing out a room that seemed to exist only to store old and broken bits of furniture. She sorted out what could be sold or given away, then put aside the rest to have broken down for firewood. That accomplished and the room empty save a serviceable bedstead, a mostly functional wardrobe, and a couple of other odds and ends, she dragged up the mattress from the tiny ground-floor bedroom that had been too cramped for Rob to sleep in. This room was much bigger and airier than the room downstairs and perhaps wouldn't make Rob feel quite so closed in. She liked the idea of him sleeping in this room she had arranged for him with her own hands.

He might not come at all, of course. He might have decided that he preferred being in London, where he belonged, not in the country in a ramshackle house with a woman who caused him nothing but trouble. That would be eminently sensible of him. She would congratulate him on having finally allowed reason to prevail for once in his life.

When night fell, Marian lit a lamp and read aloud to her father, who thought it peculiar that a literate stranger was in his midst but treated her with the cordiality and kindness with which he had always treated everyone. Occasionally she caught him looking at her as if he thought she was just a little familiar, like someone he had met in passing a long time ago. She caught a glimpse of herself reflected in the darkened window and had what she imagined was the same sensation, catching a glimpse of the person who had once been Marian Hayes.

When her father fell asleep, she extinguished the lamp, and the landscape outside the window suddenly became visible. The moon wasn't full, but it reflected brightly off the snow, giving Marian a view clear down the length of the drive until the wind picked up, concealing everything but a veil of swirling snow. She was debating whether to run out to the stable to check on the cart horse, when she saw a dark figure silhouetted against the white of the snow.

She didn't know how she knew it was Rob, and perhaps it was just that whoever it was had to be foolhardy and impetuous, but she ran down the stairs and flung open the door, letting in a gust of wind and no small amount of snow.

"The back door was blocked with snow," Rob said. His cape was caked with snow and ice, but at least he had had the sense to wear the cape in the first place. "Had to go to the front. About to ruin your parquet, Marian."

"To the devil with the parquet." Marian shut the door before the entire hall filled with snow. "What is wrong with you? What possessed you to travel on such a night?"

"Wanted to see you, love. The roads are in a state, let me tell you." His voice sounded ragged and his face was red with cold. He didn't even have a muffler, the idiot. She wanted to kiss him—she wanted to check him for frostbite—she wanted to yell at him for traveling in dangerous weather and for all the other risks he had ever taken in his life.

"Get in the kitchen so I can pour some brandy down your throat and then slap you."

"Promises."

She bullied him through the house and into the kitchen, where she divested him of his outer layer of clothes and shoved him into a chair before the fire. Then she did kiss him, even though she really ought to be carrying on with warming him up, or scolding him, or both. His lips were cold against hers, but they warmed up as she kissed him, so maybe she was accomplishing something after all. When the hand that had settled on her hip began to slide lower, she returned to her senses. "How did you get here from the coaching inn?" she asked as she knelt to build up the banked fire.

"Hired a pony cart to bring me to the end of the drive." She could feel his eyes on her. "I didn't tramp through the snowbanks, if that's what has you worried. I wouldn't do you much good if I were dead, now would I."

She sniffed skeptically. "There's brandy in the cupboard on your left. Pour two glasses and tell me what news you brought." Something occurred to her—something she ought to have realized the minute she saw him at such an hour, in such weather. "I suppose it can't have been good news, if you were in such a hurry to—"

He took hold of her hand with fingers that were icy cold. "It's fine news, Marian. Eliza's well. Percy's well. The duke is dead, and nobody got a good look at the highwayman who shot him."

She went rigid. This was the best possible news, and she supposed she ought to be happy, but instead the relief hit her like a blow to the head. Everything was as well as it could be, which was far more than she deserved. For a week now, she had been doing whatever she could to ignore her worries and instead concentrate her efforts on doing what had to be done. And now that it was over, she felt like a marionette whose strings had been cut.

The hand holding her own became an arm wrapped around her, a solid body holding her close. He didn't say anything, which was good because there was probably nothing intelligent that could be said to a grown adult who was, it had to be admitted, sobbing on the kitchen floor.

A glass of brandy somehow found its way into her hand and she drank half of it in one shaky gulp, spilling some onto her chin. Rob swiped it away with the cuff of his shirt, as if tidying up people in the throes of hysterics was all quite ordinary, nothing remarkable at all. To her side, the cat eyed her with grave distaste, and Marian was glad that at least someone in this kitchen had standards.

She had spent a long time—months, the better part of a year—trying very hard not to have any feelings at all, except for anger, which was highly motivating, after all. And now that she no longer had a reason to be so ruthless with herself, all her emotions came rushing back uncomfortably, like sensation returning to a limb. With those feelings came a wave of—of affection, of fondness, of something terribly like fascination with the man beside her. She wanted to shove it far away, back where she had been keeping all the other things she didn't want to feel, but it was too late for that.

He took the glass from her hand and drained it himself. "Now you look cross, which I suppose is an improvement over bereft. I have one other bit of news. Lord Holland has been making merry with the Clare estate. I don't know the details, but the Tories are scandalized and even the Whigs don't quite know what to think."

Marian frowned. If Percy was acting as the rightful inheritor of the Clare estate, then it sounded like he didn't plan to reveal his father's bigamy to the world after all. Well, good for Percy, she supposed. That was what he had been raised for, and if he could live with the risk of someone coming out of the woodwork with information about the duke's first marriage, then so be it. "If you don't want the duke's legitimate son to inherit, making sure Percy does inherit is your best bet. So this is good news all around." She had rather reconciled herself to the prospect of being a disgraced woman and a commoner. More than reconciled herself, truth be told; she thought she might dread returning to Clare House, returning to that life, more than she dreaded the hangman. But that was immaterial. She was being silly, that was all.

She took hold of the poker and began prodding the fire back to life. The only real problem left to her was Sir John Fanshawe. If Percy was the duke, she could rely on his help to pay the rent, but the idea left a sour taste in her mouth.

"As much as I enjoy sitting on the floor with you, I'm half starved."

Marian turned to look at Rob, because there was no trace of facetiousness in his voice. He sounded as if he did enjoy sitting on the floor with her, as if he had been looking forward to nothing so much as that very act. When he said that sort of thing, made those troublingly earnest allusions to his feelings for her, she knew he wasn't toying with her, but she couldn't take him quite seriously and didn't know how to react. The last person who had poured that sort of nonsense into her ear had been the duke, and now it sounded both implausible and somehow ominous.

"Don't try to charm me," she said, scrambling inelegantly to her feet and pushing open the door to the larder. There was steak and kidney pie somewhere in there and she hoped she could contrive to heat it up.

"I'm not trying to charm you. You'd know if I were trying to charm you. Do give me some credit." He stepped into the larder behind her and relieved her of the pie. "I charm strangers, and people I want to go to bed with, and strangers I want to go to bed with. And also people I've upset. And, all right, you fit in at least two of those categories, but the fact is that you'd have my bollocks off if I tried it on you."

"I have no interest in your bollocks."

"Evidence suggests otherwise," he said lightly, ignoring her sound of protest. "Besides, charming you wouldn't suit my purposes." From one of the hooks near the hearth, he removed a pot, dropped the pie into it, and hung it over the fire.

She refused to rise to the bait and ask him what his purposes were, because no doubt all he would give her would be a load of moonshine. "Are you certain that's how you're meant to heat a pie?"

"Not in the least. Do you have a better idea?"

Hester was long since asleep so there was nobody to ask. "I think we're meant to use the oven." They both regarded the box-like space set into the wall beside the stove as if it were a mysterious relic of a forgotten age. "But I can't see how it would be hot enough yet."

"I feel enormously relieved that you're as ignorant as I am. Kit is forever mocking my ineptitude in the kitchen. In any event, I don't want to charm you." He regarded her with eyes that were somehow sharp and warm all at once. "I want you to know my worst possible self, Marian."

She swallowed and looked away. "Why?" she asked.

"Because I don't want you ever to be disappointed in me."

"Considering the circumstances under which I made your acquaintance, my opinion of you could only improve." She took out a second glass, filled both with brandy, and sat at the table.

"I really am tired of disappointing people," he said, sitting beside her. "Do you know, I couldn't work up the courage to see Kit? He was with your Lord Holland, and all I could think was that I'd interrupt them and have to watch his face fall."

She grimaced, understanding this sentiment all too well. As much as she missed Percy, a part of her dreaded seeing him because of all the explanations and apologies their reunion would require. She lifted her glass of brandy to Rob in a wry salute. "I don't think Kit would really be disappointed in you. He's known you since you were a child, yes? I doubt that you've done nothing but impress him since then."

"True. But at some point I—I don't know. I started keeping secrets."

She thought about what he had said about wanting her to know his worst self. "And you want me to know all your secrets?"

"I wish you did, without my having to go to the trouble of telling them to you."

That was always the trouble, wasn't it? The act of confession took private shame and guilt and made them irrevocable. Once one gave voice to one's more sordid truths, there was no ignoring them anymore. Perhaps that was why the Catholics thought it was a sacrament; perhaps it really was a sacred mystery, or perhaps it was just the horror of having one's worst parts exposed.

"You already know my worst secrets," she said. Maybe that was one explanation, at least, for why she felt so bound to him.

He knew the worst and he was still there. He would probably always be there, by her side, if that was what she wanted. That was terrifying—it felt like more responsibility being shoved in her direction, as if she didn't already have enough. There wasn't going to be an *always* between them and she didn't want his—devotion, or whatever it was—if instead he could bestow it on someone more worthy and less troublesome.

"I also know your best secrets," he answered.

When she took hold of his collar and pulled him down for a kiss, she told herself she was doing it to stop him from saying anything even worse.

Chapter 21

Rob had returned at breakneck speed, spending the night in the godforsaken stagecoach, all while telling himself that he was in a hurry only because he owed Marian information, and that his urgency had nothing to do with how much he wanted to see her.

But he had thought of her the entire time he was gone, and now that he finally had her in arm's reach he didn't want to let her out of his sight. And she had been thinking of him as well—she had brought him up to a sparsely furnished but large bedchamber that was a vast improvement over the tiny room by the kitchen.

"Thank you," he said, dropping his satchel onto the carpet.

She made an impatient noise and waved her hand dismissively.

He began removing items from his coat pockets so he could assess the worst of any damage the snow might have inflicted. The knives would need to be cleaned to prevent rust, but when he patted the pocket that held Marian's letters, he found that they were dry. "I brought you intelligence about Sir John Fanshawe."

"Oh? From your mother, I suppose."

He looked up from the knife that he was polishing with a soft piece of chamois leather and raised his eyebrows. "What do you know about my mother?" He didn't think he had mentioned much about his mother to her.

For a moment, Marian looked caught out, but she recovered herself. Probably she felt guilty about snooping. "I didn't follow you about for two weeks without gathering that your mother is who she is."

"Are you fishing for information or are you too delicate to say 'brothelkeeper'?"

"I wasn't certain if 'brothelkeeper' was disparaging," Marian said primly. "What did you learn about him?"

"He's the usual sort of bastard. Stingy with his servants, late with his bills, a trial for the women in his household. She doesn't know of anything especially horrible about him but doubts that anyone would shed a tear if he parted ways with some of his coin." Before leaving London, Rob had asked his mother to collect a bit more information, just the usual sort of details anyone might want if they planned on a bit of burglary. But that information would concern the Fanshawes' London house—if Marian wanted to steal anything from Fanshawe's house in Kent, they would need their own intelligence.

He took the final weapon, the pistol, out of his coat pocket, meaning to clean it along with the rest of his weapons. This was the weapon Marian had taken from Lord Holland's hand and used to shoot the duke, and he hadn't paid it much attention beyond making sure it was safely stowed in his coat pocket. But now he regarded it in the firelight. He might have expected Holland to have a fancier pistol than this one, probably one of those jeweled dueling pistols that gentlemen bought in pairs. This was an old sea service pistol with a walnut stock and a twelve-inch barrel, very much like one he bought off a sailor a few years ago and gave to Kit. In fact—he held up the pistol to catch the light. And there it was, a scratch near the trigger guard that he'd have known anywhere and a faint *W* carved into the stock.

That meant Kit had given Holland his own pistol to use during the robbery, trusting that Holland wouldn't drop it or leave it behind and effectively cast a trail of breadcrumbs from the duke's carriage back to Kit. And Holland *had* left it behind—not on purpose, but he had left it nonetheless.

Christ, but Kit should have known better than to get mixed up with Holland. He could have been hanged for this, for this scheme Holland and Marian had cooked up between them. It was reckless and dangerous, and here Rob was doing the exact same thing: walking headlong into danger in an asinine attempt to be of service to a person he shouldn't care for half as much as he did.

And yet, that night he was probably going to have the first uninterrupted night's sleep he had managed in ages, all because Marian had seen to it that his room was large and airy. Because she had not only remembered that his poor lunatic mind required a constant reminder that he was not imprisoned, but she had also made sure that he would feel safe.

He trusted her. He was probably a fool but, God help him, he was Marian's fool. And when he looked at that pistol, all he felt was a rush of relief that she had used it to put an end to the duke. He placed it beside the knives that he had laid out on the hearth rug, at the hem of Marian's skirt, where she sat beside him on the floor. It was fitting, he thought, that he had laid all his weapons at her feet.

She was sitting very close to him, and it wasn't an accident. Nothing with her—nothing with either of them—was ever by chance. Every time he moved, the linen of his shirt brushed the wool of her gown, and whenever he turned his head, he caught her looking at him. Which, of course, meant that she was catching him looking at her, so at least they were on the same page regarding enjoying the looks of one another.

"It's getting late," he said.

"Do you want me to stay?"

"Of course I do," he said immediately. "I think I'll always want you to stay. I think that, given a choice between more time with you and almost anything else in the world, I'll always choose more time with you."

Marian looked like she didn't know whether to be amused or alarmed. "I really was just asking if you wanted to—"

"I know what you were asking. My answer is yes, to anything you could possibly ask of me."

She made a sound of acute exasperation and kissed him.

Chapter 22

arian had watched Rob meticulously clean each of his knives, his long deft fingers going about their business as if handling deadly blades was second nature. She had watched him stretch his legs out before the fire, watched him peel off his coat and shove his sleeves up. The firelight glinted off him—off the freckles on the bridge of his nose and the copper hair on his arms, off the worn leather of his boots and the scars on his hands.

He was pleasing to look at. She had known that as soon as she saw him in that little room where she had imprisoned him. It was perfectly reasonable to find him attractive; if one believed even half the contents of that ballad people persisted in singing about him and Mr. Webb, many people agreed.

But when she looked at him, what she felt wasn't attraction. Or it wasn't only that. It was a bright spark, something warm and glowing that took up residency in her chest and refused to budge. It was something like contentment, only sharp and with teeth. It was the urge to wrap her hand around his arm and not let go. It was the knowledge that he would let her.

It was foolish, of course. She didn't know if, after everything, she was capable of falling in love, or indeed if she ever had been, but she knew she could lose things, and she didn't want to lose him. She didn't know what her future held but she could be sure it didn't hold any more of this—a closed door, a quiet house, weapons and firelight and the steady rumble of his voice. But what good had ever come of her trying to be sensible? Reason had got her nowhere.

If she wanted him, and he wanted her, it seemed the most uselessly indulgent self-flagellation not to do precisely as they pleased. What a luxury it was to think about what she wanted and not have the answer be a matter of life or death.

She pressed up into his kiss, digging her fingers into his shoulders, feeling his muscles shift beneath her touch. And in response he moved closer, one hand on her jaw and the other on her hip. As he leaned in, she felt the length of his erection press against her.

Well, she hoped it wouldn't be a matter of life or death. With any luck, she could manage things so that the troublesome part of his anatomy stayed clear of places where she didn't want it. If she explained as much to him, he would listen. She was almost certain.

"Where did you go?" he murmured, speaking the words into her hair. The hand on her jaw was still there, but the hand on her hip had slid to the small of her back, where it rubbed gentle circles.

"It's nothing," she said quickly.

"What do you need from me? What do you like?" He kissed under her jaw. "Or what do you not like?"

Marian didn't want to talk about what she didn't like. She

didn't want to ask for something not to happen and then have
it happen anyway. She didn't want to think about that, so she
took hold of his collar and pulled him down hard for another
kiss, pressing her body against his until his breaths were shallow
and needy and so were her own. This was what she needed, the
scratch of his stubble against her skin as he kissed her neck, the
feel of his hands as he sought out the places that made her breath
hitch.

In one movement he scooped her up, one hand under her
backside and her legs around his waist, never breaking the kiss
until he deposited her onto the bed. Rob braced above her, and
for one moment it was exactly what she wanted. Then everything
came crashing back, this room shifting into another place, another time. It looked like this was something else the duke had
taken from her—just the simple ability to go to bed with the person she fancied.

Rob rolled so she was on top of him and suddenly everything
was all right again—it was just the two of them.

"You didn't answer my question," he said, his voice low and
rough. He was in total disarray—his hair unbound, his coat off,
and the picture he made against the clean white sheets was almost enough to distract her from the words he spoke. "What
would you like? My hands? My mouth?"

"Yes," she answered before he could suggest more. "Those
things. Not anything else."

"Excellent. That's exactly what I want as well, then."

She doubted that, but wasn't feeling particularly argumenta-
tive, so she bent down and kissed his neck, breathing in that scent

of woodsmoke and leather that he somehow always carried with him. His heart was racing, his pulse fast and urgent beneath her lips, and she loosened his collar to expose more of him. "What do *you* like?" she whispered, judging it only fair to return the question.

"Marian. Literally anything."

She refrained from rolling her eyes. "I was honest with you."

"I'm being honest. I really just want to please you. That's what I like." He looked away, his cheeks stained red. "I like being"—he scrubbed a hand over his jaw—"I like being what my partners need."

She raised an eyebrow. "Very well, then," she said, because it sounded rather like he was asking her to tell him what to do. "Take off your shirt."

She must have got it right, because he complied.

"I've wanted to get my hands on you," she went on, running her fingers over the lean muscle, the hair, the scars. She skimmed a thumb back and forth over his nipple and watched in satisfaction as he tried to twist into her touch. He made a picture like this. He looked debauched. Desperate, even. "Look at you," she murmured.

Rob swore and sat up, pulling her with him, to settle her in his lap. Then he began rucking up the hem of her skirt, sliding his hand underneath, along the inside of her thigh until his knuckles brushed between her legs. It felt so good, just that whisper of a touch, that she wanted to push against his hand, make him do more and better things with it.

"Marian, you're so . . . is that all just from . . . Christ—"

A very stupid question, but she would forgive it. "I don't know what else you think I've been about this evening."

She felt his smile against her neck. His thumb skimmed against her and she rocked into his hand. She could feel how wet she was against his palm as they moved together. "Good," she said. "That's what you're meant to be doing." She had intended the words to be brisk and sure, because hadn't he said that he wanted to do what pleased her? But instead she sounded breathy and fervent. It must have not gone amiss, though, because he swore again and drew her close into another kiss. Then he moved a little, and she felt him brushing against her entrance. "Yes or no?"

Must he keep asking her these things? "Yes," she decided, because if it was unpleasant or unseemly she would tell him to go find something more useful to do. He slid a finger—two fingers?—into her, and she wasn't sure why she was gritting her teeth, as there was no resistance or pain, of course there wasn't, it was just—

The fingers were gone but the stroking continued, only over the outside of her body now. He wanted to make her feel good, he had said. He wanted her to feel safe, to *be* safe. And that was how she felt—safe, as if all it took was one well-intentioned man to shelter her from the wrongs of the world. It was nonsense, but it was intoxicating nonsense. "You're so good," she whispered, because he seemed to enjoy hearing that sort of thing, and she enjoyed the mortified pleasure that swept over him at hearing the praise. One of his hands found its way to her breast, and she realized she was rocking her hips into his hand.

He shifted beneath her and she felt how hard he was. He hadn't taken his breeches off, nor unfastened them, nor even adjusted himself. Embarrassingly, that was what did it. The knowledge that Rob was probably uncomfortably hard and desperate to do something about it, but that he was enduring it for her, tipped her over the edge, and she reached her climax as if she had fought for it.

She collapsed gracelessly to the side and Rob had the gall to laugh at her. She kicked him half-heartedly in the stomach, then slid her foot lower to prod at his erection. It was as hard as an iron bar and he groaned at the contact.

"Merciless," he said, taking hold of her ankle. She thought this was when he'd unfasten his breeches, but instead he kissed the inside of her knee. "Another?"

"Don't ask silly questions. Find something useful to do with your mouth."

He laughed, his breath warm against her thigh as he kissed his way slowly up her leg, shoving the fabric higher and higher.

"Do take your time. I can't see any reason why you'd be in a hurry," she observed, nudging his shoulder with her toe.

His only response was to hitch both her knees over his shoulders and bury his face between her legs. When he gave a little hum of satisfaction, she could feel it as much as hear it, and she had to cover her mouth with her hand to keep from crying out as he licked and stroked and kissed. She imagined him still hard and untouched.

"You'd better not finish in your breeches," she said. "I don't want to have to explain that to Hester when she comes to collect the laundry."

He laughed, his shoulders shaking and his mouth momentarily stopping what it was doing, his breath hot and teasing against her skin.

"I didn't tell you to stop."

He glanced up at her. "Darling, we can either talk about Hester or I can resume what I was doing. Not both."

She raised an eyebrow, then tangled her fingers in his hair and gave his head a little push in the right direction.

He groaned. "Do that again." She pulled at his hair, not too hard, but enough so that he'd feel it, and he moaned into her oversensitive skin.

"Don't stop," she said, trying to make sure it sounded like a command and not like begging. "I'm going to—" And she fell apart under his touch, one hand fisted in his hair.

As she got her breath back, he lay with his forehead against her stomach.

"You've been so good—"

"Oh Christ," he said, covering his eyes with his hand.

"—so good that you probably deserve better than my hand. But my hand is what you're getting."

"God, Marian—"

She sat up and pushed him onto his back, then set about unfastening his breeches. "There, hush, I've got you," she said as she wrapped her hand around him. His jaw was clenched and his length so hard that she almost felt bad for him. "You did so well to wait," she said, because she liked seeing that conflict between embarrassment and pleasure play out on his face. She liked the way the muscles in his neck and shoulders tensed when he was momentarily embarrassed, then relaxed with the praise.

She bent down to kiss him, stretching her body alongside his, so she could feel his arm wrap around her as if it belonged there, heavy and sure. She had always enjoyed bringing pleasure to her bedmates—of course she had, it was only fair. But with Rob, she felt nearly possessive of his pleasure, proprietary, as if she somehow owned it. Feeling his muscles tense against her, hearing the soft sounds he made, she felt like she was almost about to come again herself. He muttered something garbled and nonsensical, which she took as a warning. So she bit down on his shoulder and snaked an arm around his neck to pull at his hair again, and felt his body go rigid beside her before he came, biting back any sound he might have made behind clenched teeth.

Chapter 23

The next morning, they had a robbery to plan.

"It's not a robbery," Marian protested. "I only mean to talk to the man."

Rob held his best knife up to the light, inspecting its blade before returning it to its sheath and handing it to Marian.

"I'm giving him a chance to be reasonable," she said, sliding the knife into the bodice of her gown.

Marian wasn't dressed for robbery. She wore a costume of a gray so dark it was nearly black, and which seemed to absorb all the light in the room until Marian was wrapped in her own private shadow. Tucked into her neckline was a white neckerchief, and beneath the hem of her skirts he could see white petticoats. Her sleeves tied up somehow at the cuffs, exposing maybe an inch of the sleeves of her chemise. And then there was the black of her hair, the white of her skin. The ultimate effect was that she cut a swath of unyielding black and white across the gently muted and faded kitchen furnishings. Everything about her was crisp and uncompromising, from the straightness of her back to the tilt of her chin. He thought he could stare at her all day and never tire of it.

"I found it in the attic," she said when she caught him looking. "It must have been my mother's and somehow was never remade into something more fashionable."

Rob could see that there was something faintly old-fashioned about the ensemble. There was also something else. "It's mourning attire." The idea that she was planning to go into mourning for a man she had killed with her own hands, while—regardless of what she said—robbing, extorting, or otherwise dealing feloniously with another man, made Rob feel faintly dizzy.

"I could hardly wear anything else, could I?"

"Do widows typically call on gentlemen in the first week of mourning?"

"Gentlemen typically don't extort money from their tenants," Marian retorted.

"That is precisely what gentlemen do," he pointed out, exasperated. "It is practically the entire point of gentlemen."

She opened her mouth as if to protest, then frowned. "Fair."

She had left him alone in bed last night. Not that he had expected her to spend the night with him. It was just that he didn't quite like that he could miss someone who was across the hall. And now he felt like he missed her even though she was two feet away from him at the kitchen table. He didn't know how that was possible.

The snow hadn't melted, but it was packed into something navigable, so Rob had no trouble getting to the village and hiring a pair of horses to pull the earl's ancient carriage and bring Marian to the home of this blackguard. Because even though the two houses were a scant mile apart, Marian naturally couldn't go on foot—she was making this visit as the Duchess of Clare. The notion set Rob's teeth on edge.

While Marian went inside, Rob took himself to the kitchens, where he found Fanshawe's servants preparing for the following day's festivities. Somehow, what with all the running back and forth between London and Canterbury, Rob had lost track of the calendar. He was vaguely aware that the moon had been full when he and Marian set out from London, and that now the moon was nothing but the thinnest sliver of a waning crescent. But it seemed that the following day was Christmas. Nearly a fortnight had slipped away from him, two weeks during which he had thought of little other than Marian. Two weeks during which he had, unaccountably, been something like happy.

It wasn't that unaccountable, he supposed.

Rob accepted a cup of ale from Fanshawe's cook and listened as the staff discussed their plans for the following day. Aside from servants, the house would be largely empty. Even if Marian didn't plan any burglaries, Rob had half a mind to do so himself, just on principle.

He hadn't done much in the way of housebreaking, truth be told. He and Kit were both too large to consider windows a reasonable means of entering or leaving buildings, and charming the servants was the sort of trick that people caught onto eventually. But Marian was an old hand at helping herself to dainty bits of silver, and also at climbing in and out of windows, if it came to that. Rob was happy to let her take the lead.

Meanwhile, Rob did what he did best. He engaged the servants in the sort of idle conversation that drew out more than they meant to tell. He played the part of an interested well-mannered stranger. He complimented the cook, he flirted with the gray-haired housekeeper, he slipped a farthing to the boy who turned the spit.

"He was not reasonable," Marian said crisply as he handed her into the carriage.

"That's too bad for him," Rob remarked, but he didn't think he mistook the light in Marian's eye. She was looking forward to this and so was he.

"I plan to see that it is."

After depositing Marian at home and returning the hired horses, he walked back to Little Hinton. The snow had stopped falling and the lane to the village was already packed solid, but whenever Rob stepped off the path, his boot crunched through the top layer of snow, which had frozen into a sheet of ice. Anything they did would leave footprints; there would be no silently sneaking through the grounds of Fanshawe's house. They would have to rely on means other than the usual subterfuge.

When he stepped into the kitchen, he found Marian sitting at the table, her somber black gown exchanged for breeches and a coat.

"He had a manuscript that belongs to my father," she said, handing him a cup of tea. "There's no possibility that my father gave it away, not after spending what he did to acquire it in the first place. Heavens, when I think of how Richard carried on about its purchase."

Rob had lived five and twenty years on God's earth without knowing that manuscripts were something one would want to spend any money whatsoever on, but he supposed rich people had to think of new and inventive ways to fritter away their money. "What kind of manuscript is this?"

"It's a fourteenth-century map of Roman Britain and some accompanying text."

Rob's knowledge of history might be lacking but he knew the Romans had been well and truly gone from these shores some thousand or so years before the fourteenth century.

"It was written by a monk," Marian went on, "based on the writings of a Roman general that are now lost, as well as various ecclesiastical histories that were in the monastery's library, one imagines."

Rob bit back a comment along the lines of how normal people had better things to do than imagine anything of the sort, and instead enjoyed the sight of Marian going on about things. When she had finished talking about some fellow who apparently had a single-minded obsession with calculating the correct date of Easter, which Rob would have counted the most boring topic in the world if anyone but Marian was talking about it, he spoke. "And you're certain this is your father's?"

"Of course. There's only one. And I could hardly fail to recognize it, seeing as I spent an entire summer translating the confounded thing. Sir John left it out in plain view, even though he knew I was calling on him. I don't know if he didn't realize that I'd recognize it or if he meant to throw it in my face that he stole it. Either way, it makes me despise him more."

"See anything else worth taking?"

"Oh, all the usual things. I saw a pair of gold dolphins on the chimneypiece and a few pieces of silver."

"The silver will be easier to sell than whatever gold dolphins are. Bringing Betty a pair of gold dolphins to fence will be more than my life is worth."

"Betty?"

"The fence Kit and I worked with. Terrifying woman. You'd love her. Now, about tomorrow." A plan had been shaping itself in Rob's mind since he had listened to Fanshawe's servants talk among themselves. "Tomorrow is Christmas. There will be all kinds of commotion. Mummers coming and going. Wassailing all day long. People will be in and out of the house constantly. Half Fanshawe's servants have the day out. It would be nothing at all to create a distraction in the kitchens to draw the remaining servants there. That would leave the field clear for you to grab what you need and get back out."

"The only thing that worries me is that someone else might be blamed for the theft."

Rob had thought of this as well. "That's the advantage of drawing the servants down to the kitchen. They'll be able to verify that the others were with them."

Marian didn't seem convinced, and Rob was pleased to see it. He didn't think she had been terribly worried about who would be blamed for her thefts when she had stolen from those houses in London, and maybe if she was thinking that way now it meant—

He stopped himself. It was a dark day indeed when he wanted to congratulate an aristocrat for simply remembering that servants were human beings. Just because an aristocrat learned to be less of a nuisance to everyone around them didn't mean she was any less an aristocrat; it didn't mean there was anything for the two of them when this was over.

Chapter 24

*M*arian would have been lying if she said she didn't get a visceral thrill when she slipped inside the garden door and into Sir John Fanshawe's house.

Early that morning, she had set about tidying her father's papers. He had never been an organized man, and Marian spent years attempting to impose order on the stacks of papers and indiscriminately filled pigeonholes that housed her father's work. She remembered sheets of vellum covered in monkish Latin piled alongside unpaid bills and sternly worded letters from the solicitor. Even when she was a child, it had been enough to send her organized mind into throes of despair.

Now there were no letters from the solicitor or unpaid bills, because Marian had seen to those matters. The chaos was confined to incomplete translations wedged inside novels, unanswered letters stacked beneath dripping candles. But she needed to make sense of her father's papers in order to see if anything was missing beyond the manuscript she had seen at Fanshawe's house the previous day.

And there, right inside the crimson-bound *Iliad* where she had placed it over a year ago, was the inventory she had written with her own hand. Referencing it, she was able to identify three other missing manuscripts, but also, infuriatingly, her own translations of the missing manuscripts.

When she thought of the hours she had spent poring over those blasted manuscripts and how pleased her father had been with the results, she could have screamed. There were no copies. If Fanshawe had taken the originals, she wanted them back.

So when she slipped inside the garden door, she was spurred on not only by the desire to make things right for her father, but by something smaller and pettier yet somehow more pressing— the urge to take back what was hers.

As Rob had predicted there was no small amount of chaos with mummers and wassailers coming and going, and they had been able to approach the house without anyone questioning their presence.

"Do not even think about climbing out of any windows," Rob hissed. "Nor up any chimneys or down any drainpipes. There's ice all over everything."

"You don't want me to have any fun at all," Marian complained.

Rob gave her a long look and took off in the direction of the kitchen, carrying a basket of some sort of pies that he had shamelessly convinced Hester to bake. "They're all going to have a very trying time when Fanshawe discovers he's been robbed. They might as well have some pie beforehand," he had explained, which she supposed made some degree of sense. He wore one of the earl's old wigs and an ancient black coat they had found in the attic. He carried a Bible and a handful of pamphlets he had procured from heaven only knew where. And just like that, he was a dissenting clergyman, ready to annoy the revelers with warnings against overindulgence and hard spirits.

Marian waited in the dark corridor, listening to footsteps descend the back stairs toward the kitchen. Eventually there were no sounds at all and it was time for her to move.

She was wearing the breeches and coat she had worn on their journey from Kent, partly for ease of movement in case they needed to make a quick escape, and partly as a disguise. If anyone caught a glimpse of her, they would see a slender young man, she hoped.

On her visit the previous day, she had paid close attention to the house, mapping its corridors and passageways in her mind. She hoped her memory was correct, as it would do her no good to get lost. The library where Sir John had received her was on the east side of the house, one story off the ground. So that was the direction she headed, remembering her way back to the door that she had used to enter the house.

And there it was, the library door. She stood with her back flat against the wall, listening for any sounds coming from within. No light shone from under the door, and every sign indicated that the room was empty.

Holding her breath, she stepped inside the library. It was pitch dark and she waited for her eyes to adjust to the gloom. The only sound came from the singing of carols downstairs.

Slowly, careful not to trip over any furniture that might still be invisible in the dark, she made her way toward the window, where she pulled back the curtain just enough to let some pallid winter light fall on the writing desk, which was where she had seen the manuscript the previous day. But when she approached the desk, she saw that it was empty of everything except a blotter and an inkwell.

She tried the desk drawers, even though she was sure they would be locked. But the top drawer opened on her first try. Its contents were veiled in shadows, but when she put her hand in the drawer she could feel for herself that there was no manuscript, nor were there any signs of the translations.

She tried the other drawers with the same result. The manuscript was not on or in the desk.

Grimly, she looked at the walls of the room, all lined with bookshelves. If Fanshawe had put the papers inside a book, she would have no chance of ever finding them. She would need hours to properly search every book in this room. But she remembered the sight of the manuscript on Fanshawe's desk: it was smooth, or as smooth as it could be after a few hundred years of being passed around among antiquarians. It hadn't been folded and stored in a book, and Fanshawe—if he understood the value of the manuscript he had taken the trouble to steal—would understand that such a priceless piece of vellum could not be folded up and stuck in a book like the bill from one's tailor. The manuscript had shown no signs of being rolled, either, which meant she didn't need to search the pigeonholes.

Perhaps he took it to bed with him? Perhaps he stored it in some other room? If so, she couldn't find it now, because she didn't know any other rooms in this house, and she was running out of time. Rob had said that he could maintain a distraction in the kitchen for a quarter of an hour, and Marian had already used up nearly all of it.

This trip had been a waste. She reached for the golden dolphin statues but at the last moment stayed her hand. The last thing she wanted was to alert Fanshawe that there were thieves in his midst. He might decide to keep his treasures better hidden in the future. Worse, he might blame some hapless servant for the theft. She knew that Rob thought luring the servants to the kitchen would keep them all out of suspicion, but Marian had spent enough time in large households to know that there were always servants who couldn't or wouldn't leave their posts no matter how tempting the distraction—nurses who tended to babies or the elderly, upper servants who always stayed within reach of the lady or gentleman they served. During the last several months of her marriage to the duke, her lady's maid had followed her like a shadow.

Disappointed, she left the house the same way she had entered it and did exactly as Rob had instructed her earlier that day. When a group of carolers emerged from the house, she stepped in with them, walking with them as far as the lane that would eventually lead to the village.

When they approached the wood that bordered the Fanshawe property, someone fell into step beside her. It was Rob, of course. She looped his arm into hers.

"I don't see your pockets bulging with golden dolphins," he murmured. He smelled of mulled wine and plum cake.

"Don't be cross."

"I'm not. It was an observation." He pulled off his wig and handed it to a confused mummer. He handed his remaining pamphlets to a caroler, who stopped singing long enough to spare a few choice profanities for Rob. Then he guided Marian off the lane and into the wood

"The manuscripts weren't there," Marian said. "As for the rest, I couldn't go through with it."

"Moral crisis?" Rob leaned against a tree.

"Not the sort you're thinking of. I just can't stand to think of someone being arrested and punished for my own crimes."

He looked at her for a long moment. "Fair. Well, according to the butler, Fanshawe returned to London late last night. I hoped he might leave your manuscript behind, but it seems he took it with him."

"Well, where does that leave us?" Marian asked, annoyed.

"I suppose we'll have to catch up with him in London. How annoying. I wish Kit were here. He was always better than I am at figuring these things out. He'd know at which inn we could intercept Fanshawe and how many of his outriders were likely to be in their cups."

"Then I suppose we go back to London," Marian said, trying not to think about how dismal this prospect left her feeling.

Chapter 25

On their way back to Little Hinton, they passed the village church that Marian remembered from her early childhood. "Do you mind if we go in?" she asked Rob. "It's Christmas."

"You don't need to ask."

"I will, though." They looked at one another, the light glinting off Rob's eyes, the moment stretching out between them until it held more than Marian knew how to say.

They found a pew in the far back of the church, nearly concealed by shadows, which suited Marian fine. She had spent many an hour in this very church. And maybe she had thought that sitting in one of its pews, listening to the familiar canticles in a familiar place, she would feel herself again, in the same way she had the night of the shooting when she first sat in Gwen's saddle. She had thought that maybe everything would make sense—or failing that, that maybe she would make sense.

Instead she felt alienated not only from her past but from her future. She didn't know how she was meant to pack up everything that had happened in the past fortnight, store it tidily away, and go back to being the Duchess of Clare. She had made her peace with walking away from that title, that life, and—God forgive her—she didn't want to go back. She would, though. She'd go back for the same reasons she married the duke in the first place.

There were too many parts of her, and none of them good—daughter to a man who didn't know her, mother to a child she barely knew, wife to the man she had killed, sister to a man she counted as an enemy. She knew there was more to her than that, that she was more than the sum of those roles, but she couldn't put a name to any of those other parts, so it was hard to believe that they counted for much.

She gripped the edge of the pew, curling her fingers around the scarred and polished wood, as if maybe if she squeezed hard enough she could drive the confusion out of her body through pain alone. It seemed as good a plan as any.

But then, instead of squeezing the seat, she was grasping a hand. Rob had pried her fingers off the bench and clasped her hand in his, beneath the folds of their cloaks. She tried to listen to the chanting, but it was the Magnificat, which used to be so lovely but now only made her feel uneasy and unwelcome. Her gaze skated around the church, from the wooden cross that hung above the altar, to the painted altarpiece, to the cold stone statues.

"I'd like to leave," she murmured, and Rob was on his feet in an instant.

It occurred to her for the first time, at the back of a cold church on Christmas Day, exactly what it meant to have a man like Rob jump to his feet the minute she opened her mouth. She had seen him, time and again, reach absently for his coat pocket, ever ready to put his hand on a weapon. Sometimes she forgot that he was a dangerous man, because she knew that not only would he not harm her, but that he would do what it took to protect her.

That was something they had in common—they were neither of them, perhaps, especially good, at least not by any standard Marian had ever heard of. But they would do what it took to protect the people who were theirs. They would do what needed to be done, maybe because nobody else would do it.

"Would you mind going around the side of the church with me?" He hadn't let go of her hand, so she led him beneath the tall windows, where they could still hear the singing. "There," she announced. "That's nice."

Rob coughed out a laugh, his breath fogging the air between them. "I don't know why I'm surprised that your idea of a good time is lurking in a boneyard on a cold and moonless night."

"It's not quite moonless," she said, because she really couldn't take issue with the rest of it. The sun had set while they were in the church and darkness descended as abruptly as it always did in midwinter.

"It's been a long time since I set foot in a church."

She squeezed his hand and it had the effect that she had hoped gripping the pew would: some of the doubt and confusion that had been chasing her seemed to recede into the background. She wasn't any less confused or doubtful, but she felt like she could live with it as long as she had something to hold on to.

"My mother—not my adoptive mother, but the woman you know about in London—was very young when I was born, so she arranged for me to be fostered by a childless couple. The head gardener at Cheveril Castle and his wife, in fact."

Marian raised an eyebrow. "You were raised by the duke's gardener?"

Rob nodded. "She wrote to me a few times a year and paid for my schooling, but I never met her until after my adoptive parents died and Kit and I went to London. By that point, we had been living rough for the better part of a year, and Kit had come down with a cough that I didn't like the sound of, so I swallowed my pride. It wasn't easy to go for help to the mother who had given me away, you understand?"

"I can imagine," Marian said, trying not to think of Eliza, who she had left some fifty miles away.

"To be clear, I didn't want to ask anyone for help, but especially not someone to whom my existence was . . . complicated. But it turned out that it wasn't complicated at all. She was glad that my mum and dad looked after me, and later she was pleased that she could afford to educate me."

"Why are you telling me this?"

"Because my mother wasn't whatever we mean when we think of good mothers. But she was a good parent. There are plenty of fathers who never bother to see that their children are looked after, let alone loved and educated. When I went to her for help, she gave it to me." He was silent for a moment. "I saw you looking at the altarpiece. Madonna and child, and so forth. There will come a time when you haven't recently killed on your daughter's behalf or nearly died bringing her into the world, and you'll likely settle into something a good deal less complicated than whatever it is you're feeling now."

Marian swallowed. She hadn't realized that her thoughts were so transparent, nor had she realized exactly how much Rob knew about her history. "I know that I didn't abandon Eliza," she finally said. "It's not that. It's more that I know I don't feel whatever a mother is meant to feel for her child." She knew there were reasons for that, but none of them were good enough. "And I didn't shoot the duke for her. You don't know what you're talking about."

"I don't know the details, but I suspect the duke found out that you knew about his bigamy and threatened Eliza so you'd keep quiet."

Marian felt hot despite the chill in the graveyard. "If he had threatened Eliza, he would have been dead much sooner. And I wouldn't have been satisfied with a single shot. I'd have unloaded every pistol I could get my hands on."

Beside her, he went silent for a moment. "Holland, then."

"The duke found—he found out that I knew about his bigamy the morning of the highway robbery. The truth is that he had always hated Percy and made no secret of it, and I think he was rather looking forward to being rid of him. And, sure enough, he recognized Percy during the hold up and shot him. So I shot the duke, because even though he had aimed badly that day, he wouldn't the next time." That wasn't the whole truth, but it was enough, and it felt good to say it aloud, in all its bleakness, and to know that Rob understood.

Rob nodded, as if this all made perfect sense, which Marian was fairly certain it did not.

"It wouldn't only have been Mr. Webb's cough," Marian said, mainly because she didn't want to think about that charnel house of a carriage or the duke's labored breathing. Instead she recalled her realization when they had left the church. "I don't think you would have gone to your mother just for your friend's health." It was a shot in the dark, but Rob opened his eyes wide for a moment, so she knew she was close to the truth.

He shifted his body so there was suddenly space between them, and until the cold air reached her, she hadn't realized how close they had been. "We got into some trouble with a smuggling gang in Rye," Rob said. "I needed to take care of that in a way Kit wouldn't approve of, so I left him with my mother for a few weeks."

"Did Kit know?"

He shook his head. "He may have suspected, but I doubt it."

"Was that the only time?"

"No, love. When there were people who wanted to hurt us, I dealt with it. And one thing I learned to a certainty is that when you're busy trying not to starve or freeze, there are plenty of people who want to hurt you in all kinds of interesting ways."

"You made sure they didn't, so Kit didn't have to."

Now he looked sharply at her. "Don't make it out to be noble."

"Fine, then make sure you don't do that, either." Their breaths met in white puffs between them. "Am I right, though?"

"He's a better man than I am. He'd have been eaten up by guilt."

"And you aren't?"

"I used to think I was more pragmatic, but really I just didn't want to see my friend hurt. In any event, it's been a while since I needed to do anything of the sort. At some point we got better at avoiding trouble, and Kit figured out his own ways of making sure nobody bothered us."

She remembered what he had told her that first night, when she was still rattled and raw. He had said that it didn't get any easier. "I'm glad you don't have to do that anymore."

He snorted. "You say that as if you're glad I no longer have to use bad roads or put up with a smoky chimney, rather than that I've given up the practice of committing murder."

Hearing that word spoken aloud sent a chill down her spine, but she supposed she ought to get used to it.

"For what it's worth," Rob said, "I don't think that what you did is murder. He was going to kill somebody. Maybe not that minute, but he was going to. Then again, I'm not exactly an expert on morality, so what do I know."

"I don't think it matters, because I'd do it again," Marian admitted. "So if it's murder, then I'm a murderer, and so be it. And if that makes me an evil person, then I'm an evil person, because I still wouldn't change what I did. I'll do my duty. I'll do what needs to be done and leave deciding whether it's right to other people." Putting it as baldly as that made her feel exposed, but she remembered what Rob had said the previous night about there being comfort in someone knowing the worst you were capable of.

The doors of the church opened and the few congregants who had come to evening services on a cold Christmas night emerged into the darkness, wrapping their coats and cloaks around them. Marian and Rob held still and silent, waiting for the last of them to disappear into the night.

"Would you mind if I stepped inside again?" Marian asked.

It was hardly warmer indoors than without, now that the building was empty. She reminded herself that churches had offered sanctuary to worse than her.

"Who was the patron saint of thieves and vagabonds?" Rob asked in a low voice.

"What a Romish notion," Marian murmured, amused. "Saint Nicholas, I believe. He has all the interesting people."

Rob crossed the church, his boots clicking on the stone floor and his cape fluttering behind him, and Marian momentarily lost her breath at the sight of him. Then she saw him reach for a taper and she nearly laughed. Sure enough, he lit a candle.

"I mean, it can't hurt," he said, coming back to her.

"Indeed not," she agreed, and together they left the church.

Chapter 26

As they walked home, they pressed close together to ward off the cold. The sun had long since set, taking with it what little warmth it had brought to the day. Rob couldn't have said whether he reached for Marian or she reached for him, but her gloved hand wound up in his own, as if it belonged there, as if they would have days and months and years of reaching for one another.

They didn't, though, and Rob didn't want to waste a minute of what time they did have. In the distance, he could see a few dim lights in the windows of Marian's father's house. He pulled Marian behind a stand of trees. "May I?" he asked, bringing a hand to the small of her back.

She nodded and came close, and he bent down to meet her lips. And, Christ, their faces were cold. If he were any kind of decent person he would have waited until they got back to the house, but Marian wouldn't let a little thing like frostbite prevent her from doing precisely what she chose, so neither would he. She gripped his shoulders and kissed him hard, and he kissed her back, putting as much intent and honesty into it as he could.

There were a thousand things he could say, endearments and promises and more, but he didn't think she'd believe him, so he wanted to show her instead. He was already trying to show her, with everything he did, but he didn't know if it was enough, and he doubted this kiss would do a damned thing to help matters, but it felt good anyway.

Marian pulled back long enough to take the fingers of a glove between her teeth and tug it off, and God help him but that shouldn't have looked half so good, and then her freezing cold hand was at the back of his neck, her fingers threaded in his hair, holding him close, keeping him still. She tasted of the brandy-laced tea they had shared earlier that day and she smelled of the lavender and other herbs her clothes must have been packed away in. In his arms she felt as sharp as a knife and as sure as a promise and he never wanted to take his hands off her.

A clump of snow fell from a tree branch and landed beside them, and as neither of them wanted the next clump to land on their heads, they ran the rest of the way home.

In the kitchen, they ate cold ham for supper and hurriedly cleared the table before Hester could return and be scandalized about a grand lady washing the crockery. The warmth of the kitchen did something to dispel the strange, hard intimacy they had shared outside, or at least to shift it into something more mundane. They stood side by side, their shoulders sometimes bumping, their hands sometimes brushing. Rob scoured the dishes and pots with wood ash from the hearth, and Marian rinsed them in a basin of hot water and dried them.

"Shall we leave tomorrow morning?" Rob asked, handing a bowl to Marian.

"First I have to make sure that everything is in place for Father to move. But I ought to be ready to leave a little after noon."

"Move where?"

She sighed. "I don't know where, or how, or with what money. But if I'm going to make an enemy of Sir John Fanshawe, then my father can't be his tenant."

She sounded dejected, so he changed the topic. "What I want to know is how we're going to travel with that cat."

The cat was engaged in his favorite pastime of winding himself around Marian's ankles, and whether he did this out of affection or in a bid to trip her was anybody's guess. "He'll be a perfect lamb, just you wait."

Rob gave it even odds that the beast tried to slit his throat before they got so far as Rochester. "I'll be honored to be slain by such a worthy foe."

"I wonder, though, if we ought to leave the cat here for the time being. He seems perfectly content, and it seems cruel to bring him to his third home in a fortnight." They both turned to look at the cat, who was dozing by the fire, sated by the bits of ham Rob had sneaked him under the table in an ongoing but probably doomed bid to win the creature's affections. "Besides, I can't imagine that any cat would want to rattle around Clare House."

She sounded as if she wasn't relishing the prospect of returning to Clare House herself. He didn't know what to say—he had no solution to suggest, no alternative to offer. She was the Duchess of Clare and that was her home. It wasn't as if he could ask her to instead wander the countryside with him; he certainly couldn't ask her to take her daughter and decamp to the room that Rob sometimes used over Kit's coffeehouse.

He couldn't offer her a better life or even a decent life; he couldn't even come up with a way for them to spend much time together, unless Marian wanted to resume sneaking about London at night, and he didn't think his nerves could handle the idea of her doing that.

This was the first time that he had ever felt that his way of life was in any way unsatisfactory. He didn't wish that he had a house and a respectable position, exactly, but he felt every inch of the gulf that separated him from Marian.

He thought that if anything could have tempted him to confront his inheritance, it would be Marian. But that wasn't even a choice—the idea of living as a duke was anathema to everything he thought was right and good. He imagined walking into a tavern or an inn and being recognized not as a friend, not as a fellow patron, but as the Duke of Clare. The idea made him feel faintly sick, as if he were killing off the person he wanted to be.

"What would you do if you didn't have to go back to Clare House and you didn't have to worry about anyone but yourself?" he asked.

"What a depressing question."

"Indulge me."

She dried a platter on her apron. "I've never thought of it."

"Never?"

"You must have guessed that I'm not much given to flights of imagination." She swirled the tips of her fingers in the cloudy water in the basin.

"Try."

"Well, I'd say that your friend who runs the stables seems to have a plum job. He charges a king's ransom and spends his time looking after horses."

"What we paid was his special rate for pretending he never saw us."

"As if I couldn't do that, too," she scoffed. "I'd make a specialty of hiring horses out to all manner of scoundrel."

"I don't think you'd much like most scoundrels," he said darkly. "Neither would your horses."

"I'd be very selective. Only the finest scoundrels."

"You'd be good at it." She'd be good at anything she turned her hand to. He only wished she were able to choose what that was. "Take the damned cat to London, Marian," he said. "Just because a decision makes you miserable doesn't mean it's the right thing to do."

"I beg your pardon." God help him, he loved that she could say the most innocuous phrase in a way that sounded like the type of insult that usually preceded street brawls. "Are you accusing me of being a martyr?"

"I damned well am not. Martyrs seem to enjoy suffering. In all the paintings they seem to positively get off on it. But you certainly don't. When you can't make up your mind what to do, you choose the option that results in the least happiness and pleasure for yourself. It's the damnedest thing I've ever seen."

"This is utter nonsense," she said, but he didn't think she sounded like she believed it. "Come upstairs with me," Marian said when they put the last dish away. "And I'll show you just how well I can make choices that please myself." She cleared her throat. "If you like, that is. It was meant as an invitation, not a summons."

"Summon me anywhere you please." He meant it, even if he wished he hadn't sounded quite so fervent about it, and he was pretty sure he was blushing when she glanced up at him.

"I thought we could have our tea in my room. It's small but nice and warm." She said this as if he needed any additional enticements.

Marian's bedchamber wasn't by any means small, unless you were used to living in palaces, which he supposed Marian was. The ceiling was low and slanted because the room was tucked under the eaves. But that meant that as soon as they got the fire going, the room warmed up almost straight away. Still clutching the fire iron, Marian sat on her heels. Rob arranged himself beside her on the hearth rug, his legs stretched out toward the fire, a cup of tea in his hand.

He tried to believe that they would have more nights like this, more time to be warm and safe, with no questions hanging over their heads. But he had never been any good at convincing himself of falsehoods. Instead he told himself that they had this night, and that this night was what mattered.

"I wonder if you're going to keep holding that fire iron," he murmured. "That would make things interesting." She gave a very unladylike snort and he nudged her leg with the toe of his boot. "Do you want to come over here?"

"I have a plan."

"Do you?" he asked with great interest.

"You have to lie down."

He lay down, not wasting any time about it.

She came closer, kneeling beside him. Her hair had come down from its pins and fell over her shoulder. "You shaved." She moved her fingers along his cheek and bit her lower lip. "I don't know why I find you so attractive."

Rob, who had known since he was fifteen that his looks were sufficient to attract just about anyone he pleased, almost laughed. "Is that so?"

"I think I thought you were attractive even before I had seen you."

"The letters?" When she nodded, he laughed. "You have terrible taste."

"Well, not the first letter. That one only made me furious. But the other ones. Rob, it was fun. You were fun. And we could be honest with one another because it didn't matter."

He caught her hand in his own and kissed it. "I wasn't entirely honest with you."

"It doesn't matter," she said, and it sounded like she believed it, like she trusted him.

He wanted to tell her that it mattered a great deal. He was tempted to tell her the truth about his parents now, but before he could work up the courage, she bent her head to kiss him.

She kissed him as if she were trying to solve a riddle or do a complicated sum, or as if his mouth contained the answer to a puzzle. He brought his hands to her waist and gave a little tug, just a suggestion, and she followed him to the floor.

Then her thigh slid between his legs, pressing against him, and he groaned. She went rigid.

"I don't wish you to put that inside me," she said, pulling away from him.

"I wasn't planning to."

She made a disbelieving sound. He sat up, putting a little distance between them but keeping hold of her hand.

"Marian, I know that you mustn't get pregnant."

"You do?" She raised both eyebrows.

He sighed. "My mother. Don't even ask. In any event, I know that your health depends on not getting pregnant. Did you think I'd risk it anyway?"

By her silence, she plainly thought he would. And of course she did; her experience with men was skewed toward abject evil. She looked both sad and skeptical and he felt his heart break a little.

"Sweetheart. Just to be clear, I don't want to do anything that will harm you. I wouldn't find any pleasure if I knew my pleasure might kill you. That prospect does not make me feel amorous, Marian. And even if you could bear a dozen children without consequence, I still wouldn't do anything you didn't want. I— you must know this, but I love you."

Her gaze flickered away from his. "The duke said that as well."

Rob hadn't thought that anything she said could shock him,

but this did. There was nothing he could say; he couldn't tell her that he was different, that the duke's love was false—she already knew the latter and he hoped she knew the former. "Have I ever touched you in a way you didn't want?" he asked.

"No," she said, managing to sound both irritated and reassuring at the same time.

"Do you think I enjoyed what we did last night and that evening in the stables?"

She sniffed. "I gather you found those encounters acceptable."

"Marian. Acceptable doesn't begin to cover it." He realized what she was really asking and debated how to best answer. "I don't need to put any part of myself inside you," he said.

"Well, obviously you don't *need* to."

"I mean that it isn't even at the top of my list of things I'd like to do with you. Or with anyone, for that matter."

"Pfft. You're telling me that you don't do that with most women you lie with?"

"I suppose I have, not that I've kept much track of which specific acts I did and didn't do with various people. And even if I did that with most of the women I lay with, I didn't with the men."

She gave him a very skeptical and long-suffering roll of the eyes. "I do know how men lie together. Percy told me." She said this with such an air of expertise that he had to bite his lip to keep from smiling.

"I didn't realize I was dealing with a regular expert in buggery. In that case I'll point out that while, yes, I sometimes stuck my prick in the men I lay with, sometimes it was the other way around. Usually, in fact." He scrubbed a hand over his face. "Christ, I cannot believe I'm talking about this with you."

She looked over at him with an indecipherable expression. "I see."

"And now I've shocked you."

"No," she said slowly, licking her lips. "I would not say that I'm shocked."

It was true that she didn't look shocked so much as intrigued. In fact, she looked like a person who was getting ideas, and Rob very much wanted to be there when those ideas came to fruition.

"But that's not the point," he said. "The point is that I wish you believed that I won't hurt you."

She gave him a faintly pitying look. "You want me to trust you."

"Yes. I don't expect you to, though. What happened to you—"

"Rob, I've never been a trusting and open-hearted person. I've never been affectionate and loving. I've been cold and prickly my entire life. The past year forced me to make use of those traits, but they've always been part of who I am."

"I understand that."

"I don't think you do. You want to be with someone who loves you the way you love, without any reservations, without holding anything back. And that can't be me. That's never been me. Maybe you think that beneath all this is someone sweet and—"

"Oh, for Christ's sake, Marian. If you acted sweet, I'd think you were a changeling. I'd call for the doctor. I love every prickly, sour, difficult inch of you." He could see, though, that she had been telling the truth—she didn't love him the way he loved her.

He supposed he had known that already. Not that any of this mattered, since in less than a week they'd be in London, in their separate worlds.

"Do you want to go to bed?" he asked. "Just to sleep, I think."

She glanced at the bed and he could have sworn that she looked tempted, as if seeing a cake or—he didn't know—a mean cat or an old map that she had her heart set on. But she shook her head. "I think not. Good night, Rob." She kissed him on the cheek and he accepted his dismissal, leaving the warmth of her room.

Chapter 27

"A re you quite certain we can't take the stagecoach?" Marian asked Rob for the dozenth time as they piled their meager baggage in the kitchen.

"I'm quite certain that people will not know what to think if the Duchess of Clare is seen in a stagecoach."

Marian increasingly did not give a fig what people thought about the Duchess of Clare. "People are already going to be dismayed by the Duchess of Clare not traveling with a lady companion and a full retinue. What if I dressed as a man again?"

"That disguise isn't going to work if you're crammed into close quarters with eight other people." He tapped his fingers on his thigh. "If it's money you're worried about, I'll stand the expense."

"How?"

"I have a bit of money put aside." He seemed awfully shifty about this, and Marian assumed he had acquired this money in some disreputable fashion. "Not a lot. Certainly not enough to gallivant about in post chaises whenever the mood strikes me, but it occurs to me that this trip will be vastly more pleasant for myself—and also for the cat—if we use a private post chaise."

She recalled that night he had spent in the kitchen after being unable to sleep in the cramped room. Perhaps the stagecoach was unpleasant for him for similar reasons. "I'd hate to inconvenience the cat," she conceded.

And then she set about saying goodbye to her father without crying, as he would surely be distressed and confused by a weeping stranger. She thanked Hester, Netley, and Nurse, scooped up the cat, and let Rob hand her into the carriage that was to bring them to the posting inn.

"I'll be glad to see Eliza and Percy," she said, as if saying it aloud would make her less distressed about leaving her father, or less guilty about having left Eliza and Percy in the first place, or even less miserable about the prospect of returning to Clare House. "I suppose you'll be glad to get back to your usual life."

He gave her a look she couldn't decipher. "I'm not sure I have one of those anymore." He reached out and poked the nose of the cat, who had stuck his head out from the folds of Marian's cloak as if eager to participate in the conversation. "Before I ran off to France last year, Kit and I were holding up carriages and that sort of thing, and then we'd come back to London, where he'd run the shop and I'd dispose of our takings. But now he's not doing that anymore and I won't work with anyone else. So I'm rather at a loose end."

"Last night you asked me what I'd do if I had nobody to consider but myself. Now I'll ask you the same."

"Marian. Do you really have to ask?"

She felt herself flush. She was not prone to blushing and it was terribly annoying that Rob had this effect on her. "Obviously I have to ask or I wouldn't have done."

"I wish I could stay near you. I wish I could eat at your table and sleep in your bed, or you in mine. I wish there were even a half measure that I could think of. I suppose I could dress in my best coat and call on you and perhaps drink tea in your parlor once a fortnight."

The image this conjured was too appalling for her to accept: Rob, stiff and uncomfortable in the Clare House morning room, making polite conversation, never once picking anybody's pocket, never kissing her the way he had last night, never again using that low soft voice that sounded like it was all for her. "I don't want you to drink tea in my parlor once a fortnight!"

"Well, darling, that's the best we can do."

Marian thought that two intelligent, resourceful, unscrupulous people could do a sight better than that if they put their minds to it. She didn't know whether to be pleased that Rob was disappointed that he wouldn't be able to see as much of her as he wanted, or severely annoyed that he couldn't see his way to solving the problem. "May the devil take your best and you with it."

The cat, evidently enjoying the quarrel and deciding to join in, began howling. "Oh, you can be quiet until you have something useful to say," Marian scolded the beast, and for some perverse reason known only to the cat, he promptly went silent.

Rob started laughing. "I really do think that animal believes he's your familiar."

"Maybe he *is* my familiar and you've just insulted him."

"I beg your pardon," Rob said to the cat.

When they reached the coaching inn in Canterbury, Marian retired to a seat by the fire, the cat bundled in her cloak, while Rob set about hiring a chaise. It was a pleasure to watch him. It was always a pleasure to watch someone do what they were good at, whether they were a blacksmith or a painter or a man who enjoyed charming ostlers and innkeepers. Marian felt quite secure in the knowledge that they would have a very comfortable chaise, good horses, and competent postilions.

She let herself acknowledge that she also enjoyed looking at Rob simply for the sake of looking at him. He cut a dashing figure in his boots and cape. He'd probably cut a dashing figure in just about anything, but he had a way of making that cape swish about his calves that she found strangely beguiling.

As if he knew he was being watched, he threw a look over his shoulder at her and she felt caught out, as if she had been doing something far more shameful than only looking at him. But then he cast a quick, appraising look at her, which transformed what she had done into something they were doing together and carried with it a promise of more to come.

They had tonight, and then tomorrow night, unless the roads were far better than she had any right to expect. After that they'd be in London and effectively separated. Of course, these next two nights would be nothing like the nights they had spent at inns on the way to Little Hinton. She was traveling under her own name—well, as Marian Hayes—and he under his and they would take separate rooms. It was all disconcertingly aboveboard.

"It's all set," Rob said, now standing beside her, one hand resting on the back of her chair in a manner so casually proprietary that Marian felt her face heat.

She got to her feet and shook out her skirts, readjusted the cat in her arms, and proceeded outside to their waiting chaise.

The carriage that had taken them from Little Hinton into Canterbury had been large and old-fashioned, but this light, fast, two-wheeled chaise was very similar to the one the duke had owned, but stripped of all ornament and embellishment. When she stepped in, she realized it was similar on the inside as well. It would seat only two with any comfort, so after handing her into the carriage, Rob sat precisely where the duke had, so near her that their legs touched.

She tried to think of the differences: the duke's carriage was equipped with velvet cushions and decorated with rather more gilt than one might think appropriate for an object that spent most of its time encrusted in mud. The principal difference was that in this carriage, the duke was not sitting beside her, calmly threatening her friends and family. Instead Rob was here, alive and well, and that was because in the other carriage Marian had seen what the duke was about to do—she had seen his hand move for the case that held the second pistol, she had seen the frozen look on Percy's face, and she had done the only thing she could think of doing.

She supposed nobody would ever use that other carriage again. That much blood would never wash out.

"Marian!" Rob said, low and urgent. Marian realized he was

holding one of her hands. The carriage was already moving, rolling down the frozen London road.

"It's nothing," she said quickly. And since that was manifestly not the case, she went on. "This carriage is similar to the duke's carriage and I was startled by the resemblance, but I'll be well in a moment."

"I'll arrange for another one at the next inn."

"Please don't. I expect all post chaises are similar enough. And it really was just the initial shock. I'm already feeling better." That was true; her heart had calmed down and she no longer expected to see blood all over her.

He gave her a narrow look, then nodded his head.

As it was apparent that unless she did something about it, he was going to spend the rest of the journey watching her for signs of imminent mental collapse, she decided to take action. "I find myself filled with curiosity about the business of robbery," she said. She tilted her body toward him, angling herself on the seat, so she kept him fully in sight and would not forget that she was in *this* carriage with *this* man. "What did you mean when you said that after a robbery, you customarily disposed of your takings? I was under the impression that you used a fence."

"Ah." Rob looked embarrassed, of all things. "My part comes after things have been fenced."

"You're being mysterious."

He rubbed his palm over his face. "Not deliberately. My job is to make sure the money is properly distributed."

"Meaning you give it away."

"Not to put too fine a point on it, but yes."

"To the worthy poor," she guessed.

"I don't much care if they're worthy," Rob said. "None of my business."

"And you give all of it away?"

"No, no, of course not," he said hastily. "We keep some back for expenses—horses, bed and board, and so forth. And anyone who works with us gets a share, naturally. A few years ago, Kit held on to enough to buy the shop. I buy some things for myself, sometimes, too."

"Like what?" she asked.

"Clothing." He was blushing furiously now and she was delighted. "Not a lot! But I won't go about in shabby clothes if I can help it."

"I've been admiring your coat."

"Shut up, you," he grumbled.

"I have! I noticed it yesterday." In truth, all his clothing was made of good fabric and tailored to fit him. She was charmed to realize that he indulged what was either vanity or rich tastes in this one small way. But she also noticed that he seemed to regard this coat—which was a simple brown woolen thing—as an extravagance.

"I wonder," she said carefully, "what your plans were for the five hundred pounds you meant to have from me and Percy."

His gaze darted over her shoulder to the window and then back to her. "The same as I do with everything else."

"You would have just given it away." She found that she was surprised, not that he meant to give it away, but that he hadn't a grand plan for how to give it away. "I thought that perhaps you had debts to pay, or more likely that a friend had debts to pay. Or that you meant to do something more . . . more official, I suppose. Such as start a school or fund an orphanage."

He made a face. "There are plenty of people funding those things. Irritatingly noble-minded individuals who want to inflict their prayers onto the people they deem worthy of their largesse. I'd rather get money into the hands of somebody who needs to pay his landlord."

This seemed a frightful waste. How could one know that the recipient of these funds wouldn't spend it all on the bottle or other vices? Rob put a good deal too much trust in his fellow man. "Aren't you worried that the money will be spent on drink?" she asked.

"If you recall, I spend money on drink from time to time."

"I see," Marian said, even though she didn't. She was trying to, though.

"For that matter, you spend money on drink as well. And so does everyone you know."

"I suppose that, by your logic, my money isn't any more mine than it is anybody else's," she said.

"I wouldn't go quite that far," he said, "but that's about right."

She nodded. It still sounded fairly mad to her, but she could see how it didn't to Rob. When Rob had first explained his philosophy to her, calling robbery a targeted tax on the wealthy, she hadn't quite known whether he was being entirely serious. But that was before she had really known him. Oh, she had known the Rob who wrote to her; she had known that he was clever and oddly sympathetic and a terrible blackmailer. But she hadn't yet known that he regarded robbery as a sort of vocation.

"You look like you're about to launch into a speech telling me why I'm wrong," Rob said, in the tone of a man who had heard many such speeches and enjoyed none of them.

"No," she said. "That would be a waste of my breath. You clearly know what you're doing. I was only wondering whether there was a way to rob your targets without anyone risking their necks."

She found that she very much disliked the prospect of Rob endangering himself. It might not be an exaggeration to say that she would not know a moment's peace if she believed Rob to be in a prison awaiting the hangman.

He gave her an odd look. "But darling, that's half the fun."

Chapter 28

*T*his trip had been a mistake. Even though they had spent the entire day side by side, Rob somehow missed Marian anyway. He missed her preemptively; he regretted any future where he couldn't simply turn his head and see her.

And now he was standing outside her door, his fist raised, already knowing that whatever happened inside would only make it worse.

When he tapped at the door, he held his breath. Perhaps she already had gone to bed. Perhaps she had more common sense than he did—she could hardly have less—and recognized this for the terrible idea that it was. But she answered the door wordlessly and he slipped in before anyone could see him.

The only light came from the hearth, and the room was warm enough that he knew she had paid for extra firewood. Her hair was unpinned, falling down her back in smooth waves, as if she had just brushed it, and she wore a faded woolen wrapper. She looked soft and touchable in a way she seldom did, all her hard edges temporarily put away, and he almost couldn't believe that he got to see her this way. He was sure nobody else did.

For a moment, he didn't know what to do. There was no tea or supper with which they could occupy themselves while working up to anything more; there was no pretense that could explain his visit. They both knew why he was here and why she had let him in. They held one another's gaze for long enough that Rob nearly started in on some small talk, but Marian reached out and slid her fingers between the buttons of his waistcoat, not pulling him close, but holding him in place. Then she stepped near and kissed him.

Christ, the way she kissed. It was as if she had a job to do, and that job was to memorize his lips, to map out every place that made him draw in his breath or tighten his grip on her waist. It was as if she wanted to take him apart, and he didn't think he had ever wanted anything more than to let her.

She put her palm flat against his chest and gave him a push until he stepped backward, his back landing against the wall, his breath almost knocked out of him. Her fingers were on his waistcoat buttons, deftly popping them open until she reached the linen of his shirt and began to ruck it up. And all the while she kissed him, devastating soft kisses that left him gasping and hungry for more.

He let go of her for long enough to shrug out of his coat and waistcoat and to help her get his shirt free of his breeches, then over his head. She smoothed her hands over his chest, through the hair that ran down the center, pausing each time she encountered a scar. The room wasn't bright enough for her to see, but he was familiar enough with the geography of his body to know that she could hardly miss them with her fingertips, touching him as she did.

If she spent much more time on his scars, that would probably put her right off the idea of doing anything else with him. So he slid a hand up her back and into her hair and then bent to kiss her. She kissed him back, but then hooked a finger into his waistband and tugged him toward the bed. There she gave him a shove and he landed on the mattress, looking up at her.

She hesitated, a little uncertain. "Is that . . . acceptable?"

"Yes," he said, even before he understood that she was asking whether it was all right for her to manhandle him a little. In which case, "God yes please definitely," he said on a soft exhale.

She settled onto the bed beside him, holding herself up on an elbow, and this time when they kissed there was nothing between them but the threadbare fabric of her wrapper and whatever she had on beneath it. He could feel her heart thudding against his own chest.

"I want to make you feel good," he said, as if answering a question she hadn't quite asked. "That's all I want."

"Surely that's not all you want."

"I think you want to make me feel good, too. I think you like having me at your mercy," he ventured, really hoping he had this right. "I think you'd like that again."

Her eyes were wide and dark and a little shocked. She nodded.

"I'd like that, too," he said. "I think it'll be easy. It'll be so easy, Marian. How about this. I can't unfasten my breeches or take myself in hand until you let me. Would you like that?"

She gave him a quick nod. Good. And then something passed over her face, something decisive and mischievous. "That's enough talking, Rob. Now. You said you wanted to bring me pleasure, but so far all you've done is run your mouth." She flopped back onto the pillow, one hand crooked behind her head.

"I do beg your pardon," he said, and unfastened the sash of her wrapper. Her shift was snowy white but so worn as to be nearly transparent, her nipples visible as dark shadows beneath the fabric. He cupped one breast, running his thumb over the tip and feeling it harden beneath his touch.

He lay beside her, his hand still on her breast, and resumed kissing her—first her mouth, then her neck, then a spot beneath her ear that always made her moan. When he reached for the hem of her shift, she arched up into his touch. When the hem was high enough to bare her breasts, he paused.

"You're staring," Marian said.

"Yes," he agreed, and did it some more. He bent his head to take one pink nipple into his mouth, caressing the other with his thumb. She made a needy little sound and he kept going. He already knew that she liked his mouth on her, and he liked it, too, liked the taste of her and also the way she arched up into his touch. So he took his time with her, sucking and biting and licking, coaxing sounds out of her that he didn't think she knew she was making. When he pulled back, her chest was flushed, wet where he had kissed, red where he had used his teeth. His erection strained uncomfortably against his breeches, so he sat back on his heels and reached down to adjust himself.

"Tsk," she chided, taking hold of his wrist and returning it to her breast. "I didn't say you could do that yet."

He felt his face heat with an unexpected mix of lust and embarrassment, and he skimmed the thumb of the hand she still held over her taut nipple. "I apologize."

"I'm sure you can find a way to make it up to me."

This time when he kissed her breast, she twined a hand in his hair and with the other caressed his shoulder and arm as if she wasn't sure she was allowed to.

Slowly, he smoothed a hand down her stomach, between her legs, and found her already hot and wet. She had been so easy to bring off the last time, arching against his hand, tilting her hips so he was touching where she wanted. And she did the same thing now, but this time he knew what she liked and stroked her steadily. He didn't try to slip his fingers inside, just petted at her and kissed her until she went tense beneath him, her nails digging into him as she hovered on the edge of her climax. Then she let out a contented sigh.

By now he was incoherent with want, his cock painful, his mind frantic.

"You can do as you please," she said lazily, and he tore open his breeches with a desperation that would surely mortify him when he thought back on it. When he got a hand around himself, he groaned. She regarded him, curious and a little hungry, watching his fist move as if studying how he pleasured himself. The idea of her touching him instead, as she had the last time, made him need to squeeze the base of his erection to hold off his climax.

"Stop," she whispered, and he groaned as he complied. "I think you ought to kiss me while you do that."

He opened his mouth to argue that such a thing would result in his promptly coming all over her, then realized this was probably what he wanted more than anything else in the world at that moment, so he braced himself on one forearm and kissed her. His erection slid against her sweat-slick belly and he had to bury his face in her hair to muffle the sound he made.

"Can you . . . will that work for you?" she asked.

He nearly laughed. "Darling, a swift breeze would bring me off right now," he said into the soft skin where her neck and shoulder met.

"Prove it," she said, her hand on the small of his back, urging him on.

And so he did as he was told, thrusting into the warm space between their bodies, feeling her lips on his throat and one hand splayed at the base of his spine, the other tangled in his hair.

Afterward, he collapsed half on top of her, trying to catch his breath.

"Get off me, you oaf," she said, pushing at his shoulder. But when he rolled to his side and looked at her, she had a smile playing over her lips.

He found a cloth so they could clean themselves off, then got back into bed beside her, pulling the covers up to their chests.

"What's this one?" Marian asked, skimming her fingers over his shoulder, her touch disappearing as she reached a scar. "It's larger than the rest."

"Pistol shot. And it's not the largest. That would be the scar on the back of my calf from a dog bite." He slid the covers down, exposing his flank. "This is just a knife wound, but it festered and . . ." He trailed off, noticing that her face had gone pale and her body stiff. "Ah, yes. It's all a tad gruesome." He covered himself up, feeling like he ought to have known better than to take Marian on a tour of his grisliest injuries. "I apologize."

"No, you daft clod. It's not gruesome. Nothing about you is gruesome. I simply hadn't realized that you had been shot in the chest."

"It's really more my shoulder than my chest, and I was assured by the surgeon that it was as good a place as any to be shot. It looks much worse than it was."

She trailed her fingers down from his shoulder and across toward the center of his chest. "That's where I shot the duke," she said.

Rob took her hand and held it in place. He didn't know whether she was distressed by the memory of what she had done, or by the fact that if she had been a few inches off the duke could have walked away.

Her eyes were dark and hard. "Somebody could have killed you," she said. "I find that idea completely incompatible with my happiness."

Oh. He kissed her knuckles, because there was nothing he could trust himself to say.

"They weren't the first to try. But I've been lucky."

Marian—there was no other word for it—growled. Then she appeared to come to a decision. "What's this one?" She placed a finger over his left eyebrow.

"Fell out of a tree and hit a branch on the way down."

"And this one?" This time she tucked a strand of hair behind his ear and touched his temple.

"That's one of about six I got jumping out a window. A miracle I didn't break a bone."

"You jumped out a—"

"You, madam, are in no position to judge my means of exiting buildings. Nor, frankly, are you in a position to judge any of my riskier ventures. Capering around town past midnight on your own. It gives me gooseflesh just to think of."

"Poor Rob," she teased, and then yawned.

"Go to sleep. I'll see you in the morning." He dressed silently before slipping out and returning to his own cold room.

Chapter 29

$\mathcal{M}$arian had never been particularly fond of carriage travel. At best, it meant being cooped up in a small space with no means of escape and no useful means of occupying one's time. In the winter, when traveling over heavily rutted roads, it also meant being jostled about to a bone-rattling degree.

But it was amazing how quickly a few hours passed, even in a bouncing carriage, with someone whose conversation one enjoyed. She and Rob already knew the basic outlines of one another's lives, and now all that was left was to shade in the detail. Marian had never imagined that this process could be anything but tedious.

"Now, her father was the best fence in all of London," Rob was saying, "and he did all his business with this scrap of a child by his side. Betty was eleven, maybe twelve, when Kit and I first met her."

"And you must have been all of seventeen."

"Yes, exactly. I was a man of the world. I could not believe I had to do business with a little girl."

"The indignity."

"She had pigtails, Marian. She also had a knife that she kept up her sleeve and a mean right hook. Well, when her father died a few years later, she took over. There was never any question of it. Her brothers didn't quarrel about it, her mother didn't try to stop her, and any pawnbrokers or jewelers who wouldn't give her a fair price soon realized they had alienated the most powerful fence in London."

He spoke with naked pride and fondness for this Betty, but also with a degree of wistfulness that made little sense until Marian recalled that Rob had been away from his friends for a year, and then back with them for only a few days before leaving again with Marian. "You miss her."

"I do. I miss her and Kit. Even though I know they'll both be there in London when I return."

On the list of things that Marian liked about Rob, a list that was increasing at an alarming pace, the fact that he was so openly fond of the people he cared for was toward the top. He didn't conceal his fondness, whether it was for someone he had just met or for someone he had known his whole life. And he didn't try to hold it back, either. His friendship was like a creeping ivy—all one had to do was let it be, and it covered the whole barn.

She had experienced it herself, as unreal as it felt. He had seen something worth liking in her letters, and the next thing Marian knew he was devoted to her. She could no longer pretend that he was simply saying those things to her without meaning it; he had traveled back and forth across the country four times now for her. He had shown his fondness with word and deed since that first night, and maybe even before it.

He claimed he loved her. A better woman would cherish the sentiment; Marian wished she had never heard it.

"You love your friends," she said, mainly because she knew she would enjoy hearing him agree.

"Very much," he said firmly.

She looked out the window for a moment, watching the dreary countryside roll past. "I'm certain they love you as well," she said, not taking her eyes off the empty fields, the muddy verge. She didn't know how anyone could help but love him. He was easy to love. Everyone he met must fall a little bit in love with him; she had seen it herself, again and again. She shouldn't be surprised that it had happened to her.

"I hope they do," he said, and she knew he was looking at her, but she didn't dare turn her head.

They hit a rut that sent them both careening to the side, and he wordlessly braced her with one arm, steadying her so she didn't hit the door. Then, just as casually, he let his arm drop.

"Once," Rob said, precisely as if they were continuing their earlier conversation, "Betty stabbed someone who tried to start a fight in Kit's coffeehouse."

Marian raised an eyebrow. "That would seem to escalate the fight, rather than stop it."

"Oh, she didn't want to stop it. She wanted to win it. And she only stabbed the fellow in the arm."

"No harm done then," she said, amused.

"Precisely."

"And what did Mr. Webb say to all this?"

"He begged her to come work for him. She accepted, and there hasn't been another fight on the premises since." He smiled at her, wide and guileless, as if he were talking about sweets and kittens rather than stabbings and brawls, and she couldn't help but smile back. "I'd like for you to meet them."

The smile dropped from her face. He had to have forgotten that she was returning to Clare House and would be in no position to mingle with fences and highwaymen. And even if she were free to do as she pleased, she didn't know whether she wanted to be welcomed into the bosom of this criminal family Rob had assembled. These were the people Rob truly belonged with, and part of her couldn't help but think that she would matter less to him once he had his real friends back.

Mercifully, they reached a posting inn and stopped for a meal. Rob, as ever, was willing to let uncomfortable topics drop. The meal, when it arrived, was splendid. All meals were when taken with Rob. People wanted to give him their best dishes, wanted to keep his cup filled to the brim.

When they stopped for the night, she let Rob into her room when he knocked. His hands were warm and callused and gentle and she gave herself up to his touch. And then she watched, fascinated, her heart in her throat, as he did the same for her.

Later, Rob fell into a doze, his face burrowed into her shoulder, his hair glowing copper in the firelight. From where she lay, she could see at least half a dozen scars on his arms and back. He spoke of them as if he didn't mind them, and she thought she understood—what were the pair of them, after all, but a collection of things gone wrong and then, slowly, made right again.

Rob woke up in the small hours of the morning.

"Why are you awake?" he asked, his voice rough with sleep.

"I haven't slept much." She hadn't slept at all. Instead she had alternated between watching him and chastising herself for watching him. In her defense, she told herself, he was remarkably pretty and anyone in their right mind would want to look at him, and this night would likely be her last chance to do so.

"If you keep looking at me like that, you're going to give me ideas," he said.

She swallowed. "Well. This is me, continuing to look at you."

He raised an eyebrow and pushed the covers off her.

He made the question of sex so easy. She had thought that of all things, her limitations in this area would finally be the thing that served as a check on his affections. She had even been a little relieved to know that something would happen to restore some semblance of sanity between them.

"I could fall asleep like this," he said dreamily afterward, his head pillowed on her thigh, when she was trying to catch her breath. "And then I could wake up and do it again."

And, good God, he sounded like he meant it. She didn't think that she could take it—the raw affection in his voice, the way his hand rested on her hip, not any of it. She swallowed. "You have to go back to your room," she snapped. "You can't be discovered here."

He pressed a kiss to the inside of her thigh and got to his feet, as if she hadn't just been rude and cruel.

"I can't let you go in that state," she said, no less rude, and with a vague gesture in the vicinity of his obvious erection. "What will people think? You should probably let me do something about it."

"Whatever you say," he said, sliding back into bed and forbearing from pointing out that there wouldn't be anyone awake at this hour to think anything at all about any part of his body.

"My hand is all you're getting," she said, aiming for aloofness but instead sounding regrettably eager.

"Oh no," he said dryly. "That'll be terrible. If you really want to make me suffer, you could use your mouth."

She went momentarily still, imagining it. "Not, I think, this time," she said, but she couldn't help but lick her lips.

And then he lay beside her in bed and showed her exactly what he liked, coaxing her in precisely the same voice he used on horses, except now it was somehow arousing, and it all ought to have been sadly lowering but instead when he finished, he slid his hand between her legs and she managed to climax again. It was terrible. How was she supposed to think reasonably about any of this when he persisted in kissing her shoulder like that?

The next morning she made a valiant effort to be cool and rational, and she sat with especially rigid posture and spoke in single syllables. This resolve lasted about four miles, at which point the cat woke up from a doze and Rob began teasing him with a bit of string. She didn't know how anyone could be cross with him.

"Marian," Rob said when the carriage pulled to a stop before Clare House, and she avoided his eyes because she knew he was going to ask her something she didn't have an answer to. But then he let out a confused laugh. "I'll write to you, all right?

By now, my mother ought to have more information about Fanshawe, and Kit will likely have some ideas about how to get into his house."

And that wasn't quite what she wanted, but she didn't know what it was she did actually want, other than some improbable way for two lives that didn't seem to have any smooth edges to somehow fit side by side. But it was something. She was still furious that Sir John Fanshawe thought he could take advantage of a sick old man, and part of her would not rest until she had got some kind of revenge. She liked knowing that Rob would help and that she had another letter from him in her future.

She nodded at him. "Thank you," she said as she descended from the carriage, knowing it wasn't enough, but hoping she'd find time and a way to say something better.

Chapter 30

*B*y this point in his life, Rob was used to how his friends reacted to one of his cock-ups. He had, after all, plenty of experience observing how they responded to his impulses and his schemes and his brushes with death. Kit was always exasperated but fond, like a tired parent. Betty liked to yell a lot and see if he'd let her get in a couple of punches. His mother sighed in disappointment and barred his access to the brothel's kitchens. It was all comfortingly predictable.

"It's really anybody's guess what's wrong with you," Betty said conversationally when Rob got back to their table with three pints. She had been going on in this style all afternoon. "Could be that your brain never worked right. Could be that you just enjoy scaring the piss out of your friends every couple of weeks. Me, I can't be bothered to worry about it anymore."

"That's the spirit," Rob said, lowering himself into the chair that Kit had kicked out for him. This was their second round and he still hadn't explained anything—not why he had disappeared a year ago, not why he had run off earlier that month, not the blackmailing, nothing.

"God forbid you leave a note before you decide to fuck off for a fortnight," Betty went on.

"I think you both ought to finish your beer, because I have news that you aren't going to like one bit," Rob said. "It might go easier if you're sozzled. Honestly you both usually drink faster than this, so get to it. Act lively."

Betty eyed him suspiciously but drained her tankard. Kit pushed his untouched cup across the table to her.

"Out with it," Kit advised Rob, not unkindly.

"Twenty-six years ago, my mother was the Duke of Clare's mistress." Rob forced himself to look his friends in the eye. "He brought her to France on some jaunt he was taking with his friends. For reasons I can't even begin to comprehend, she married him. It was never annulled. I was born some nine months later."

Rob watched Kit closely, but his friend only nodded. Betty made a strangled sound and drank Kit's beer.

"When my mother told me, I . . . did not take it well," Rob went on. "It was right after I was shot and I thought you were dead," he said, directing these last words at Kit.

"I recall," Kit said dryly.

"I immediately went to France to see the parish records for myself. When I came back, I learned you were alive, of course, but I let you believe I was dead, because I didn't want to admit that I might be the legitimate son and heir of a person I reviled."

"A person *we* reviled," Kit amended softly.

"Right. So I was a coward about it, not to mention thoughtless and cruel, because it was so much easier not to deal with any of it. I can't even tell you how sorry about that I am. I know it was—"

"Rob," Kit interrupted softly. "We already did this. It's forgiven. Now, out with the rest."

Rob took a deep breath. "Then I made things worse by deciding that I ought to at least get something out of the mess, so I blackmailed Lord Holland and Marian."

"Marian?" Betty repeated. "Who?"

"He's talking about the Duchess of Clare," Kit said.

"Oh, right. Somehow I forgot that we're all on a first-name basis with lords and ladies," said Betty. "Now everything makes perfect sense."

"Well, she did leave me tied to a bed all night," Rob offered as an explanation.

"It's how I make all my friends," said Betty.

"Can we get back to the part where I'm apparently the legitimate heir to some fucking dukedom?" Rob turned to Kit. "Why aren't you more upset about this? I thought for sure you'd be upset."

"Mainly because I already knew. Percy figured it out last week." The bastard sounded almost smug about his horrible paramour's acuity. "But also I don't really give a shit who got your mother pregnant and it's a little insulting that you thought I would."

"But. The Duke of *Clare*. It makes my skin crawl to think that he might have been my—" He shuddered. Rob really didn't want to think about how much of his belief that his friends would hate him for an accident of birth was actually due to his hating that accident enough for all three of them. "Anyway, it might not be true. My father could be anybody."

Kit and Betty both raised their eyebrows in identical expressions of skepticism.

Kit narrowed his eyes. "You do look—"

"Don't mention my cheekbones," Rob pleaded. "Marian already did and now I want to go about with a sack over my head."

"You told her?" This was the first time in the conversation that Kit sounded surprised—and pleasantly so, if Rob had the right of it.

"No, she mentioned the resemblance in passing."

"So what are you going to do about it?" Kit asked.

"*Do* about it? I'm going to bloody ignore it and let your Percy do what he pleases. He can ponce about in ermine all he bloody well likes, and I can . . . not do that, and everybody lives happily ever after."

"I meant, what are you going to do after Percy tells the world that you're the true Duke of Clare?"

Rob paused with his tankard halfway to his lips. "And why in hell would he do that?"

"He and the duchess didn't much care for the idea of always being vulnerable to blackmailers," Kit said. "They reckoned that if one person knew the truth, there would always be somebody knocking at the door. And what they're doing *is* telling the truth, which I'm not sure needs an explanation."

Rob put his head in his hands. These were the wages of sin

people were always going on about. He was furious, and only more so because he had only himself to blame. "I already told my mother that I'd deny having ever met her and insist that my real mum is some nice lady who never married any dukes."

"That's one way of going about it, I suppose," said Kit. "I don't know how much your mother would like it. But I reckon they can't make you inherit a fortune and a title if you insist that it's a case of mistaken identity." Kit paused, as if weighing his words. "I might have hoped that after the past year you'd have thought twice about running away from your problems."

"Running away?" Rob scoffed. "I'm not running away from anything. I'm refusing to participate in inherited wealth."

Kit sighed. If Rob didn't know better, he'd think that Kit was trying to shame him into inheriting gobs of money. He changed the topic as best he could, asking Betty about a pawnbroker who was the bane of her existence, which set her off on a monologue.

While Rob listened, he thought of what Kit had said a moment earlier. He'd said that Lord Holland *and Marian* had intended all along to expose the duke's bigamy. He was hardly in a position to blame anyone for keeping secrets. But her title and position were what stood between them and any kind of future. If she had meant to rid herself of those encumbrances, her choice to keep that information from him was tantamount to saying that she didn't want anything more to do with him.

Except—no, that was all wrong. She had definitely believed that she was returning to London to live at Clare House and resume being the Duchess of Clare. And she had been miserable about it. He couldn't make it add up.

"Well, I'm off," Betty said, rising to her feet. "God knows what's become of the shop without me or Kit there for an hour." They had left the coffeehouse in the hands of some lad Rob had never met, the sight of whom viscerally reminded Rob of how much he had missed during his year away.

When he and Kit were alone at the table, Rob went and fetched another pair of pints from the publican, perversely wanting to delay whatever would happen when he was alone with Kit. Kit had always had a way of seeing through him and Rob shuddered to think of what Kit would be able to see now.

"You really all right?" was all Kit asked, though.

"Not really, but I'll do, all things considered. What about you?"

"Percy's buying the house next door to the coffeehouse," he said, as if this were an answer to Rob's question. And Rob supposed it was, in a way.

"I hope he'll be very happy in it while I'm dragged kicking and screaming into a Chancery suit that'll no doubt take the rest of my life to be resolved."

"I think you should talk to Percy," Kit said.

"I'm sure we'll have plenty of opportunities to talk when we start spending all our time in court," Rob grumbled. "I'm not going along with it. You might as well tell him that. I'll deny it with my last breath."

Kit didn't ask any more questions, and they settled into an old and familiar rhythm of pointless conversation until finally Kit sighed. "I'd better help Betty close up."

"I'll stay and finish my beer. And probably get another one, if we're honest." And probably another one after that, but nobody needed to be *that* honest. "Do you wish he had been a commoner?"

Kit raised his eyebrows. "Percy? At first, maybe. But I—I love him, and I wouldn't want to change anything that made him the person I love." He scowled and got to his feet, leaning heavily on his walking stick. "To hell with you for making me say that aloud."

"It was worse for me," Rob said with feeling.

Kit squeezed Rob's shoulder. "You've always been brave. You can find a way to be brave about this."

Rob looked up at his friend. "I've never been brave. I'm just reckless."

Something sad passed over Kit's face. "No. You find a way to be brave for everyone but yourself. When I think of the things you did for me when you were a child, Rob."

It probably said something that Rob couldn't immediately tell whether Kit was referring to Rob helping him bury his family or Rob killing those smugglers in Rye—the latter of which Kit definitely wasn't supposed to know about. But Kit had always been more observant than Rob gave him credit for. "I want to take care of my—of the people—of my family, I suppose. That's all."

"Well, you're my family, too, and I'd love it if you could find a way to take care of yourself in the same way that you've always taken care of me."

Rob wanted to point out that there was nobody to threaten, nobody to hurt, just one future he couldn't have, and one he didn't want.

Instead he watched his friend head out into the cold.

Chapter 31

$\mathcal{M}$arian shouldn't have been surprised to find that Clare House was quiet and somber with mourning. But she hadn't been expecting the black crepe, the drawn curtains, the closed-in feeling that comes from too little light and too much silence.

And there was no sign of Percy.

"His Grace has business that often lasts until late at night," lamented Percy's valet. "Sometimes even until the next morning," he added, for all the world as if he and Marian didn't both know perfectly well what sort of things were keeping Percy occupied until all hours.

Marian wrote a note to Percy announcing her arrival in London and sent it with a footman, instructing him to check for His Grace at Mr. Webb's coffeehouse as well as the solicitors' chambers and anywhere else that seemed a likely destination. Next she wrote a similar note for Marcus.

And then she went upstairs.

"I just got her to sleep, Your Grace," Alice said, dropping into the hybrid curtsey and bow that she seemed to think appropriate for greeting her charge's mother. "She's working on a new tooth and is ever so displeased about it. But I can wake her if you like."

"No, no," Marian said, watching her daughter sleep. Her hands were balled into little fists and the remnants of an imperious tantrum were still on her face. She looked remarkably like Percy, and the resemblance only increased the crankier she became.

"I'm glad to see that you're well, Your Grace. We were worried, ma'am, if you'll forgive me for saying so. I thought you might have been injured by the villains who killed His Grace."

"I ought to have left word, but I needed to—" Marian broke off. She had nearly repeated the line she had been formulating as her official excuse, that she was so distressed by witnessing her husband's injury that she sought comfort in the home of her father. But anyone who knew her, and anyone who had spent months in the duke's household certainly knew her at least slightly, would know that she wasn't prone to fits of nerves. "The truth is that I needed to see to my father in Kent. He's old and unwell."

Eliza grumbled in her sleep, rolling from her back to her belly with an air of great suffering. Marian and Alice remained perfectly still and silent until the baby's deep breathing resumed.

"Is that a new trick she has?" Marian asked. "Rolling over onto her belly?" She had seen Eliza roll onto her back, but not the other way around. But perhaps she had always done this and Marian had failed to notice.

"Yes," Alice said proudly. "And at not even five months, too."

"She's a regular prodigy," Marian said, momentarily filled with a pride she knew to be irrational.

"Will you be returning to Kent, Your Grace?" Alice asked.

"I'm not certain about my plans. But as soon as I know, I'll tell you." The household servants would need to know whether Percy and Marian intended to stay, or whether they too would have their lives thrown into turmoil if Percy revealed himself not to be the true Duke of Clare. Marian ought to begin writing their references now, as there were dozens of servants who would need new places. That reminded her of something. "Alice, where do your parents live?"

"Kentish Town," the maid said with some surprise. "By St. Pancras."

"Thank you."

Marian watched the baby sleep for another moment, then returned to her bedchamber. Her own maid wasn't there, thank heavens. Now, that was one member of the household who could look for a new post immediately, as she wasn't spending another night under this roof. Marian would pay her the fortnight's wages she was owed and even double it, as long as doing so meant not having to see one of the duke's informants.

Come to think, there were probably other spies in the household besides the lady's maid. And while they could no longer spy on her for the duke, she still couldn't trust them. She didn't think she could trust anyone in this house, except Alice and possibly Percy's valet. She glanced around her apartments and knew she would never be comfortable here. She certainly never had been, although that owed more to her illness and the duke than anything else. But this place was poisoned for her. Her skin crawled at the prospect of spending another night here, let alone weeks and months.

It occurred to her that she didn't have to. Percy could do as he pleased, but she didn't have to go along with it. She could leave him up to his own devices, and—well, that was the problem. She had very little money of her own, and no way of getting any more unless she married again. And that was simply out of the question. She had made one ill-advised match, and she wasn't ever again making the mistake of giving up control of her fate and fortune.

If Percy meant to conceal the duke's bigamy, there would be a small widow's portion left to Marian in the duke's will. But she couldn't let herself touch it. Whether for good or ill, she had killed the man and couldn't profit from his death.

Perhaps Percy could help her hire a modest house, big enough for her father, Netley, Hester, and Nurse, along with Marian, Eliza, and Alice. That seemed like a paradise, almost impossibly ideal. And yet—it was a house. She remembered Rob's embarrassment over spending money on his brown wool coat. He didn't like spending money to indulge himself, and she didn't like indulging herself full stop.

She walked around the perimeter of her sitting room, stepping softly on the plush carpet, her fingertips tracing along the polished woods and gilt surfaces. She didn't have to stay here. She heard Rob's words, telling her that just because something made her suffer didn't mean it was the right choice.

She was out of the habit of wanting things. What was the

point of wanting anything—anything that actually mattered, that was—if one wasn't going to get it? What was the point of wanting anything if she had only a few years left?

But now she at least knew what she didn't want, and it was to be in Clare House. She wanted a chance to figure out what she wanted, because right now all she could think of was that she wanted more time with Rob. She had dismissed that as ill-advised and impossible for a dozen reasons, but she was getting to be an old hand at doing things that were ill-advised and impossible.

She was about to ring for a bath when she heard footsteps outside her door. She braced herself to have to face her maid, but when the knock sounded, it was loud and impatient, not at all the quiet scratching she was used to from servants. "Come in!" she called.

Percy entered, dressed in an ensemble of a peacock blue so eye-wateringly bright that it nearly distracted her from the fact that Percy had to be terribly displeased with her.

"Percy," she started, "I'm so sorry for running off like that. I can't—"

"What *are* you wearing?" He stared at her in horror. "What is the meaning of this? What can be the provenance of these—these garments, Marian? Did they come from an attic?"

Marian glanced down at her gown, which was one of the gray worsteds she had found in the attic at Little Hinton. "Why, yes, they did. I thought they rather suited me."

"They'd suit you perfectly well if it were twenty years ago."

He sank into a chair by the fire. "And if you were a provincial spinster who drank tea without any sugar and terrified all the neighborhood children."

Marian, momentarily impressed with this aesthetic success, preened a little before remembering why she needed to speak to Percy. "Are you well? The last I saw you, you were bleeding and . . ." She trailed off. She hardly needed to remind Percy of the circumstances of their last meeting: him shot, her holding a smoking pistol, the duke bleeding.

"It was nothing more than a scrape," Percy said, waving his hand dismissively. "I'm not even going to have an impressive scar. Those leather breeches are quite ruined, though, which is a pity, but Collins has already got me a new pair."

Percy shifted in his seat, as if he didn't quite know what to say next, and then got to his feet. Marian thought he meant to leave, so she automatically stood. The next thing she knew, his arms were around her and her face was being pressed into the peacock-blue silk of his coat. "I do apologize—I know we don't ordinarily do this, but I'm so pleased to see that you're well. You had me worried. When you disappeared after—after what happened, I thought you might have done something drastic."

It was true that they didn't ordinarily embrace; Marian wasn't in the habit of embracing anybody and Percy was loath to wrinkle his clothes. She didn't know what to do with her hands and settled for patting feebly at his back.

"I'm sorry that I—" She stopped before she could finish that statement with a lie. "I'm sorry that you had to see it." She swallowed. "I didn't plan to do it. That's not why I was in the carriage that day."

"I know that," Percy said quickly, pulling back to look Marian in the eye. "I knew that all along. I know you better than that."

She wanted to say that she was glad that he did, because at some point she had lost all sight of who she was. She wanted to tell him that the idea of leaving this life behind and starting something new—something she chose for herself—terrified her.

Instead she managed a watery smile and they both sat down again.

"What if we don't talk about any of that," Percy suggested. "And you don't have to tell me where you've been this past fortnight if you'd rather not."

Marian instantly felt guilty. This kindness was more than she deserved. He had to at least wonder why she had been in the carriage during the robbery, rather than safe in London. And she wanted to explain that to him—she wanted to explain everything to him—but right now he seemed light and happy in a way he seldom was, and she didn't want to interfere with that. "It's not a secret. At least, it wasn't meant to be. I was with my father."

"You went to Chiltern Hall?" Percy looked baffled.

"No. My father is in Kent. He's been there for over a year. He's not well, Percy. His mind wanders." She could get into the details of her brother's threats later on; for now she had more pressing matters to discuss. "Mr. Brooks was kind enough to take me to Kent. I wasn't thinking clearly after the incident, and he was kindness itself."

Percy looked faintly stunned. "And here I thought you had kidnapped him."

"Oh, I did," Marian said, abashed, "or at least I meant to, but we've made up. He told me that you're acting as the Duke of Clare." She smoothed her skirt over her knees and then immediately snatched her hands away, annoyed with herself to have resorted to nervous fidgeting while talking to Percy, of all people. "I suppose that means you've reconsidered your plan?" Her heart was pounding beneath the heavy wool of her gown and she hoped her anxiety didn't show. "Because if you are, I'm happy for you, Percy, but I need to get out of here. This"—she gestured around them—"isn't what I want and I don't think I can stand it for another minute."

"I haven't changed my mind," Percy said, a strange look on his face. "I'm arranging things so the estate's assets are all being used in a way that's less horrible than before. On the first of January, I'll publicize my father's first marriage, precisely as we planned, but by then I ought to have the estate in enough of a tangle that whoever inherits won't be able to undo any of the changes I've made."

"I see." She was almost lightheaded with relief. The first of January was only a few days away. She could wait that long. "Good."

"Marian, I would have checked with you if I had known where to find you. But even so, I've never known you to waver, and so I didn't think you would this time."

"I haven't. I don't want to go back to this. I don't know what

I'll do instead, or where Eliza and I will live, but I'll think of something."

"About that. I bought a house. It's on the small side but it'll do for the two of us, Eliza, and a handful of servants."

Marian tried to imagine living in a house with only Percy and Eliza. It seemed almost heavenly, too good to be true. "Where?"

"Covent Garden. Well . . . you see, it's next door to Kit's coffeehouse."

She raised an eyebrow. "Is it, now?"

"I don't want to talk about it," said Percy, sounding all of six years old.

"Rob told me that the two of you were quite disgusting together."

"He's Rob, now, is he?" Percy raised an eyebrow, then suddenly adopted an earnest mien. "Marian, you need to know that Mr. Brooks is—confound it, there's no delicate way to put this— but I believe he's the duke's only legitimate son."

That, Marian supposed, was the secret Rob had been keeping from her. She didn't know why she wasn't more surprised. It added up: his foster parents had lived on the duke's estate; he looked like Percy; he was the right age. His mother could certainly be Elsie Terry. Most of all, he seemed to have a personal vendetta against the duke.

"That does complicate things," she said. He should have told her. Why on earth hadn't he? She supposed it was for the same reason he hadn't wanted to tell Mr. Webb and Betty. He wanted people to look at him and see Rob, not a title and station he found hateful. She was aware that perhaps another person would have been annoyed or even hurt that Rob hadn't confided in her, but when she thought of Rob believing he had to keep this secret to himself all she felt was an ache in her heart and a furious urge to protect him.

"I don't suppose he'll cooperate with the court and let me hand the whole estate over to him in one tidy but morally complicated package?" Percy asked.

"Ha! No."

Percy looked at her for a long moment. "Do you love him?"

"Yes," she said immediately.

"And is he in love with you?"

Marian swallowed. "He says that he is."

Percy sighed with relief. "Well, he could marry you. That would be very convenient for you and Eliza."

It would be. There would be no loss of status for her and very little for Eliza. And Marian would be on hand to show Rob all the things he didn't know about his new position. The thought made her feel acutely ill.

"And even if he's not interested in wealth or station," Percy went on, "being with you might sweeten the bargain."

Now Marian thought she might actually be sick all over Percy's fine suit. "I never want to be part of anyone's bargain ever again. Not my hand, not my body, none of it. Just—don't ever say that again, all right?"

Percy looked shocked and mortified. "I didn't mean—I'm sorry."

"You couldn't have known," Marian said when her heart stopped racing.

"It was not a good year," Percy said, and it was such an understatement that Marian started to laugh. Then Percy started laughing, and Marian had to bury her face in her skirt so she didn't frighten the servants.

"It wasn't all bad, though, was it?" Marian asked when she finally recovered. "There's Eliza, and you've made a new friend in your Mr. Webb. And . . . well."

"Well, indeed. Definitely not all bad," Percy agreed.

Chapter 32

The fire at the Royal Oak was blazing and the ale was very good, so Rob saw no reason to peel himself off his chair and return—well, he had no idea where he would go. His luggage was in one of Kit's spare rooms over the shop, so he supposed that was where he'd sleep.

He had a passing notion that he probably ought to do something about that. At his age, it was high time for him to have a steady address. He probably ought to find work, as Kit was done with thieving and Rob didn't want to work with anyone else. He needed to find something to do with himself.

Rob had finished two more pints and made respectable progress on a third when the chair across from him scraped across the wooden floor. A person dusted the seat with a handkerchief and gingerly lowered himself into it.

"Kit said I'd find you here," said Lord Holland, surveying his surroundings. He wore a blue suit of clothes so fine that Rob wanted to set things on fire. "You're pouting. The Talbot bone structure isn't made for pouting, I'm afraid, so you only look slightly louche. You really ought to cultivate a glare, or possibly a glower, if you're up to it."

"What do you want, Holland?"

"Do I need a reason to further my acquaintance with my own brother? I think not."

"First of all, shut up. Second, I'm not your brother."

Holland had the nerve to give him a pitying look. "I had hoped that you might be clever enough to keep up with Marian, but it seems you aren't clever at all. I suppose she's found some use for you, though."

Rob gripped the edge of the table. "Don't talk about her like that."

"Good Lord. You're either very drunk or very deluded if you think Marian would object to my talking about her like an adult human being with free will who's able to do as she damned well pleases."

And, well, Rob actually was pretty drunk, now that he thought about it. But Holland's words rankled. "Free will? Do what she pleases? I wish Marian would do as she pleased. Instead she does her duty," he scoffed.

Holland looked at him as if he had just barked like a dog. "Her duty? Marian? Marian Hayes? Black hair, bad attitude? Of course she does her duty. But she also does precisely what she wants."

Holland made a gesture to someone over Rob's shoulder, and a moment later another pair of pints appeared on the table. "When we were about thirteen," Holland said, "we took out one of my father's hunters. The horse bolted, and only Marian's talent for a quick dismount saved her neck. I was in for a hiding and Marian knew it. So she took the blame, saying that she took the horse out over my protestations. I was furious with her. I didn't need anyone to take my punishments, what did she think of me, et cetera."

"What did she say?"

"She said that if I thought she was going to let me get whipped without even trying to stop it from happening then I was a bigger idiot than I looked. And then she told me never to pester her again with trifling considerations of pride."

"Oh Christ." Rob could imagine a younger Marian saying exactly that.

"And then she kicked me in the shins."

Rob ran a hand over his jaw. "Naturally."

"I was whipped regardless, but my father said it was for not shouldering the blame for Marian. Meanwhile, Marian's father was very indulgent and never laid a hand on her, although he made her copy out some tiresome passages of Plato. My point is that Marian has always made choices that put the comfort and safety of the people she loves above her own, and often without their permission. She has her own ethics. It comes from too much time with untranslated Greek, I'm afraid."

"Why are you telling me all this?"

"Because this afternoon, when Marian was telling me about all the horrible things that befell her in the past two weeks, she never stopped smiling. Not once. Most disconcerting. She referred to you as 'kindness itself,' which, I will tell you, nearly made me quite sick. And evidently you traipsed up and down the Canterbury road simply to do her bidding. Very gallant. Now, onto less pleasant matters. Do you have a trade? A source of income? Some kind of profession?"

Rob stared for a moment. Was Holland sizing him up as a candidate for Marian's hand? No, the thought was too absurd. "Are you mad? Of course I don't. I'm a thief."

"Oh good. That *is* a relief. I couldn't bear to see Marian settle down with someone who was in trade."

"For Christ's sake, Holland. She's not settling down with anyone! And neither am I, for that matter."

"It doesn't matter to me whether you call it marriage or settling down or whether the two of you start a traveling circus. I will point out, though, that most people wouldn't consider falling in love and inheriting a dukedom to be bad things, per se."

"Dukedom," Rob spat.

"There's no law saying that you have to touch the money or use the title. Give the money away. Refuse to use the title. Turn Clare House into a foundling home and Cheveril Castle into a leper colony."

Holland had gone pale as he spoke and there was a forced lightness to his voice. The title and legacy meant something to Holland, but he had decided not to fight for it—partly on principle, but partly, Rob guessed, for Kit. Holland had made a choice he didn't entirely like. So had Kit, who couldn't have been delighted about falling for an aristocrat, no matter what he said.

Rob didn't know how to explain that the money and the title—both of which were despicable, obviously—weren't even the crux of the problem. "I don't want anything that was his," he said from between gritted teeth.

"Ah. Well. You already have plenty that was his, if you'll forgive my saying so. Your nose and your cheekbones, notably. Your height. Your ability to look well in even the most appalling of garments."

"Enough." He scrubbed a hand over his chin. "I understand your point. I just—it's going to take a while to get used to it." He had spent a year fiercely denying it to himself.

"Excellent. You're not an idiot, even if you do wear your hair like that," Holland said earnestly. He drained his pint and got to his feet. "Start with what matters. Everything else is mere trifles, Rob. You have until the first of January to get used to calling me Percy, because after that I won't answer to anything else." And with that, he left.

Rob, thinking he had better sober up, waved over the innkeeper and ordered supper, and then, remembering his promise to Marian, asked for paper, pen, and ink.

Dearest Marian,

I had grand plans to write you something witty and entertaining, something to amuse you while you do whatever it is you ordinarily do all day when you aren't with me, but all I can think of is that I miss you. It's hardly a surprise; I've been dreading missing you for days now, but the reality exceeds the anticipation.

I hope you're not too miserable. I know you weren't pleased about going back. Is the baby well? Has the cat engaged in any witchcraft? I saw your Percy this evening and he told me a story that began with horse theft and ended with assault and battery, and all I can say is that you clearly had a life of crime and adventure long before meeting me.

Tonight—your tonight, the day you read this—I'll be at the Royal Oak near Charing Cross. I likely shouldn't ask you to meet me, so I won't; instead know that I'd be pleased so see you (trust that this is an understatement). I'd also understand if you can't get away from whatever it is that people like you do—and I don't even mean that in an insulting way, only that it kills me not to be able to picture you, not to know what you're about, after having been in your pocket for so long.

I want nothing more than to be in your pocket, Marian. I would alter my life in any way you required and that thought terrifies me.

There are things I ought to tell you, secrets you'll have every reason to be cross with me for keeping. I'll come clean when I see you.

This letter is an exercise in why one shouldn't write when one's been drinking. It's a poor excuse for a love letter and there's no style to it at all.

Entirely yours,
Rob

Chapter 33

$\mathcal{M}$arian didn't dare hope that there would be a letter from Rob so soon, so she didn't shuffle through the stack of correspondence looking for a boldly scrawled address as she had so many times back in the autumn.

There were five condolence letters, each using a rote formula Marian had herself employed many times. There was a letter from Richard, which Marian threw directly into the fire. There was also a letter from Richard's wife, encouraging Marian to make her home with them, and if Marian had needed a vision of a life that could be more oppressive than remaining at Clare House, it was living as a dowager aunt with Richard and his family. Marian had met her sister-in-law exactly three times, and each time that lady expressed a fervent desire to change everything about Marian's manners, morals, dress, conversation, and habits—and still, Marian vastly preferred her to Richard.

At the bottom of the pile was a letter addressed in a too-familiar hand. She broke the seal in such haste that she tore the flimsy paper, then smoothed it out on the table as if that would repair the tear.

It was indeed a love letter; however inexpert Rob believed it to be, it was precisely the sort of love letter she would have hoped to receive, if she had ever dreamed of receiving such a thing. He missed her, he thought of her, he asked after the things that mattered to her. He had evidently had a civil conversation with Percy, of all things.

She had once jested that she would press love letters between the pages of the *Aeneid*. She doubted there was a copy of that volume in this house, and even if there were, she didn't want it. Instead she folded the letter into a neat square and tucked it into her bodice.

But after visiting Eliza, she was faced with an entire day and nothing to do. She certainly wasn't going to spend a single unnecessary minute in Clare House, so she dressed for the day in her most somber gown and had the carriage bring her to a house near Covent Garden.

"Are you quite certain, Your Grace?" the coachman asked when Marian gave him the address.

"I'm starting a charitable home for fallen women," Marian said, not particularly caring whether the lie sounded plausible.

The door was opened by a woman carrying a mop and a bucket. She wore a cap and an apron and had to be at least fifty. She reminded Marian of nobody so much as Hester.

"I'm here to see Mistress Scarlett," Marian said, feeling ridiculous about using the lady's sobriquet. "It's about her son."

The woman gave her an appraising glance and wordlessly ushered her in. The house was quiet, and Marian realized belatedly that at ten in the morning most women of this profession were likely still asleep.

The parlor that Marian was shown into was furnished in much the same way as Marian's own private sitting room at Clare House: pale silks, delicately tinted landscape paintings, a plush settee with gilt legs. On the settee sat a plump, red-headed woman of indeterminate age and Dinah.

Well. For a few days, Marian had surmised that Dinah and Rob's mother were friends. That explained how Dinah was able to supply Mr. Webb's name when Marian had asked for a high-wayman and also how Rob's mother had learned the details of Marian's illness. It also might explain why Dinah had, now that Marian thought back on it, perhaps recognized Rob after Marian tied him to the bed.

What she hadn't known was that the two women were the kind of friends who sat around in peignoirs with their hair still obviously disheveled from sleep.

"I'm so glad you called," said Rob's mother, rising to her feet, for all the world as if Marian were an expected visitor. Marian remembered Rob saying that his mother knew everything.

"I wanted to make your acquaintance," Marian said, trying to sound warm and interested in the way Rob did when meeting people. "I've heard so much about you."

"Do take a seat, Your Grace."

"Marian," Marian said, sitting in a chair by the fire. "I'm not a duchess, and all the world will know that in less than a week. I'm not certain what to call you. I don't think you go by Elsie Terry any longer."

"Scarlett will do just fine, my dear," said Rob's mother, not betraying any surprise that Marian knew the name she had used when she married the duke. "And what is it that my son said to make you wish to see me?"

"He said you were a good parent."

Both the women on the settee went still, as if they had been prepared to hear anything but that.

"He told me that you paid for his education, and that can't have been a small expense, considering how well educated he is. And he told me that when he was in trouble, he went to you."

"These are trifles," Scarlett said, and Marian *knew* that tone, knew that way of brushing off accusations of kindness. She hadn't previously noted more than a superficial resemblance between mother and son, but there it was.

"Why did you tell him about the duke?" This had troubled Marian since Percy told her about Rob's parentage. Surely Rob's mother knew how her son would react to such a thing, and if she had kept it a secret for over twenty years, why not continue to keep it a secret? "Why not let him remain blissfully ignorant?"

"Because the truth has a way of making itself known, whether we like it or not."

"You might have told him at any time. But you waited until last year."

"Because," Scarlett said slowly, "of you."

"I beg your pardon."

"The duke married you. It was one thing when he married Holland's mother. She was the duke's equal. And I don't entirely mean that as praise, however much I admired that lady. She had her own reasons for putting up with his ways. But you obviously didn't know what you were getting yourself into. Sometimes, if I get wind of an inadvisable marriage, I try to make sure the lady gets warned off. Not that she always listens, mind you, but I can try. In this case, however, he went off to the country and came back a month later with you. There wasn't the slightest hint of a courtship."

"But," Marian said, her mind reeling, "how did telling Rob about the duke help me?"

"Because, dear, she knew Rob would go to you with the information. He can't resist helping people," said Dinah, speaking for the first time since Marian entered the room. "And then you could choose whether to do something about it."

Scarlett made a disapproving sound. "I did *not* expect him to blackmail you. That was badly done."

"It worked out well enough, I suppose," Marian said, a little stunned. "Except for the duke dying, I mean."

"That is the very definition of *well*," Scarlett said firmly. "Not that I have any idea who pulled the trigger."

"Such a mystery," Dinah agreed blandly, dropping a lump of sugar into her tea.

Marian supposed that she could choose to be upset that all along, Rob's mother had been manipulating circumstances to her own ends. But that, she decided, would be a waste of emotion. And besides, it was oddly comforting to know that there had been a plan, even if it hadn't been hers.

"Before I leave," Marian said, "You may be aware that I plan to retrieve a few of my father's belongings from Sir John Fanshawe's house."

"Is that all?" murmured Rob's mother.

"I'll also help myself to some trifles in order to repay the amount he took from my father unfairly." Marian reasoned that there was no point in attempting to conceal anything from Rob's mother; she already seemed to know everything that happened in this town. "Rob mentioned that you were going to give him some information to help with this plan."

Mistress Scarlett regarded Marian for a moment, then exchanged a glance with Dinah. "That does tend to be my role in the operation."

From this, Marian gathered that Rob's mother played a regular part in Rob and Mr. Webb's criminal enterprises, along with Betty the fence and heaven knew who else. Interesting. "Well, I wonder if you have any information that Sir John Fanshawe might find embarrassing to have revealed to his friends."

"Are you going to blackmail him?"

"Nothing so vulgar," Marian said. "The secret is only a small incentive for him to behave himself."

Scarlett looked thoughtful, then went to her writing desk. A moment later she returned, handing a piece of paper to Marian. "I wonder if giving people incentives to behave themselves is something you'd be interested in doing on a more regular basis?" she asked. When Marian didn't respond, she went on. "Never mind. You can get back to me later."

Her next stop was Mr. Webb's coffeehouse. It was high time for her to meet this man Rob loved as a brother and for whom Percy had rearranged his life. She looked to either side of the coffeehouse in an attempt to guess which house Percy had purchased. One wasn't a house at all, but a greengrocer with a few rooms on top; Marian doubted that Percy would consider that in any way suitable. On the other side was a neat brick building, three windows across and four stories high, although that final story was an attic. It was probably only a little larger than Little Hinton, but with the space arranged vertically rather than horizontally. It would do for Percy, Eliza, and herself quite well, although Marian could see that it was really meant for Percy and Mr. Webb. That didn't mean that she'd be unwelcome there, but it did give her pause.

It would not, however, accommodate Marian's father and his household, and indeed the idea of cramming an elderly earl, a highwayman, a baby, the bigamous wife of a duke, and whatever on earth Percy considered himself these days under one roof was too farcical for Marian to take seriously. She would still need to somehow hire a house for her father. Somewhere near enough at hand for Marian to keep an eye on him, fine enough that she wouldn't be ashamed to house her father there, and not ruinously expensive. This seemed fantastical, but fantastical things were happening every day.

Before she could think better of it, she opened the door to the coffeehouse. She was immediately assailed by the smell of tobacco and coffee. The pipe smoke was so thick that she could hardly see clear to the back wall of the place. A glance around the room confirmed that all the patrons were men.

There were two people who stood out as distinct from the customers. One was a dark-skinned woman slightly younger than Marian who wore a cap and apron that were both immaculate and highly starched; this had to be Betty. The other stood near the hearth, gazing at a pot in a way that was somehow both proprietary and menacing, as if the contents of that pot had better start cooperating or else. He was broad shouldered and tall, with dark hair that looked like it had never known what it was to be tidy. Even if he hadn't been leaning heavily on a walking stick, Marian would have known that this was Mr. Webb.

Having never been inside a coffeehouse, she wasn't sure about the etiquette. Did one simply take any seat one wished, cramming oneself between strangers? Where did one pay? How much did one pay? Pondering these questions, she dithered too long in the doorway and was nearly run down by a group of rowdy young gentlemen entering from the street. To avoid getting trampled, she pressed her back against the wall.

When she looked up, Mr. Webb was staring at her even more menacingly than he had looked at the coffeepot. But when his eyes flickered to the raucous gentlemen, she realized his baleful gaze had been directed at them all along. This made her feel in perfect sympathy with the man. She, too, wished to direct her most malign of stares at men who jostled past strangers in places of public accommodation. This gave her the courage to cross the room.

"I beg your pardon. You are Mr. Webb, are you not?"

He gave her a quick up-and-down look. "Depends who's asking," he grumbled. Good heavens, was this how he treated all prospective customers? She very much feared that it was.

She lowered her voice. "I'm Marian Hayes. Percy's—"

"I know who you are. He's not here."

"I came to see you. I wished to make your acquaintance. I

believe we are to be neighbors." She tried to pitch her voice into a sufficiently friendly register, but she was afraid that her voice simply didn't do that. Her words came out clipped and chilly. "Any friend of Percy's is a friend of mine," she added, somewhat desperately, in the hope that her words might stand for more than her manners.

"Afraid I can't say the same," said Mr. Webb. "Percy likely has any number of silly, idle, useless popinjays for friends."

"Percy *is* a silly, idle, useless popinjay," Marian protested. "And that hasn't stopped you."

The corner of Mr. Webb's mouth hitched up in something that might have almost been a smile. "He isn't idle."

"Perhaps not anymore, but I witnessed ten years of uninterrupted idleness on his part. I'm quite certain he accomplished nothing at all until last month and would have been mortally offended by anyone who suggested otherwise."

He nodded thoughtfully, as if this were a sensible response— which, of course, it was, but Marian hadn't expected him to think so. "How many animals did he take in?"

"I beg your pardon?"

"Rob. How many animals did he attempt to rescue while taking you to and from Canterbury? I've never known him to travel more than ten miles without finding a three-legged hedgehog, a blind puppy, or a litter of kittens abandoned by their mother."

"Only one," Marian said, marveling at the image of Rob rescuing a hedgehog. "A rather unfortunate cat."

Mr. Webb nodded, as if satisfied by this explanation. "Rob's not here, either," he said, as if all their previous conversation had been a test of some sort. "He's at the Royal Oak."

Marian already knew that but thanked Mr. Webb for the information anyway. "It's been a pleasure to meet you," she said before turning toward the door.

Mr. Webb didn't return the compliment, but he very nearly smiled, and that, Marian suspected, meant much the same thing.

Chapter 34

*R*ob was watching the door, so he saw the exact moment Marian walked into the Royal Oak. She was wearing one of her aggressively somber getups and she had brought with her some kind of manservant, who she dispatched in the direction of the taproom as soon as she saw Rob. He was on his feet before she reached his table.

"Percy told me this was an establishment women could enter without attracting too much notice, but I have to say I'm surprised." She looked around before sitting. "It's not a public house at all, but an inn."

He was oddly embarrassed by how reputable this place was. "There are twenty rooms. And stalls for a few dozen horses."

"More horses than people?"

He shrugged. "I think the people who used to run the place knew which species they preferred."

"Evidently, we're to be neighbors," she said. "I'm going to keep house for Percy and it's all going to be terrifyingly respectable. I'll be right next door to Mr. Webb, so it would be convenient for anyone who might wish to call on me, even at unconventional hours."

"Is that an invitation?"

She glared at him. "Of course it is. Don't be silly."

"I'm glad you came."

"I just told you not to be silly."

"I thought you might have trouble getting away. Duchess duties, I don't know." He regretted the words almost immediately. Things were easy enough like this, almost like they had been on their trip out to Canterbury; they were two equals sitting across the table from one another.

"Yes, well, you might be aware that the duchess duties will be coming to an end on the first of January." She sounded pleased, but there was something shuttered about her expression that he didn't quite like the look of.

"Three days from now," he said.

"Three days," she agreed. "So, let's have that truth telling you promised me."

Rob took a deep breath. "My mother is Elsie Terry. And my father—"

"She doesn't go by that anymore. I had tea with her this morning and she told me to call her Scarlett."

"I mean—you did *what*?—what I'm trying to say is that I'm probably the Duke of Clare's heir."

"I know."

Rob knew he was gaping. "How long have you known?"

"Since yesterday. You ought to have told me before."

"I know, but—"

"And then we could have spent the past two weeks coming up with a plan. Instead you've been pouting."

"I have not!"

"Sulking. And you, a grown man. Have you told your friends? Oh, I'm glad you did. I assume they're completely unbothered by this?"

"Yes," he muttered, unmoored by this conversation. "Although they seem to think I shouldn't be so opposed to . . ." He made yet another vague gesture.

She raised an eyebrow. "That surprises me. They think you should . . . be the Duke of Clare?"

"You don't?"

Marian took a drink from the tankard Rob had before him. "I won't insult your intelligence by pointing out that the Duke of Clare would have a substantial fortune at his disposal. That's a lot of innkeepers' wives and crossing sweeps whose pockets you could fill. Percy's cousins, or whoever the estate would fall to absent a legitimate son, wouldn't do anything noble. Of that I can assure you."

Rob could feel the walls of the room closing in on him. "I can't spend the rest of my life tied to that—"

Marian's patience seemed to snap. "You don't want to be *tied* to something? You don't want it simply because you didn't *choose* it? What a world we would live in if everyone were able to choose which burdens and duties they were to bear. You are aware, are you not, that most people do what they must, rather than run away?"

"Most people! Marian, how have you lived over twenty years and still believe that?"

"Most people who aren't cowards and scapegraces, then! You already know this, Rob. You aren't going to pretend that you've spent five and twenty years without ever doing a single thing you didn't want to do simply because it was your responsibility. You told me about how you went to your mother when Mr. Webb was ill and you needed someone to mind him while you went off and—"

"And murdered two members of a smuggling gang?" He laughed, dry and bitter. "I don't think that example bolsters your point, darling."

"Of course it does," she said, much in the manner of a put-upon schoolmistress. "I imagine that joining a smuggling gang is much like joining an army and that it's rather a kill or be killed situation. I already know those killings eat up your peace of mind. You did something horrible and which you did not want to do because you decided that your higher duty was to your friend."

He chose not to engage with what he was certain was faulty logic. She was trying to rile him up and he was annoyed with himself for taking the bait, but, as always, it pleased some inane part of himself to do as Marian wished of him. "I have no duty to the estate of the Duke of Clare."

"Somebody must! How else will the roads be repaired? Or fences mended? Or disputes settled between neighbors? Who will see to the churches? Who will—"

"I don't know! I don't care."

She was silent for a moment. "I think you do care."

He drained his tankard, then regarded the woman who sat across the table from him. Her expression was utterly uncompromising, stark and severe and—hopeful. She believed he was a better man than he was, or maybe she had tricked herself into believing as much. Or maybe he somehow was a decent person according to whatever twisted principles Marian held; maybe they both were decent people. She was every bit as ruthless as he was, and he knew her to be the best person he had ever met. He would laugh in the face of anyone who suggested otherwise. "Of course I care. Ugh. Marian. There has to be another way."

She flashed him a rare smile and all at once whatever lunacy he was about to embark on was worth it. "Naturally there's another way. We just haven't come up with it yet. Meanwhile, I wanted to make sure you understood exactly what the stakes are if you simply pretend that you aren't who you are."

"Cold-blooded," he said admiringly. "You don't blame me for not wanting to inherit?" He took her hand, half expecting her to pull it away, but she didn't. "My mother thinks I ought to marry you."

Now she snatched her hand away. "Oh, for heaven's sake. Percy said the same."

"The theory, as I understand it, is that you'd remain the Duchess of Clare."

"A role I've enjoyed so very much," she said, her voice dripping with scorn.

"Right. That's what I thought. I just needed to make sure."

She stared at him. "Are you saying you'd go through with inheriting if I wanted to remain a duchess, of all things?"

Rob swallowed and felt his face heat. "I'm not saying I'd like it. But I think I might go through with it if that was what it took to keep you happy."

"Happy," she scoffed, as if the concept was laughable. "After everything you said, you think I could possibly be happy if you were miserable? I hadn't realized that I fell in love with a simpleton."

He wanted to ask her to repeat that, to demand if she meant it, to ask for it in writing. But Marian never said anything she didn't mean. If she said she loved him, she loved him. She had once said that she didn't love people the way he did, whatever that meant. Nothing could have mattered less; if Marian loved him, then that was precisely the sort of love he wanted. "I want to be with you more than I want . . ." He didn't know how to finish the sentence, because the fact was that he could end it with just about anything and it would be true. "I've never thought about the future. Hell, I've avoided thinking about the future. But now when I look at time stretching out before me, all I can think is that I want you with me." He brought his hand to the pocket where he still held her letters and he watched her gaze track his movement. "Everything else is secondary."

She gave him a look that was somehow both warm and knife sharp. "Rob. You idiot. You were so fundamentally opposed to being a duke that when you were in a position to ask me for anything, the one thing you wanted was my assistance in making sure you never inherited. At the time I thought it odd, but now that I know you better, I see that inheriting a title and money would go against everything you stand for. Don't tell me that you'd put that aside."

"I'd do just about anything for you."

"I can't believe you think I'd let you!"

"I don't! But I had to ask. I didn't think you wanted the title and the money. I do know you, Marian. But I want to spend my life with you, and I thought I ought to at least ask if you had a preference as to how we go about doing that."

"You didn't think that maybe you ought to start by asking me *whether* I want to spend my life with you in the first place?"

"Christ, no. You'd have given me some tedious answer that would've bored both of us. Instead, my plan is just to do the thing, and then if you want to tell me to go away, I'll cross that bridge when I come to it."

She looked like she was trying to muster up a glare but her face wasn't cooperating. "This is entirely backward."

"Backward suits us." He grinned. "I want to show you that we can do it. Let me prove it to you."

Chapter 35

"I don't care," Marian told Percy yet again. "I won't take so much as a splinter from Clare House. You can do as you please but nothing there is mine and I won't have it." She stepped over Percy, who lay on the bare floor of the bedchamber that was to be Marian's at the new house.

"Perhaps a mattress?" His words resounded in the empty room. "At least let me bring some things for Eliza."

"That's entirely different. I'm bringing the contents of the nursery as well as whatever furnishings Alice desires for her quarters."

"Oh, so you're the only one who isn't worthy of furniture. I see." He dragged himself up to a sitting position. She forbore from pointing out that he was sadly dusty and disheveled. She was feeling gracious this evening.

"Worth has nothing to do with it." Marian smoothed the fabric of her own pristine skirt.

"I wish this room were furnished so I could pick up a vase and throw it at you."

"Should we check on Eliza?" Marian asked. It was Alice's day

out, and Mr. Webb had offered to look after the baby while Percy
and Marian quarreled next door.

"Let Kit have her for another half hour. As a treat."

Marian leaned against a wall and slid down so she was sitting.
Now they would both be dusty and disheveled and Percy would
be less embarrassed when he realized what a state he was in. "It's
been years since we've been able to do this."

"Quarrel in an empty room?"

"Be together without worrying that we're being spied on or
plotted against."

Percy crawled over and sat beside her. "I missed you."

She took his hand and squeezed it. "Me too."

"Sometimes I worried that you wouldn't be able to stand the
sight of me."

She turned to stare at him. "Why on earth would you think
that?"

"Because I look like him."

"Oh no, Percy. You look like Eliza."

"That's just another way of saying that I look like him."

"Pfft. You'll allow me to decide who my daughter looks like.
And I've already determined that the duke is not worth another
moment's thought."

The weather was damp and drizzly, so when they decided it
was time to relieve Mr. Webb of the baby, they went via a covered passage in the back that Percy claimed to have discovered
but which smelled of sawdust and whitewash and had probably
been completed that very day. So it was that when they entered

the coffeehouse, it was from the back, rather than from the street, and their arrival went unnoticed.

The shop was closed for the night, but cups and dishes were still scattered on every table and the fire was bright in the hearth. Mr. Webb leaned against a closed door while Rob held Eliza. He was in his shirtsleeves and held Eliza up over his head. As they watched, he brought the baby down fast, ending with her against his chest.

Eliza screamed with laughter. When Rob started laughing, she only laughed harder.

"You're going to make her sick," Mr. Webb cautioned.

"I don't care. I'm already drenched and covered in half the mud from Piccadilly. Baby sick can only be an improvement." He poked Eliza's belly and she laughed again.

Try as she might to cultivate more suitable maternal feelings, Marian's foremost emotion regarding Eliza was an acute sense of relief that no harm had yet befallen her. From shortly after the child was born, Marian had known a rush of relief every time she saw Eliza and was reassured anew that the baby was well. She experienced it as a temporary interruption in the worry that simmered all the time at the back of her mind and which she suspected would never go away. After all, it seemed unlikely that something so infinitely precious would not eventually come to grief.

She was certain that most women felt something warmer for their children, something less sharp and jagged. Marian wasn't much given to warmth, but whatever she felt now—a champagne lightness mixed with the usual knife-sharp protectiveness—felt like enough.

Eliza beat her fists into Rob's chest, apparently demanding another toss. Mr. Webb spotted Percy, but Percy put a finger to his lips, and Mr. Webb nodded. But Rob must have caught the movement, because he turned to face Marian and Percy, Eliza clutched safely to his chest.

"Kit let me share the fun," he said.

"It sounded like you weren't the only one having fun," said Marian. "Why am I not surprised that you charmed her already."

"She's the charming one." He turned Eliza face out, as if to demonstrate how charming she was. When Eliza saw Marian, she made a happy burbling noise that made Marian want to laugh.

Her thoughts were interrupted when Eliza grabbed Rob's hand and shoved a surprisingly large portion of it into her tiny mouth with more determination than Marian might have thought possible. And then she bit down with all her might. As she had only one tooth, she likely didn't do much damage. Evidently dissatisfied with her experiment, Eliza let Rob's hand drop. Across her little face passed an expression of high consternation that Marian at first thought she must recognize from Percy, but which she then realized she knew from the looking glass.

"You poor darling," Marian said, trying not to laugh. "You'll have more teeth soon and you'll be able to do plenty of mischief with them. Just you wait."

"You aren't supposed to encourage her cannibalistic tendencies," said Percy, who was looking back and forth between Marian and Rob with a curious expression. "I'm certain parents aren't meant to do that."

"She's been attempting to devour us for an hour now," Rob said. "Kit's forearm is covered in very adorable bite marks."

"For heaven's sake. Give her a crust of bread," said the woman Marian assumed was Betty. She stood in the doorway to what must have been the kitchen, carrying what looked like one of Percy's swords in one hand and a Bath bun in the other. She tossed the bun to Rob, who gave it to Eliza to gnaw on, and handed the sword to Percy. "Got the emeralds out of the hilt and I'll bring them to a couple jewelers tomorrow." She turned to Marian. "So you're her ladyship's mother."

"You shouldn't call babies rude names," said Rob, covering Eliza's ears.

Betty rolled her eyes.

"I'm so glad to finally meet you," Marian said, trying and probably failing to sound warm. "I've heard so much about you."

Betty pinched Rob's arm. "How am I supposed to make your new friends like me if you fill their ears with malice?" She shot an exasperated look at Marian and then went over to talk to Kit and Percy.

Eliza began wriggling in Rob's arms and making grabbing motions at Marian, so Rob passed her over. She settled against Marian's chest with a sigh.

"I have something for you," said Rob. "I spent last night drinking with one of the footmen from Fanshawe's London house and I learned all kinds of interesting things. And that's in addition to the information we have from my mother." He drew a paper from his coat pocket. "I drew up a map of the entrances to Fanshawe's town house. That's the mews behind it, and you can see Jermyn Street over there."

He presented this paper to Marian with the air of a man presenting his lover with a posy. And that's almost what it was, she realized—a courtship present.

"Let me see," said Mr. Webb, crossing the room to bend over the map. "Who are we burgling?"

"Oh, are we doing burglaries now?" asked Percy, looking over Mr. Webb's shoulder.

"*I* am doing the burglary," corrected Marian.

"He cheated Marian's father and stole some fancy old pieces of paper. She means to get them back and then some," said Rob.

"If you expect me to fence old pieces of paper, you can guess again, lads," said Betty.

"She'll bring you something lovely," Rob assured Betty.

"No fucking diadems," Betty said.

"I really don't think it was a diadem, Marian," Percy supplied in a loud whisper. "Just a tiara. I don't know why they keep calling it a diadem. I suppose they think it sounds fancier."

"You're all mad," said Marian. "I'm taking some things that belong to my father and a bit extra to cover the amount Fanshawe raised my father's rent. There will be neither diadems nor tiaras."

"I really don't see how this is supposed to be any fun at all," said Percy.

"What I don't see is how you mean to burgle a house you've never set foot in," said Mr. Webb. "A map of the neighborhood is all fair and well, but you need to know the inside of the house—that way you can get what you want and make an easy exit."

They all frowned at the map. "I could call on Fanshawe," suggested Percy. "As far as he knows, I'm the Duke of Clare. For two more days, at least. He'll receive me. I'll get lost in the house a few times and report back."

"There's really no need," began Marian, but stopped when she found four pairs of eyes trained on her.

"Nobody's talking about need," Mr. Webb said gently. "It's an offer."

Marian realized that Rob was doing precisely as he had promised at the inn the previous day: he was showing her how they could go on together. He was showing her that there was a space for them—not her old world or even his, but something new, something they could build together.

She didn't know if it could work. She didn't know if she was capable of the trust it would require to build a life with anybody. But she found that she wanted to try.

"All right. Fine," agreed Marian. "Do as you please."

Rob grinned at her.

Chapter 36

The following night, Marian and Rob met in the lane behind Fanshawe's house. Darkness had long since fallen and the air was heavy with cold.

"What in hell are you wearing?" Rob asked, unable to pry his eyes from what appeared for all the world like a pair of leather breeches.

"Percy insists that this is the proper attire for crime," Marian said primly.

Rob found that he wholeheartedly agreed. Marian snapped her fingers in front of his face.

"All right," he said. "Two footmen have the night out. The butler will be asleep by the fire and the cook will have finished with dinner and gone to bed. There will be a handful of maids about the place but all you have to do is keep to the shadows and leave them to me."

"I remember," said Marian. "You don't need to go over it a hundred more times. I enter the servants' stairs on my right, go up two stories, turn left, and enter the second door to my right. That will be Sir John's study. I have a quarter of an hour and then

I'll be waiting for you at the back door, where you'll make sure I get out unobserved."

"If anyone sees you, what will you do?"

"If I'm at the back of the house, I'll go out the window and make my way to the neighbor's roof. If I'm at the front of the house, I'll signal to Kit, who's waiting across the street."

"Excellent."

Rob proceeded to work open a narrow, high window leading to a small stillroom that ought to be empty at this hour of night. Once it was open, he gave Marian a boost, and she disappeared inside.

A quarter of an hour. All he had to do was remain reasonably calm for a quarter of an hour and not think about how the woman he loved was risking her neck for a couple of moldy old maps. It would be fine. Marian was clever. Marian was also armed to the teeth—he had supplied her with a pistol and a pair of knives.

Once he had given Marian enough time to make it up the stairs, he rapped on the kitchen door and played his part, introducing himself to the maid as the country cousin of John the footman, who, as Rob knew, was at the tavern he customarily visited on his nights out.

"Ah, a pity I missed him, and after I came all this way," Rob lamented, and in short order was supplied with a cup of ale and a heel of bread.

A quarter of an hour later he thanked the kitchen maid for her troubles and insisted that he could show himself out. Instead he went directly to the stillroom, where Marian would be waiting for him. He would take the manuscripts so she could escape without any risk of ruining them, help her out the window, and then return to the kitchen, apologizing on his way for having taken a wrong turn.

Marian wasn't in the stillroom. He looked at the window, wondering if she had managed to reach it without help. But it was seven feet off the ground, and no furniture was beneath it to provide a convenient foothold. Which meant that Marian was still upstairs, involved in God only knew what kind of mischief.

While he was deciding what to do, he heard the pistol shot.

LATER, HE WOULDN'T remember running up the stairs, or turning down the corridor, or entering the study, or any of the other steps that led up to him finding Marian, the pistol in her hand pointed at a man sitting behind a large desk.

For the span of a single breath, he was relieved—Marian was fine. It was odd that she was still aiming the pistol after having fired it, but that hardly mattered. Then he saw the tear in her left sleeve, the blood trickling onto the floor.

"You've got that out of your system, have you?" Marian asked the man who had to be Fanshawe. Her voice was perfectly steady. "Excellent. Now, do you want to give me the manuscripts or would you like to see what I can do with my pistol?"

"This is lunacy," Fanshawe said. Rob was inclined to agree.

"Marian," Rob said, attempting to cross the room to go to her, but halting when she held up her hand. Instead he shut the door, thinking that the fewer people who witnessed whatever was happening here, the better.

"Leave me to it," Marian said to him. "I'm having a little talk with Sir John about what will happen to him if I ever hear the faintest whisper of his raising the rent on any of his tenants. First, Sir John, tell whoever's knocking at the door that you had a mishap while cleaning your pistol but that all is well."

Rob could not hear anything but the acid calm of Marian's voice and the sound of his own heart pounding in his ears. He wanted nothing more than to cross the room and shield her with his body. He couldn't bear the thought that she had put herself in harm's way, when he could have done it for her while she was safe at home in bed. After all, he had spent years being injured, arrested, imprisoned, and otherwise harmed. He was used to it.

And she was in plain view of Fanshawe, the light from the oil lamp shining full on her face. She hadn't even made an effort to conceal herself or keep to the shadows. Even Rob, who had dashed up here without a second thought, had kept his hat angled over his face.

Then he noticed something about her expression. Her jaw was set with what he recognized as determination, not clenched with pain. She was . . . perhaps enjoying herself was an exaggeration, but satisfied was not. She was doing what she believed was right and necessary. Not only was she doing it, but she was able to do it—she was able to right wrongs and protect people who needed help. She looked, he realized, powerful.

Fanshawe hesitated, clearly deciding whether to call for help. In the end, the pistol Marian aimed at him was the more compelling argument. "There's nothing to worry about," he called. "My pistol went off unexpectedly."

Marian waited while they listened to the sound of footsteps receding down the corridor. Fanshawe remained perfectly still. He was somewhere between thirty and forty, had hair the color of sawdust, and wore a coat so ugly it had to have cost a fortune. He looked like any other gentleman and probably acted like them, too. There was nothing especially villainous about his appearance, but then there hadn't been anything about his actions that most people would count as villainy: he had simply raised the rent on someone who wasn't in a position to refuse him and had taken some papers whose owner would never notice were missing.

"I had an entire speech planned," Marian said.

"Oh *did* you," Rob cut in. "Did you now."

Rob thought he saw the corner of Marian's mouth lift into a smile. "You can scold me later," she said, never taking her eyes off Fanshawe. "But now I've been shot and nobody's in the mood for speeches. So, listen here, Sir John. I simply don't have any more patience left. Does anything you've seen tonight make you think that I'd hesitate to sneak into your bedroom and smother you in your sleep? Because you don't look terribly bright but you also don't seem an utter incompetent."

"You'll hang for this."

"I really won't, though. What will you say? That the Duchess of Clare broke into your house and threatened your life? Nobody would believe it. Besides, I came here to take exactly what you stole from my father, not a penny more, and you shot me for my trouble. I haven't committed even the tiniest crime."

That was true if one forgot about the breaking and entering as well as the pistol, but Rob wasn't going to point that out.

Fanshawe sputtered. "That's a gross—"

"Are you really going to argue with me at a time like this? Of all the foolish wastes of breath. If you need an added incentive to be a decent human being, understand that if you say a word about what happened here tonight, I'll tell all your friends about that card game."

"What do you—you can't possibly—"

"Let's take it as read that I do. Don't be tedious. Now, we need to cut this short before I ruin your carpet with even more blood. Give me the papers you took from my father."

Rob watched as Fanshawe opened a desk drawer and retrieved a sheaf of papers, then thumbed through until he found the ones Marian wanted. He reached out to offer them to her.

"Not to me, you buffoon. Do you think I want to get blood on four-hundred-year-old vellum? You may be willing to ruin your possessions," she said, gesturing to the steadily growing puddle of blood on the carpet, "but some of us were raised better. Give it to him." She gestured at Rob, who took the fragile manuscripts. "Now give me ten pounds."

"Ten pounds!"

"That's the amount you increased the rent, you great lummox."

And that, Rob supposed, was true if Marian was collecting interest at a usurious rate, but he wasn't going to point that out, either.

With a shaking hand, Fanshawe handed over a banknote.

"Well, I daresay we're done here. I'd ask for your word that you aren't going to increase rent on any of your tenants, but I doubt your word is worth much. Instead you may have *my* word that

I'll find out if you do. Now, you'll stay put while we leave, just to let your temper cool," Marian told Fanshawe and then finally, finally she was walking toward Rob.

"Don't even think of exiting by the window," Rob told her under his breath. "Not in your state."

They left by the front door.

ROB HELD IT together until they were outside.

"Let me look at it," he urged her.

"It's scarcely bleeding at all," Marian said, not breaking stride. "I just couldn't put pressure on it because then I would have had to let go of the pistol. It's hardly even a graze."

"I'll believe that when I see it. There's a public house around the corner. We can go there and see if they have—"

"I'm going home. It's a five-minute walk."

"What's going on?" asked Kit, crossing the street from where he had been keeping watch on Fanshawe's house.

"Marian's been shot in the arm."

"The merest scratch!" Marian called, continuing to stride away in the direction, Rob realized, of Clare House. She and Percy hadn't yet decamped to the house next door to Kit's.

"Percy's going to kill me," said Kit.

"He's going to kill all of us," called Marian over her shoulder.

Rob caught up with her. There was no way Kit could keep pace with them, not with his limp. He turned and saw that Kit was already making his way in the opposite direction, where he would presumably inform Percy of what had happened.

Rob took out his kerchief and wrapped it tightly around Marian's arm. "Don't even consider complaining," he warned. "You had a speech ready? Exactly how much of our plan had you decided to ignore? And why didn't you let me in on what you meant to do?"

"Look," Marian said, pausing long enough to let Rob knot the kerchief, "I wanted to make sure Fanshawe knew that he couldn't get away with what he had done."

"Rich people get away with things like that all the time! Do you plan on robbing them all?"

Marian wheeled on him. "Only some of them. Same as you."

"Oh Christ."

"You were right," she said, continuing to walk. "It was rather fun."

"Oh *Christ*. You're going to do this again."

"Not all the time. I'm a busy woman."

This struck Rob as inordinately hilarious and he let out a burst of laughter.

"Oh, you've lost your mind," Marian said tartly as she climbed the steps of Clare House. "It was bound to happen. All the signs were there."

And thus Rob entered the front door of his ancestral home for the first, and hopefully the last, time.

Chapter 37

"You realize he's still going to tell everyone what you did," Rob said while attempting to clean Marian's wound—which was entirely negligible, truly a glorified scratch, thank you very much.

"Of course he will," said Marian, wincing as he poured some gin over the wound. "That business about the card game—he cheated, by the way, and one of your mother's girls saw it happen—was just to make him think I wanted him to keep it a secret. A card game," she repeated scornfully. "Imagine caring about who cheats at cards. Imagine *not* cheating at cards. Percy and I always cheat. How boring it must be otherwise. Anyway, he's going to say that I demanded that he return the amount he charged my father in excess of our agreement as well as a couple of old maps and some translations I completed as a child, and that he subsequently shot me. Most people will think that he's making a mountain out of a molehill, but after I give the same treatment to a few other gentlemen, I daresay the point will get across."

"The point?" He opened a jar of salve that he had found in the kitchen.

"That if anyone chooses to ride roughshod over people who have no recourse, I plan to do something about it."

"You're not worried about, oh, I don't know, being caught and hanged?"

"Robert, darling. I plan to be more discreet in the future. This time it would have been pointless. I couldn't very well go to him and demand that he return the items he stole from my father if he didn't know who I was."

"Naturally," Rob said faintly. With the pad of one finger, he gently spread ointment on the wound. Now *that* hurt, there was no denying it. But the pain felt irrelevant; she was almost euphoric with her success. The dose of laudanum and willow bark Rob had advised was certainly not harming matters, either, she supposed.

"You could have been killed," he said.

"As I said, in the future I'll be more cautious."

"I can't stand it, Marian." He wrapped a piece of linen around her arm a few times and tied it off but didn't take his hand away. He really was very good at tending to wounds, which figured.

"You spent years risking your life. You've been shot and stabbed and I don't even know what else. You can't hold me to a different standard." Marian held her breath. She knew that Rob wouldn't like this, which was partly why she hadn't told him of her plan beforehand. But he had to understand why she wanted to do this, why she *needed* to do this, and that her reasons for risking her safety weren't any less important than his own reasons had been for all those years. "I want you to be safe all the time," she went on, "and I know you want the same for me. But that isn't who we are."

"When I was risking my neck, it was because I was angry and sad and grieving, Marian. My life had been taken away and so had Kit's. I wanted revenge."

"I'm angry, too, Rob." She didn't know what she would do if he didn't understand. She didn't want to say this next part out loud, she didn't even want to admit it to herself, but it was important. It was perhaps the only secret she had kept from him. "I'm angry and sad and grieving."

For a moment he looked at her searchingly, and then he sighed. "Of course you are, darling." He held her close, careful though not to jostle her arm. "I'll do whatever you need."

"I wasn't asking for anything."

"I didn't think you were. But you have it anyway."

And she knew he meant it. She knew, by now, that not only was he serious, but that he wanted to give her anything she needed. She wanted to say no, to insist that she didn't need anything from him, that she didn't ever want to trust anyone or need anyone.

"You already do trust me," he said, as if he understood the direction of her thoughts. "I think you've trusted me for weeks. After you shot the duke, you came to me, Marian. You came to the one place where you might find me."

She couldn't deny it. She hadn't been thinking clearly that night, but some part of her knew who she could rely on—and it was a thief, a blackmailer, the person who had set out to upend her life.

All she could do was nod against his shoulder, and then he was kissing her, hard and fervent. She kissed him back and he groaned. She glanced down at his breeches.

"Are you hard? Don't tell me it's from dressing wounds."

"I've been half hard since I saw you in those breeches."

The leather breeches were, in fact, all she had on. She gave him a shove and he lay back on the bed, then she swung a leg over him. "You like them?"

He made an incoherent noise and then seemed to collect himself. "Your arm. We can't."

"Is that a challenge?"

"Christ, no. It's—all right, danger takes some people this way. I understand that."

"It certainly seems to take you that way," she said, pressing the palm of her hand to his growing erection. He made a helpless sound that made her mouth go dry. "Get your clothes off." He complied swiftly, his clothes landing in a pile at the foot of the bed. She took her hair out of its plait and let it fall around her shoulders, because she knew Rob wouldn't be able to resist getting his hands on it, and sure enough, he reached for her, pulling her down, tangling his fingers in her hair.

"What would you like?" he murmured, speaking the words against her mouth.

She shook her head. "Just lie back." That had come out far too sweet, so she cleared her throat. "And behave."

She had been paying attention to all the little things he liked, greedily amassing information, storing it away with the goal of rendering him a shivering, begging, helpless mass of muscle and longing. "You were so good tonight," she said, pausing to bite his collarbone, "letting me get what I needed from that horrible man and then taking care of me." Propping herself up on her unin-jured arm, she moved her mouth lower, giving some attention to one nipple, and then the other, teasing him until he tried to twist on the mattress beneath her, the muscles of his shoulder and chest bunching and shifting with the effort of remaining still.

When she moved lower, he swore. She kissed his lower abdo-men and the top of his thigh, never quite reaching his straining erection. Only when she saw him reach above his head and grasp the headboard did she take the tip of his cock into her mouth.

He was breathing heavily now with the strain of not bucking his hips, but she kept her kisses light and insubstantial. This was part of the pleasure for him, she knew. He liked being made to wait, he liked the knowledge that his discipline pleased her.

"You can touch me," she said, and in an instant one of his hands was in her hair, not pulling or pushing but just feeling her, and she could sense the effort it was costing him, too. She rewarded him by taking him a little deeper.

She felt his fingers on her cheekbone, tracing her lips, pushing the hair out of her face. It was as if he couldn't stop touching her. She pressed into his touch while at the same time moving her tongue along his shaft, and he made a noise of desperation. He likely couldn't hold out much longer, so she nudged one of his legs aside and slid a hand up the inside of his thigh. No sooner had the pads of her fingers come to rest behind his bollocks than he thrust the jar of salve into her hand.

She pulled off him and laughed. "I'd swear this was across the room a minute ago," she said, uncorking the jar.

"I think I moved it with my mind," he said, sounding a bit dazed.

She laughed again, muffling the sound in his thigh. She moved a slick finger against him and felt a shudder run through his body. "Tell me what to do," she said.

"Inside," he said, his voice rough. "Please."

She felt the heat of him around her finger, heard the strangled noise he made as his body gave way. "Do you know," she said, "Percy tells me that they sell cocks made out of glass and wood and all manner of interesting things."

"Do you need a list of acceptable topics of conversation for when you have any part of your body inside me? Because Percy would not be on that list."

"So fussy," she said, then added a finger, twisting them until he shut up. "I bet you'd like me to get you one of those so you can get properly fucked." Deciding she had been altogether too nice for the past few minutes, she added sweetly, "Would you like that, darling?"

"Yes, Marian, do you even need to ask?"

"It figures you'd want to be lazy," she said. "You'd want to just lie there and have me do all the work."

He made a sound that was somewhere between a laugh and a moan, as if he were in on the joke—Rob might have many faults, but laziness wasn't among them—but enjoyed the fiction anyway.

She might not understand the appeal of having anything inside her, but she was beginning to appreciate being on the other end—she relished the sensation of his body opening for her, the sight of his arm thrown across his eyes, his face turned to nearly hide in the pillow.

Now he was begging very prettily so she decided to relent. "I'm afraid you'll have to make yourself useful because I only have one hand and it's busy. Bring yourself off." She watched him stroke himself, his fist moving quickly over his length. "You're gorgeous for me," she said. "Look at you." And he came in his hand and around her fingers, the tension building and releasing from his body, right before her eyes.

"You're a witch," he said a few minutes later. "No other explanation."

"I don't see you complaining," she said, yawning.

"God, no. Let me get those breeches off you so I can take care of you."

"Tomorrow. I'm tired." Her arm was starting to hurt, not that she was going to admit it. And whatever surge of energy she had experienced after the robbery was now long gone. She was exhausted.

"Come here," he said, holding his arm out, and she curled into his side, her head on his shoulder. The last thing she remembered before falling asleep was the feeling of Rob's fingers carding through her hair.

Chapter 38

When Rob woke, the sun was already up but Marian was still fast asleep. He carefully extricated his arm from beneath her and dressed as well as he could, considering that his clothes were variously stained with blood or crumpled from a night on the floor.

He began looking for Percy, guessing that the man would have returned to Clare House when Kit brought word that Marian had been injured. But Rob also wanted to explore this house for his own reasons—he wanted to see what his life would have been, if things had been different. He wanted to see the house where he didn't grow up, the house where his children wouldn't play. And this morning was the first of January, the day Marian and Percy planned to move out of Clare House, so this would be Rob's last chance to see the place.

He found Percy at the breakfast table. "Good Lord," Percy said, glancing up from his toast. "You're even more unkempt than usual."

"Marian is fine," Rob said. "In case you wondered."

"Naturally." Percy took a sip of tea. "I do think highly enough of you to believe that you'd let me know if she weren't."

"I want to talk to you," Rob said.

"You're talking to me right now," Percy said.

It figured that he wasn't going to make this easy. "What if we moved Marian's father into Clare House? The house he's living in now isn't suitable. Also the landlord shot Marian, so I think a cordial relationship is out of the question."

"It's your house," Percy said. "Do as you please."

"Quit that. We both know that probate is going to take an eternity and until then it's neither of our houses."

Percy raised a pale eyebrow. "Does this mean you're going to go along with inheriting the estate?"

"Christ, no. I'm not going to involve myself with it. The court can do what it wants. If I have to testify, I'll tell the truth. My mother will, too. If I do inherit, I won't use the title and I'll give all the money away. I don't mean that I'll endow a charity. I mean that I'll bankrupt the estate. I know that you signed deeds of manumission for the people on the West Indies properties, and I'd see to it that those were honored. Also, I'd have to see how to make sure the estate's duties are fulfilled—Marian reminds me that somebody has to pay the vicar and look after the roads and so forth—but other than that, the estate won't keep any funds."

"You'd be willing to bankrupt the estate of your son?"

That brought Rob up short. "I'm not likely to have any children."

Percy stared at him. "I've seen the way you and Marian look at one another."

"Children don't necessarily follow," Rob said, and something about his tone must have got the point across because Percy didn't pursue the topic.

"She trusts you," Percy said after a long silence. "I suppose that's better than the alternative."

Rob swallowed. "I'll try to deserve it."

"Yes, yes, that's enough of that." Percy cast a desperate glance at his toast, as if it could save him from sentiment. "Is there anything else you need from me?"

Rob realized what had been wrong with this entire conversation. "Why are you going along with everything I suggest? I thought you'd fight me tooth and nail."

Percy looked chagrined. "Because it really is your choice what happens here. It's yours. I'm willing to facilitate what you want, as long as it won't harm anyone I care about."

"Please don't—"

"That's the way it is, Rob. Fair warning, I will probably always consider you the Duke of Clare in some regard, and it will probably always matter to me. Old habits and all that. But, if it makes you feel any better, I'm also trying to be kind and civil because it would please Kit. And we both know it will please Marian."

"We're family."

"Well, yes, but I wasn't thinking of that."

"I wasn't referring to the blood tie, although God knows there's enough of that to go around." The links between Rob and Percy and Eliza and Marian would make them a family by anyone's measure. "I meant that I've considered Kit my family since—well, I don't remember a time when I didn't. And if he considers you family, then so do I."

Percy momentarily looked stunned but recovered quickly. "Yes, well, I'm sure I do, too," he said, all in a rush. Then he got to his feet and pulled a cord. "I ought to have known you'd become sentimental and it serves me right for letting you in here in the first place." A footman entered the breakfast room. "See to it that Mr. Brooks has a fresh pot of tea."

"That won't be necessary," Rob said. He didn't want to drink the tea or eat the food from this place.

"Ah," said Percy as the footman left, as if he finally understood that Rob didn't want any part of Clare House. He returned to sipping his own tea. Rob didn't have much sympathy for men who thought they were going to be dukes but then learned their fathers had been bigamous, but he found that he had a bit of sympathy for Percy and what he had lost. And for just a moment, Rob felt a pang for having upended this man's life, or at least for the manner in which he had done so.

"I'm sorry," Rob said. "For the blackmail. I've apologized to Marian but not to you. I've done a lot of terrible things but that might have been the worst. You were both victims of the duke and I made it worse."

"You did indeed. Apology accepted," Percy said and then looked away. Rob took the hint and returned upstairs to Marian's chambers.

When he entered the bedroom, he found Marian sitting on the floor, wearing nothing but a shirt. Around her were scattered old papers. For a moment he thought that these were the manuscripts that they had taken from Fanshawe, but then he was struck with the truth.

"I meant to clean your knives," Marian said. "I thought they might rust from the blood. But I found—" She smoothed her hand over the papers that were covered in her own slanted handwriting. "You told me to burn mine."

"I didn't follow my own advice," Rob admitted. He didn't understand why Marian looked so bleak. He crouched down on the floor beside her. "What's wrong, darling?"

"I saved your letters, too. I hid them under a floorboard, but that morning in the carriage, the duke had them." She skimmed her finger over the paper, along water blots, bloodstains, and creases. "It was all there in the letters, all the information he needed to figure out who had written them. He recognized your mother's name. And even though she had been quiet for twenty-five years, the fact of the letters meant she might not be so quiet anymore."

Rob didn't need to ask what this meant. They already knew that the duke was more than willing to kill Percy; certainly he wouldn't have stopped at killing Rob's mother, or Rob himself, for that matter. Rob wondered how many lives Marian had saved by shooting the duke.

"That night, when I went to the hired room and found it empty, the first thing I did was burn the letters," she said. That was undiluted regret he heard in her voice and he couldn't stand it.

"I'll write you a hundred more," he murmured, and he hoped she heard all the promises he was managing not to make. He thought she did, because she pulled him down for a kiss. He kissed the hinge of her jaw, then her neck, then pulled back enough to talk to her. "Marry me. Or don't marry me. Just say you'll be with me. Every minute I spend away from you is second best."

She raised an eyebrow. "I won't marry you."

"Then we won't get married. Good." It wasn't quite a lie, because if she didn't want to marry him, then he wouldn't bother her with the notion. If she did, he'd marry her immediately. He'd devise different pseudonyms in order to marry her more than once in a succession of churches. He'd convert to different religions and travel to foreign lands to marry her in every way imaginable. "It's a boring institution."

She laughed, bright and happy, and he knew she could see right through him. Her laughter was rare and precious; it was the sound of church bells, the sound of coins dropping into a pocket, and he wanted to save it in a bottle and wear it close to his heart.

MARIAN PULLED HER cloak around her shoulders as she and Rob walked in the direction of the coffeehouse. It was windy and damp, what passed for a sunny day in the London winter. But they had endured worse; there was something almost comforting about being cold next to Rob, knowing that the warmth of his body was only a few inches away and that soon enough they'd be at a fireside.

"Would you mind if we stopped at the Royal Oak?" Rob asked, looking oddly shifty.

Marian agreed, and when they walked into the inn, they were met with a blast of heat and sound. Rob went off to talk to the couple who ran the place while Marian looked around. A pair of elderly dogs sat by a pair of equally elderly looking men; a harried looking mother tried to stop her children from jumping off their stacked traveling boxes; clusters of people played darts and cards.

Seated by the fire, she watched Rob laugh with one of the barmaids, shoot some menacing glances at a table of rowdy young men, then repair the leg of a chair. When he came over to her, he was smiling, and she found that she was smiling back at him. In the last two days, she had smiled more than she had in the previous two years, and that was with a gunshot wound. The level of contentment she was experiencing was probably unsafe.

"If you don't object, I'd like to go back to Kent and bring your father and his household to live at Clare House," Rob said when he sat beside Marian. "I'll leave as soon as possible."

Clare House would suit nicely for her father. It was comfortable and already had a full staff, and was near enough for Marian to keep an eye on him. Marian nearly insisted on accompanying Rob to Kent. But then she realized she had business of her own in London. She needed to speak to Richard and—well, perhaps not hold him at gunpoint, but do whatever the moral equivalent of that turned out to be. She needed to make it clear that if he so much as whispered a threat against their father he would be waging war not only with her, but with people more terrifying than she ever hoped to be.

"Why are we really here?" she asked when she and Rob had plates of roast pheasant before them.

"Betty and I are buying the place."

She raised her eyebrows. "I didn't know you had money saved." She assumed large coaching inns didn't come cheap.

"Well, I didn't. Not exactly. A few years ago Kit and I held up a carriage and there were too many jewels."

"Too many jewels," Marian repeated.

"Betty said it was too risky to fence so many rubies all at once. So she took half, and we put the rest behind a brick in one of the chimneys upstairs at Kit's, where they remained until two days ago."

"And you used the proceeds to buy something for yourself?" Marian asked, astonished. This was the same man who felt guilty about buying a new coat.

"Ah, well, you know me. I like ale. I like horses. I like having something to do when I'm not helping you commit felonies. And the stables are large enough so that if someone wanted to use them to hire out horses, they could do that," he said so casually, as if he weren't offering her the one thing she had been able to name when he asked what she wanted.

"I'd like that," Marian said. "I'd like it very much."

Epilogue

Clients," Marian repeated in exasperation. "I insist that we take clients. We cannot be a freewheeling band of felons."

"You say that like it's a bad thing," Rob said.

"We cannot roam about indiscriminately punishing evildoers."

All four of the other people who sat around their table at the Royal Oak—Rob, Percy, Kit, and Betty—looked at her with undisguised enthusiasm.

"She just makes it sound so fun," Betty observed to the table at large.

"And so noble," Rob agreed.

Marian put her face in her hands.

"Marian's right," Kit said. It was his turn to hold Eliza, and Rob probably thought nobody saw him sneak the watch from Percy's pocket to see when Kit's quarter of an hour was up and his own began. Marian had given up worrying that the baby was going to be spoiled; it was a foregone conclusion, and there were worse things than being spoiled. "It's one thing if we occasionally

get a tip from Scarlett," Kit went on, "or if we ourselves know
that there's someone who needs to, ah . . ."

"To receive the sort of justice we plan on dispensing," Percy
supplied.

"Exactly," Kit said. "But it's better if our purpose is helping people who come to us with problems. If someone has been harmed,
we can redress that harm in a fitting manner."

"Precisely," agreed Marian.

The idea had started with Kit, who evidently had a fundamen-
tal inability to stay on the right side of the law. Rob, who jumped
at any chance to take money from those who had too much, did
not need to be persuaded. Neither did Betty.

Percy's enthusiasm had surprised Marian at first. He had never
been particularly interested in danger and adventure—of the two
of them, she had always been the instigator. But he was still being
invited to the dinners and balls of precisely the people that Kit
and Rob wanted to go after. "I've always wanted to be a spy," he
had said, preening a little. But Marian suspected that he would
do anything to please Kit.

And Marian, well. Marian fully planned on exacting her
unique brand of justice anyway. Now she was doing it with
friends—with family. And while she didn't regret what she had
done to the duke, it was much easier to live with that memory if
she knew she was putting some good into the world. If that good
took the form of helping people who weren't able to save themselves and the people they loved in the way that Marian had, then
all the better.

"In addition to the burglary, I want to look after the money," Marian said. "It's all well and good to give the money away, distributing it among the needy like pepper from a pepper mill, but it's February. On the way here I lost count of the number of people I saw huddled in doorways and—if they were lucky— warming their hands over braziers. What we need is a house, or a couple of houses. Firewood. Food." Rob looked skeptical, and Marian took his hand. "Look, I don't know if it will work, but I'd like to try. Maybe twenty percent of the takings could go into a foundation of sorts for me to put toward larger projects."

Marian was coming to realize that she liked looking after money. It had been satisfying, arranging her father's affairs so his money stayed not only out of his reach but was put to use in a way that was unlikely to vanish in a bubble. He was not likely to become rich through the breweries Marian had bought or the horses she had brought to Chiltern Hall as breeding stock, but people were unlikely to stop spending their money on beer or horses.

She looked around the table. With the possible exception of Betty, none of them could be trusted to save money. Rob gave all his away as a matter of principle, and even now that he had the inn, he managed to hire so many people that he was unlikely to ever turn anything close to a profit; Kit seemed to have put a bit aside but, as far as Marian could tell, this was mainly a coincidence; Percy was a lost cause. But Marian could do this for them: she could make sure that whatever happened, there was enough put aside so they'd always be safe. They might not like it, but they could take their lumps.

"All right," Kit said. Percy nodded. Rob squeezed her leg under the table.

"Fine, but maybe you could sometimes steal little things for me?" Betty asked. "As a treat?"

There was one thing they had all agreed on instantly. Something had to be done to ensure that nobody was blamed for any crimes they committed. They would do that by leaving a note behind and explaining what they had taken and why.

They would sign the note Gladhand Jack.

The conversation drifted away from criminal conspiracy and toward topics that a year ago she would have found equally bizarre: prize fighting, whether Kit ought to keep the coffeehouse open later at night, and whether a girl who worked in Rob's mother's establishment was Rob's sister or one of his mother's spies. (Marian thought the smart money was on both.)

Every quarter of an hour, Eliza passed from one set of hands to another and was cooed over and admired, even when she fussed, even when she demanded part of Rob's potato.

Marian could rely on all these people, and they on her, and that thought made her feel safe in a way she hadn't known she wanted. She turned to look at Rob, who she had always, somehow, known was safe, who she had trusted when she didn't think she could trust anyone.

"You all right?" Rob asked.

Marian knew she was a bit misty and didn't try to deny it. But she also knew that there was nothing she could say that would do justice to her feelings.

"You're mine," she said. "And I'm yours." She swallowed. "It's a promise."

And Rob must have understood, because he picked up her hand and kissed her palm. "A promise," he agreed.

Acknowledgments

This is the first time I've written a book while packing up a house and moving, and neither would have been possible without the cooperation of everyone in my family with tasks ranging from labeling boxes to listening to me ramble on about plot threads.

As always, this book owes so much to the ability of Elle Keck, my editor, to zero in on what needed to be done to make this book into the story it was trying to be all along. I'm grateful to everyone at Avon for getting this book into existence and then out into the world. Margrethe Martin kept me supplied with dog pictures and reminders that I know how to write. And I want to thank my agent, Deidre Knight, for making sure my stories find a home.

THE PERFECT CRIMES OF MARIAN HAYES
BOOK CLUB DISCUSSION QUESTIONS

1. Do you think Marian had an alternative to killing the duke? Does your answer affect how you feel about Marian as a person? Would your answer change if Marian lived in a time when women were able to able to obtain a divorce?

2. At the beginning of the book, Rob is infatuated with the version of Marian he knows through their letters. When do you think he starts to know and love her as she really is—or is the version of herself in the letters her real self?

3. How do the characters transform themselves over the course of the book, and do you believe those changes will last?

4. If you were in Rob's place, would you have accepted the inheritance? Do you think he was right for making the choice he did? Did his decision surprise you?

5. Both characters have a history of hiding their problems from the people closest to them and of refusing to ask for help when

they need it. Do you relate to this? Can you think of a moment in your own life where you had to choose between pride and vulnerability?

6. Both Marian and Rob are bisexual. Do you think this affects their worldview, and if so, how?

7. Rob seems to believe that as long as laws are unfair and some people are hungry, it's permissible to break the law. Do you agree? Do you think that at the end of the book Marian agrees, or does she have her own code of ethics? If so, what is it?

8. What non-romantic fantasies are fulfilled by the book? (For example, Marian always has someone to look after her baby.)

9. There are a number of crimes committed or contemplated in this book. Which one or ones do you think the title refers to?

Don't miss Percy and Kit's road to romance in

THE QUEER PRINCIPLES OF KIT WEBB

Kit Webb has left his stand-and-deliver days behind him.
But dreary days at his coffee shop have begun to make him
pine for the heady rush of thievery. When a handsome yet
arrogant aristocrat storms into his shop, Kit quickly realizes
he may be unable to deny whatever this highborn man desires.

In order to save himself and a beloved friend, Percy, Lord Holland, must go against every gentlemanly behavior he holds dear to gain what he needs most: a book that once belonged to his mother, a book his father never lets out of his sight and could be Percy's savior. More comfortable in silk-filled ballrooms than coffee shops frequented by criminals, his attempts to hire the roughly hewn highwayman, formerly known as Gladhand Jack, proves equal parts frustrating and electrifying.

Kit refuses to participate in the robbery but agrees to teach Percy how to do the deed. Percy knows he has little choice but to submit and as the lessons in thievery begin, he discovers thievery isn't the only crime he's desperate to commit with Kit.

But when their careful plan goes dangerously wrong and shocking revelations threaten to tear them apart, can these stolen hearts overcome the impediments in their path?

On Sale Now from Avon

About the Author

CAT SEBASTIAN lives in a swampy part of the South with her family and dog. Before her kids were born, she practiced law and taught high school and college writing. When she isn't reading or writing, she's doing crossword puzzles, bird-watching, and wondering where she put her coffee cup.